"What's the big secret?"

Buck threw his napkin down in resignation and stood facing the other people at the table. "What do you all know that I don't know about Catherine Monroe?"

"There's no secret, Mr. Jordan." The voice came from behind him. "I'm as uncomplicated as you are."

A woman quietly joined them at the table. Buck stepped back, stunned, staring. This was Catherine Monroe? Every image he'd had of her shattered like glass.

The woman before him had walked out of the pages of some exotic novel. She was tall, almost as tall as he was, with brilliant auburn hair that cascaded like a river across her shoulders. But it was her eyes that held him—almond-shaped, emerald green. They made him think of the jungle, of the cool, shadowed places buried within it. *A man could lose himself in those eyes.*

He blinked, taking in the one other feature of her appearance that could make him take his eyes from hers—the veil.

It completely covered the rest of her face.

Dear Reader,

Be prepared to meet a "Woman of Mystery"!

This month, we're proud to bring you the start of
our new, ongoing WOMEN OF MYSTERY program,
designed to bring you the debut books of writers new to
Harlequin Intrigue.

Meet Erika Rand, author of *Lying Eyes*.

A lifelong arachnephobe, Erika Rand learned the true
meaning of the word *fear* while on holiday in the tropical
wilds of Peru. She also fell in love with the beauty,
mystery and romance of the Amazon Basin and started
wondering "what if" on the flight home. A graduate of
the University of Alberta with a degree in anthropology,
she lives in Edmonton, Canada, with her husband, an
untamed jungle of books and a resident ghost.

We're dedicated to bringing you the best new authors,
the freshest new voices. Be on the lookout for more
"WOMEN OF MYSTERY"!

Sincerely,

Debra Matteucci
Senior Editor & Editorial Coordinator
Harlequin
300 E. 42nd St., Sixth Floor
New York, NY 10017

Lying Eyes
Erika Rand

Harlequin Books

TORONTO • NEW YORK • LONDON
AMSTERDAM • PARIS • SYDNEY • HAMBURG
STOCKHOLM • ATHENS • TOKYO • MILAN
MADRID • WARSAW • BUDAPEST • AUCKLAND

For Elbert,
who never asked what page I was on now,
and for Peggy,
who took the bullet for me

ISBN 0-373-22259-9

LYING EYES

Printed in U.S.A.

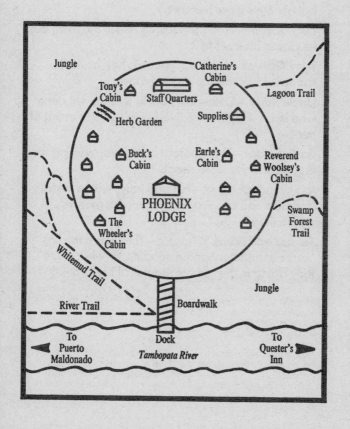

CAST OF CHARACTERS

Catherine Monroe—Her veil kept her anonymous, but her eyes gave her away.

Buck Jordan—The truth stared him in the face, but he closed his eyes to it.

Tony Garvas—Half bodyguard, half brute, he shadowed Catherine's every move.

Uncle Rudy—Catherine's uncle was the only one who knew the pain she lived with every moment of her life.

Earle Godot—This photographer was waiting for an opportunity . . . to shoot.

Reverend Woolsey—Fat and jolly, with a literary appetite—no one would question his motives, would they?

Selena and Frank Wheeler—They were the Las Vegas of honeymooning couples, so what were they doing in the remote jungles of the Amazon?

Prologue

"He's dead!"

"What—?"

"He's dead, he's dead."

"Who is this? Catherine?" Rudy Montoya struggled upright, the strangled voice on the telephone yanking him from a sound sleep. The glowing numbers on the digital clock beside his bed showed just after midnight. "Catherine! What are you talking about? Who's dead?"

At the other end of the line, Catherine Tremaine's fingers tightened convulsively around the telephone receiver as she risked a glance at the broken figure sprawled beside her. "David. It's David." Her voice broke over the syllables. "He's dead. I've killed him."

She heard her uncle inhale sharply. "What do you mean, killed him? How? Where are you?"

"At the house. At the canyon house." She shook with the effort of saying the words, bending double as the horror of the evening rolled over her. "We left the party early—drove up—he said he had something he needed to tell me—I thought he was going to propose—instead he told me—he knew about Daddy, about the theft, about the lies—"

"Slow down! Baby, you're not making any sense."

Catherine dug her fingernails into her palm, willing herself to concentrate on the pain as she struggled to put the events of the evening into words. "We left the wrap party early, right after you did. David said we needed to talk about our future together. I thought—I thought—" Her eyes darted around the room, as if seeking an escape from memories too painful to remember. Instead, she caught sight of the gaping hole in the railing of the second floor gallery fifteen feet above her head and her voice faltered.

"Easy, baby."

She forced her eyes away from the splintered wood and found herself staring, instead, at a man's loafer, teetering at the edge of the long drop to the living room. Her eyes glazed over as she focused on the fringed tassel, on the exquisite hand-stitching. "It wasn't marriage David wanted to talk about. It was Daddy. It was the arms theft. He knew every-thing—everything." She choked back a laugh, drowning in the sight of the rich oxblood leather of David's shoe. "He even had the dates right. Do you know it's been fifteen years since Daddy was shot? Fourteen years since you took cus-tody of me and changed my name?" She spoke mechani-cally, as if each word had been cut into her heart. "I've been acting for six years, three of them in feature films. And don't you think the public has a right to know?" Her breathing became ragged. "Don't you think the public has a right to know, Uncle Rudy?" She tore her gaze from the mesmerizing image of David's shoe to David himself, tak-ing in all of him, every broken, bloody inch. "Don't you think the public has a right to know who I am?"

"Catherine, calm down!" Rudy commanded, trying to make Catherine hear him. "And stay there. Do you under-stand me? Stay right where you are. I'm calling for an am-bulance—"

"Too late." She giggled, the sound partway between laughter and tears. "Too late."

"Then I'm calling the police—"

"No!" Catherine's eyes widened in horror as images from her childhood flooded through her. "No police!" Police meant flashing lights and screeching tires. "No doctors!" Doctors meant pain and suffering and death. Most of all death. She gagged as her fevered brain dredged up a picture of her father, still in uniform, being loaded into the ambulance for the frantic ride to the hospital as military police tried to clear the area. There had been so many people. So much pushing, so much shouting. She could barely breathe....

"Come alone, please." Catherine fought for breath amid the ghosts of her past and succeeded in drawing in enough air to make a sentence. "Come alone. Then we can talk, then we can call someone." She took another deep breath, concentrating on riding out the roller coaster in her head. For a moment, the world steadied itself. "I promise. We'll call the police as soon as you get here." She could almost hear her uncle frown as he decided what to do.

"You'll be all right until I arrive?"

"I think so."

"Then I'm leaving right now."

"Uncle Rudy?"

"What, baby?"

"Hurry."

Catherine let the telephone receiver slide through her fingers to the floor. Her panic had subsided, at least for the moment, although she didn't know what was worse—the frightening breathlessness or the biting emptiness that had replaced it.

Carefully averting her eyes from David's body, she tried to stand, but her cramped muscles refused to support her and she found herself back on her knees beside him. It was as though something was compelling her to take a good, long look at him.

All right, then, she would look.

David Crane lay stretched out on the parquet floor of her living room, one shoe off, one shoe on, one arm pillowing his head. If it wasn't for the pool of blood he lay in, she could almost imagine he was sleeping. Her gaze returned to his outstretched arm. He must have thrown his hands out to protect himself, she realized sickly, in the split second before his body hit the floor.

The image that thought conjured up splintered into something from a cubist painting before slowly reforming into flesh and blood. Still David. Still dead.

Or was he? She groped for a pulse at his wrist but stopped as soon as her fingers encountered his cool flesh. How long had he been lying there? How long since she had made the panicky call to her uncle? A minute? Ten? Thirty? Why was it so hard to think?

Trembling, she curled her fingers into her hair, biting off a cry of pain as she did so. Her hands came back wet with blood. She stared at them uncomprehendingly for a moment before she remembered. She and David had fallen together after their struggle on the second floor. After his shamefaced confession to her that he wasn't a fledgling screenwriter at all, but an investigative reporter.

Not a screenwriter. Not a lover. A liar. She forced her lips around the word. "Liar." It seemed to hover in the air, mocking her.

Catherine staggered to her feet, ignoring the shooting pains in her legs as she struggled to get away from the specter of David. As she lurched backward, her shoulder hit the corner of a large gilt mirror hanging on the wall behind her and she whirled around as the glass tilted crazily toward her. She gasped at her own reflection.

Was this really her, the great Catherine Tremaine? The brilliant actress? Her eyes burned back at her from behind a wild nest of hair. Lipstick curved across her cheek in a crimson slash that looked like blood. Against her will, she sought out David's body in the reflective surface of the mirror but, instead, locked eyes with herself again, this time in the self-portrait that hung on the far wall.

That was the real Catherine Tremaine, wasn't it? America's blond beauty, the one that people loved, the one they thought they knew.

Liar. The word forced her eyes back to her haggard reflection. What would they do when they found out it was all a lie?

Her gaze shifted back to the luminous woman in the oil painting and, for a moment, she actually believed that nothing had changed. She was still in control.

Liar! Like a drum pounding in her head, the word whipped her own wretched image into focus. Each time she tried to look away, her broken face loomed before her. *Liar. Liar.* The pounding built to a roar within her.

Shrieking, Catherine slammed her fists against the mirror, again and again, until the glass shattered and the blood from her lacerated hands ran down her outstretched arms.

That's when the image in the mirror shifted. She was no longer a woman, or a liar, but the frightened child she had been fifteen years ago when her father had been gunned down like a dog in the street. She tasted the warm flood of her tears as the medics worked feverishly over him. She heard the first whispers from his own men: *traitor.*

She was the daughter of a traitor. And no one must know.

"Hide me, hide me." The words tumbled from her like a prayer.

She was still moaning when Rudy found her slumped on the floor a few minutes later.

"Hide me. . . ."

Chapter One

"Welcome to paradise!"

Buck Jordan heaved the last heavy wooden crate from the motorboat onto the dock and found himself staring at the brightest pair of neon sandals he had ever seen. His gaze inched its way past the trim ankles and firm calves to the rest of the woman who stood waiting above him on the dock.

"I said welcome to paradise, Buck," the woman repeated cheerfully, squatting down to thrust her hand out to him. Half a dozen plastic bangles clattered as she pumped his hand. "The boat's a little late today. I thought you'd never get here."

"We picked up a couple of hitchhikers in Puerto Maldonado," Buck said, trying to absorb the rest of her vivid apparel. The colors in her print sundress made his teeth ache. "We dropped them off at a little village on the riverbank about an hour downstream. I guess the natives take their rides where they can get them."

"*Sí, Señor Buck.*" The old man in the stern of the boat nodded and smiled, his attention divided between Buck and the woman's vivid red toenail polish. "*Gracias.*" He managed to look away long enough to point to the pile of crates and hemp sacks standing on the dock.

"My, you have been busy," the woman remarked.

"Thought I'd earn my keep." Buck grinned, shaking the old man's hand. *"Adios, Carlos."* He dug a canvas duffel bag out from under one of the wooden seats and vaulted lightly onto the dock, watching as Carlos started the engine and maneuvered the battered old craft back into the river.

"Don't worry about taking the supplies up to the lodge. The boys from the kitchen will pick them up later on," the woman said. At closer range, she was older than she'd first appeared, probably closer to forty-five than thirty-five, though her bleached blond hair and her carefully applied makeup stripped years from her age.

"You must be—" Buck searched his memory for the name from the travel brochure that described the Phoenix Lodge "—Catherine Monroe."

"Selena Wheeler. But you can make that Selena, honey. I'm a paying customer, same as you. Catherine was a little busy this morning so I offered to bring you up to the lodge." She appraised him solemnly, as if she was evaluating a choice cut of beef. "Hmm, you're a big one."

Buck grinned at the description. Tall and broad-shouldered, he was muscled where it mattered, lean where it didn't. His thick, dark hair hadn't fully grown out after the last brutal military cut. "Vitamins," he drawled, hoisting his duffel bag over his shoulder. "I don't go anywhere without them."

Selena chuckled, motioning him to follow her up the long flight of stairs at the end of the dock. "Honey, you and I are going to get along just fine. I consider myself a fine judge of character," she called back over her shoulder. "You were a college man, right? Probably played a lot of football."

"Does it still show?"

She gave him a dazzling smile as she reached the top of the stairs. "Honey, from this angle, everything shows. Come on, the lodge is this way."

Buck shook his head, a low laugh escaping him as he watched Selena swish down the broad boardwalk that led off through the jungle. Five days ago he had been in Denver, outfitting a busload of tourists for a wilderness safari through the Colorado Rockies. Now he was being petted, scolded and cajoled in the jungles of the Amazon basin by a woman in lime high heels and fluorescent jewelry. What would the boys back in Washington have to say about that?

Probably not a hell of a lot, Buck thought, his good humor fading as he started after Selena. Tension was running pretty high in the military these days, especially after the latest theft of high-tech arms and ammunition, this time from an American base in Germany. The theft itself was a black eye to the American military machine, but the fact that it was only one in a number of sophisticated arms robberies that stretched back over twenty years was what really smarted. The top brass in special investigations had had no trouble pinning most of the robberies on military personnel gone bad, but they suspected a ringleader was responsible for coordinating all the thefts. Known in inner military circles only as the Serpent, the man, an illegal arms dealer par excellence, remained elusive.

Until now.

Until the military, in its infinite wisdom, had decided to drag Buck Jordan, formerly of special investigations, out of early retirement.

Buck dragged his fingers across the sweat-drenched front of his cotton shirt, grimacing. South America had never been high on his list of places to see. Texas had better beer. California had prettier women. The only thing the tropics guaranteed was sunstroke and, this close to the equator, that guarantee was gold. The sun beat down mercilessly from a pale blue sky, turning the boardwalk into the wooden equivalent of a forge and the jungle on either side into a green, breathing bellows. The brass in Washington must really be short on laughs these days if they were getting their kicks by sending people like him to places like this. He'd enjoyed exactly two weeks of civilian life before Uncle Sam had come calling. If they'd needed him back so badly, why couldn't they have sent him to Canada? At least there he'd have had a chance to dry off.

Buck broke into a jog, catching up with Selena just before she ducked down a side trail that wound its way through the trees. At least he wouldn't have to endure the heat for long, he consoled himself. His orders were to rendezvous at the lodge with an informant who claimed to know the identity of the Serpent and the location of his hideout in Peru. It would only be a few days until he was back in the cool Colorado mountains. Until then, he was just another tourist.

"First time in Peru?" he asked, slowing to a walk beside Selena.

She glanced sideways at him, a half smile on her face. "Honey, it's my first time anywhere. Course, I'd have sooner spent my honeymoon on a beach somewhere, but Frank seemed set on coming here."

Honeymoon. That would explain the rock-size diamond Selena sported on the ring finger of her left hand. "How long are you down for?" Buck asked.

"Three weeks. That is, if I can pry Frank away from the fishing long enough to get him on a plane." Selena made a face. "Catherine introduced him to a pole and a couple of the local fish last week and that's the last I've seen of him. That's where he is today, in fact. He and Enrique went out early this morning. Enrique's one of the staff. You'll meet him later."

"So you're a fishing widow."

"Don't that beat all?" She grinned, showing an impressive display of dental work. "The boys at the precinct bet that Frank would never make it through the first few days down here. I'll be lucky if I can get him back home."

Buck zeroed in on the one thing she'd said that mattered. "Your husband's a police officer?" It occurred to him that his informant might be Selena Wheeler's new husband.

What better cover than law enforcement for a man who, at one time, had been one of the Serpent's henchmen.

"Was. He retired from the force last year. I met him on one of those seniors' junkets to Vegas."

That would probably make Frank Wheeler close to sixty-five, Buck calculated rapidly, mentally crossing him off his list. According to Washington, his informant was closer to his own age of thirty-eight.

"Oh, left, honey." Selena pointed out a smaller path that angled sharply back toward the direction of the river. "This one winds a bit more but I think it's safer."

Buck eyed her dubiously as he edged past an enormous barrel-shaped spider's web slung beside the trail. Before he could ask Selena what she thought she was saving him from, she stiffened.

"Oh, hell and damn. I thought we'd avoided him."

"Avoided who?" The words were barely out of his mouth before Buck spotted the big man advancing toward them on the trail. "Another welcoming committee?"

Selena snorted. "Honey, this is one welcoming committee you don't want to meet. He's Attila the Hun, King Kong and the Terminator all rolled into one."

That pretty well said it all. The closer the other man got to them, the bigger he became. By the time he stopped in front of Buck, he was a mountain.

"You Jordan?" he asked, ignoring Selena. "I'm Tony Garvas. I help Catherine Monroe look after the Phoenix. You weren't down at the dock when I came to meet the boat. I didn't expect to find you out here." It sounded more like an accusation than an introduction.

"Carlos picked up a few extra passengers on the river," Buck said. "It slowed us down. Selena was just showing me the way to the lodge."

For the first time, Tony's pockmarked face turned toward Selena. "Mrs. Wheeler. You should be at dinner."

"And you should be in jail."

Buck had seen an expression like the one that came over Tony's face once before in his life: when a bulldog of a marine sergeant had discovered he'd been cheated at cards. He decided he could afford to miss the rest of Tony's reaction. "How much farther to the lodge? I wouldn't mind a cool shower and a cold drink. This heat's a killer."

The undisguised rage in Tony's deep-set eyes dampened and his throat worked furiously for a minute, as if he were swallowing a snake. "Sure," he finally muttered. "This way. It's just down the trail."

Lady, you live dangerously, Buck thought as he followed Tony and Selena along the path that led to the lodge. Both had fallen into a barbed silence, stalking one behind the other as if they were walking into a strong wind. Tony seemed to have that effect on people, Buck thought. He'd never felt a more instantaneous dislike for anyone in his entire life. Either the lodge really was paradise or Catherine Monroe single-handedly attracted guests down here. Tony Garvas was certainly no drawing card.

The trail suddenly opened out into a large clearing. The lodge stood in the center of it, a thatch-roofed two-story building built on stilts that looked like something out of *Robinson Crusoe.* A series of smaller cabins—all small, neat and thatch-roofed, with broad verandas on three sides—flanked the main lodge.

Striped canvas deck chairs dotted the verandas, and a number of graveled paths, torches plunged at regular intervals along their neat borders, ran between the cabins. Buck noticed that the boardwalk he and Selena had taken from the river led through a slash in the jungle, ending at the steps of the main lodge.

"The dining room and bar are in the main house," Tony said, nodding toward it. "You'll find your drinks there. If you don't like fruit juice and *cerveza,* one of the boys can fix you something else."

"*Cerveza* will be fine." Buck grinned, remembering the smooth taste of the local brew from the airport in Cuzco.

"Catherine has put you in cabin number three," Tony went on, pointing to his left. "Plenty of privacy. Most of our guests aren't scheduled to arrive for a few more weeks, so we've spread everybody out. The Wheelers are your nearest neighbors."

"Number seven, honey. Well within hollering distance."

Tony cut her off. "We can move you to number fourteen if you'd like."

Buck scanned the compound while Tony and Selena faced off. His informant had known exactly what he was doing when he had specified that Buck meet him here. Isolated lodge, limited number of guests. Hell, they could practically shoot rockets off without arousing any suspicion. He didn't like it. It looked too much like a setup. The closer he was to the other guests, the safer he'd probably be.

"I think I might enjoy a little company. Three sounds perfect."

Tony shrugged. "It's your dollar. I'll check on your room while you get something to drink. I'll drop your bag off while I'm at it." The knuckles of the hand he extended had been broken sometime in the past and he quickly turned his palm up when he noticed Buck's speculative gaze. "Your bag," he repeated, his own eyes narrowing as he took stock of Buck.

"I'll keep it with me. Old habit," Buck said smoothly. He'd picked up a revolver from his American contact in Cuzco that morning. The Peruvian police would probably take a dim view if they knew he had the piece. They'd like it even less if they found out he was in the country on military business. He'd just as soon miss seeing the inside of a Peruvian prison if he could help it.

Tony nodded, his eyes never leaving the duffel bag. "I'll check back later to see if you need anything else."

"Honey, if I was you, I'd make sure my needs were few and far between," Selena said when Tony was out of earshot. "On second thought, you'd be better off dealing strictly with Catherine. I'd trust Tony just about as far as I could throw him."

"Speaking of Catherine, when am I going to meet this mystery lady?"

"Mystery lady?" Selena put her hands on her hips. "Honey, you haven't been listening to any of those rumors, now, have you?"

Buck stared at her. "Rumors?"

"Because I can tell you that Catherine is just about as normal as they come," Selena insisted, "despite her appearance." She took his arm and began to steer him toward the main lodge. "And that's all I'm saying on the matter."

She'd said nothing, as far as Buck was concerned. What was wrong with Catherine Monroe? Or, according to Selena, what wasn't wrong with her? He followed her gamely up the steps to the lodge, wondering how he could reopen the discussion.

"Honey, what did you say you did for a living? You've got the same look Frank does around the eyes. I took you for a cop when I first saw you."

Buck fell back on the story they'd drawn up for him in Washington. "I outfit tourists for wilderness trips through the Rockies." At least it was partially true.

Selena stopped in her tracks, shaking her head. "I can't be that wrong."

Buck laughed, opening the door of the lodge for her. "Scout's honor."

The dining room was dark and cool, surprisingly so considering the bank of wire-meshed windows that wrapped right around the room. A massive, hand-hewn wooden table stood in the center of the floor, each of the heavy chairs drawn up to it looking as if they'd been carved from a single block of wood. Against the far wall, a lavish buffet had been set up on a serving table. Buck parked his bag next to one of the chairs and wandered over to check out the food, his thirst suddenly taking second place to a voracious hunger.

"What's good today, Jorge?" Selena asked a fine-featured young man who emerged through a swinging door beside the buffet.

Jorge grinned, showing a line of small, perfect, white teeth. "Everything, *señora,*" he said, handing her a plate. He was dressed as Tony had been, in a short-sleeved cotton shirt and neatly pressed dark pants that Buck assumed was the staff uniform.

"I don't know how Catherine does it," Selena said, spearing a slice of mango and plopping it on her plate. "She feeds us like kings out here. And she goes out of her way to accommodate her guests. Frank actually saw her in the kitchen one night after Jorge had gone to bed, cooking up something for the Reverend. Honey, I'd have told that man to go hungry." She popped a grape into her mouth. "She's even got Tony eating out of her hand, if you can believe it."

"She probably needs loyal staff this far away from civilization," Buck said absently, accepting the plate Jorge offered him. He mentally added a reverend of some kind to the list of guests he was compiling. Was that the cover his informant had taken?

"I guess if anyone could find folks willing to work out here, it'd be Catherine. She's another one I can read like a book. Of course, I usually have to be able to see a person's face to read character." Selena leaned over and knocked a piece of roasted meat off Buck's fork. "Oh, honey, you don't want that. That's guinea pig."

"What did you say?"

"That's guinea pig."

"No, I mean about Catherine's—"

"'A mask tells us more than a face.'"

Buck turned to face the portly gentleman who had just joined them at the buffet table. He was obviously the Reverend, Buck decided, judging by the beatific look of his face, and obviously not his informant. He was about sixty years old with a shock of wild, white hair that made him look as though he had just climbed down from the ceiling of the Sistine Chapel.

"Oscar Wilde," the Reverend explained, misinterpreting Buck's shrewd appraisal. "Brilliant writer. Astute man. Of course, he did have that unfortunate problem."

"Reverend, you can't be eating again! I saw you come through here not more than an hour ago," Selena said.

The Reverend's mottled cheeks grew redder. "I thought I'd take a little something back to my room for later today. For some reason, this heat seems to have increased my appetite." He fished a dingy white handkerchief from his pocket and wiped his palms with it before extending his hand to Buck. "John Woolsey. Ohio. I take it you're the new man we've all been expecting."

"Buck Jordan. Colorado." Buck grinned, taking his cue from the Reverend. "Happy to meet you, sir."

"Buck's just come up from Maldonado," Selena explained.

"I know. I heard the boat. I'm sorry I didn't make it down to the dock to meet you." Reverend Woolsey dabbed uselessly at his forehead with the handkerchief before stuffing it back into his pocket. "The heat does tend to slow one down."

"Don't let Tony hear you say that," Selena told him. "Survival of the fittest, and all. He'd probably throw you to the wolves, or whatever passes for them around here. Maybe that'd be the anaconda," she added under her breath, peering closely at another dish on the table.

Buck didn't wait to hear whether she was identifying another Peruvian delicacy or Tony's choice in carnivores.

"Reverend, what was that you said about a mask? I take it you're referring to Catherine Monroe?"

"Oh, my, yes—Catherine," the Reverend nodded, frowning. "I probably could have come up with something better from Scriptures." He squinted at the ceiling, his lips moving soundlessly as he considered his options. "Let me see...."

"Never mind." Buck was more curious about what the Reverend had meant than he was about any more quotations.

"Buck's right," Selena said. "That's the last thing Catherine needs, hearing us talk like this. I expect she's sensitive about the way she looks." She prodded the Reverend in the ribs, jolting him out of his reverie. "Wouldn't *you* be?"

Inwardly, Buck groaned. They sounded like lunatics. Either that, or he had missed something critical in the conversation. From the little they'd said, Catherine Monroe was starting to resemble something from the *Phantom of the Opera*. Not that it mattered to him, one way or the other. The elusive Miss Monroe could have horns and a pitchfork for all he cared, just as long as she didn't interfere with the completion of his mission.

He turned his attention back to the buffet, but the Reverend insisted on finishing the conversation. "I think she handles her handicap very courageously," he said, forming a steeple with his fingers.

"She's a plucky little thing, all right," Selena agreed.

"I give up." Buck threw his napkin down in resignation. "What's the big secret? What do you know that I don't know about Catherine Monroe?"

"There's no secret, Mr. Jordan. I'm as uncomplicated as you are."

The woman had quietly joined them at the table. Buck stepped back, stunned, staring. This was Catherine Monroe? Every image he'd had of her shattered like glass.

The woman before him had walked out of the pages of some exotic novel. She was tall, almost as tall as he was, with brilliant auburn hair that cascaded like a river across her shoulders. But it was her eyes that held him—almond-shaped, emerald green. They made him think of the jungle, of the cool, shadowed places buried within it. A man could lose himself in those eyes.

He blinked, taking in the one other feature of her appearance that could make him take his eyes from hers—the veil.

It completely covered the rest of her face.

CATHERINE TOOK the graveled path that ran between the cabins in long, sure strides. She could feel Buck Jordan several paces behind her, his own step measured, confident. She walked lightly up the stairs that led to the veranda of his cabin, listening for his heavier tread a second later. Was he deliberately keeping his distance so that he could observe her, the way he had discreetly watched her at lunch?

She turned to face him when she reached the door to his room. "You're staring at me."

"Yes." He dropped his bag and leaned back against the railing, his expression inscrutable. "You're not what I expected."

"You mean *this* is not what you expected," she said, indicating the strip of cloth that hid her face.

"Yes."

Yes. Was that all he was going to say? She had hardly expected him to launch into the usual self-conscious platitudes that so many other guests mouthed when she challenged them to speak about her condition, but neither was she prepared for his quiet, candid reply. The least he could do was focus on some other part of her anatomy—her hair, perhaps, or her legs—the way other men did. She could give him a label, then, stick him safely in a category with all the others.

But not this man.

This man refused to look away. He met and held her eyes in a way that both calmed and alarmed her. At least, she thought it was alarm—that tingling of her nerves whenever their eyes locked. She dragged her eyes away from the almost hypnotic pull of his and pushed open the door to his room, determined to nullify the electric effect Buck Jordan had on her. "You'll be sleeping in here."

The room was plain and simply furnished, in keeping with the spirit of the lodge, yet it exuded its own special charm. She'd seen to the decorating herself. A double bed, covered by an alpaca-wool spread intricately worked in teal and gold, took up most of the space. Two split-log chairs, made by craftsmen from the village downstream, flanked the bed, and a large, roughly finished armoire stood against the opposite wall. Catherine opened another door at the back of the room to reveal a small bathroom.

"There's only cold water, I'm afraid," she said, running the taps to the sink. "We pump it up directly from the river, so I'd keep any singing in the shower to a minimum. That is, if you don't want to come down with a galloping case of river sickness."

"I'll make my arias short and sweet."

"We're not wired for electricity, either," Catherine went on, her attention riveted to the disturbing smile that played across his mouth. "The sound of the generator disturbed the wildlife too much, not to mention our guests, so we dismantled it." She'd just noticed the tiny scar that nicked the left corner of his bottom lip. Would it heighten the potency of his kiss, she wondered, her heartbeat suddenly racing at the outrageous and unexpected turn her thoughts had taken.

She scrabbled mentally for the next item on the agenda, retreating into the safety of the memorized text as she pulled out a couple of candles from her pants pocket and dropped them on the bed. "We find these work just as well as electricity. Just be careful where you set them. The wood in the lodge has been specially treated to discourage termites, and that makes it very flammable. I'd hate to see this place go up in smoke."

"Watch the candles. Check." Again, that disarming smile flashed.

Catherine took an unsteady breath. "Meals are served promptly at seven, noon and eight." She listed off on her fingers. "Though the kitchen is always open if you want to make a midnight run. If you need anything else—" she felt her face begin to burn at Buck's raised eyebrow "—Tony will be happy to help you."

He gave her a lopsided grin. "I could use one thing...."

"That is...?"

"The key."

"Oh, I'm sorry." Catherine paused in the doorway, turning to look back at him. "I thought you knew. We don't lock our doors out here. It's all part and parcel of getting back to the great outdoors. No television, no telephone, no security system."

Buck's face lost all expression. "No locks?"

"You can latch the door from the inside," Catherine said, swinging the door partially shut to show him the flimsy hook. He didn't seem comforted by the sight of it. "Other than that, I guess we'll simply have to learn to trust one another." Her composure returned as she stared him down coolly.

"And how hard can that be?" The smile was back on his face, but this time it didn't quite reach his eyes. There was something else there instead, something that ran a finger of fear down her spine as she left the room.

She'd missed something. But what was it? Catherine slowly crossed the compound to her own cabin, her mind on the man in number three. Something about him bothered her, and it wasn't just the totally inappropriate way her body had responded to his powerful presence. There was something else there, something familiar. Or maybe it wasn't so much the man, but his actions that tickled a memory.

Or his movements.

Her confident stride faltered as she swung around. Across the compound, number three shimmered innocently in the heat of the midafternoon sun. Her mind worked furiously as she stared at it. Buck Jordan moved like her father had. The same ramrod posture. The same crisp turns. The only thing missing was the "sir" at the end of a sentence. He was a military man. She'd bet her life on it.

A sudden breath of wind swept up the bottom half of her veil, as though something ancient and ethereal had passed a hand across her eyes. Shivering, she smoothed it down. The realization that Buck was army, and probably an officer if his authoritative manner meant anything, had stirred up a barrage of old memories. Unwanted memories. Memories she'd spent a lifetime trying to erase.

She trudged up the stairs to her cabin. It was identical to all the others in the compound—same square, sturdy bed, same rustic furniture and small bathroom. A tiny addition at the rear of the cabin had been converted to a hamshack where she kept a radio and antenna. She rarely used the radio to contact the other ham operators in the area, but it was nice to know that it was there if she needed it.

An unconscious need, long denied, propelled her across the room to a small dresser beside the bed. The top of the dresser was bare, as was the top of the table near the door. She hadn't bothered to tack anything to the walls, either, though she'd used the lodge for almost five years. It was a decision she'd made when she first arrived, before she'd resigned herself to the fact that these four walls were all she could ever expect from life. Somehow, she had never gotten around to filling up the emptiness.

The fourth drawer of the dresser was full: stacks of correspondence from her uncle Rudy in California, a couple of ledgers from the lodge's first few years of operation, piles of receipts from the suppliers in Cuzco. Her fingers skimmed unerringly across the papers until they closed around the small silver picture frame at the bottom of the drawer and she pulled it free.

Her past stared back at her.

She ran one finger gently across the glass. Her father had worn his dress uniform for the photograph, as if hoping to mark the solemnity of the occasion. It hadn't been necessary. Both he and the dark-haired, green-eyed little girl who stood pressed to his side still wore their grief from the funeral. They'd clung together for sanity in those first awful months after her mother's death from cancer. Before long, he'd become her whole world.

She had been Catherine Taylor then, Neil Taylor's little girl. She had lost everything the night he died. She drew a deep breath as she continued to stare at the photograph, remembering the night of the shooting. Her father had been killed during the commission of an arms robbery at the ammunition depot he was in charge of. Soon after, he had become the target of an internal military investigation. When it was all over, he'd been linked to the thieves and to the illegal arms dealer they worked for. In the time it had taken for someone to pull the trigger of a gun, Neil Taylor had gone from patriot to traitor.

She had been ten years old. And terrified.

Catherine's hands trembled as a remnant of the old pain swept over her. Ten years old. Too young to be thrust into a maelstrom of international intrigue. What had she known about the voracious appetite of the public for scandal? She had learned, though. Oh, yes, she had learned. In the days following her father's death, the onslaught by the press had been brutal. Before she could be crushed totally by a barrage of demands for photos and interviews, she'd been spirited away by her mother's only brother, Rudy. He'd applied for permanent custody of her, changed her name, helped her establish her acting career when she had been old enough. Catherine Taylor had died the day her father did. Catherine Tremaine had been born the minute she first appeared before the cameras.

She'd been a blond then, courtesy of regular visits to her hairdresser, and the quintessential California look, coupled with the depths of emotion she was able to bring to the cameras, had guaranteed her success. No one had been the wiser. She'd survived the trauma of her childhood years by becoming somebody else. It had worked and it would have kept on working if not for David Crane and that awful night at the canyon house. How many times could her world come apart?

Impatiently, she thrust the photograph back into the drawer, refusing to torment herself any further with a replay of the past. She was Catherine Monroe now, owner and operator of the Phoenix Lodge. The blond, pixie haircut was gone, replaced by a longer, fuller style in her natural auburn. Her world was these four walls, the jungle, the veil. Most days she never permitted herself to think about her family, her friends or her former career. She was lost to them. Why dredge up so much sorrow?

She rose wearily to her feet. Work was the answer. It was the one thing that kept her going. She would keep busy for the rest of the afternoon, going through the supplies Carlos had just delivered, confirming reservations for the next batch of guests, burying memories.

Squaring her shoulders, she walked briskly into the bathroom. A cool shower would probably work wonders for her sluggish frame of mind. She rotated the taps in the shower stall and turned to the small medicine chest over the sink for soap and shampoo. The door was open. She'd obviously forgotten to close it that morning, or else Jorge had brought by a new supply of toilet articles. She frowned as she inventoried the contents. Nothing had been touched, as far as she could see, and she was still out of soap.

She swung back to the shower, snapping the medicine cabinet shut. It would have to be a soap-free rinse today— The thought died as she caught a glimpse of the bloodred words scrawled across the surface of the mirror. Transfixed, she stepped toward it, one hand going out as if to convince herself it was real.

The message was short and chilling. *I'm watching you.*

Chapter Two

"I don't like it." Tony glared at the message on the mirror, one huge hand closed around the top of the cabinet door. Metal hinges creaked in protest as he flexed his muscular forearm. "I don't like it at all."

"I don't like it, either," Catherine said gently, putting a restraining hand on his arm. She was amazed that she could sound so calm. "The point is, who wrote it? And why? Did you notice anyone around my cabin this morning?"

Tony's gaze lingered a moment on her fingers before shifting back to the mirror. "Frank Wheeler was up early to go fishing. He and Enrique left for the lagoon right after breakfast. He'd have had to come right by here to pick up his gear."

Catherine shook her head, averting her eyes from the bloodred words. They'd identified the substance as lipstick. Somehow that made the writer's intent seem all the more sinister. "I was in my room until nine o'clock. Frank and Enrique had already left by then." She ran her fingers over the nubby material of the towels hanging on the bar near the shower. "The sheets have been changed. I checked. And all the towels are clean, so Jorge has been here. That means that whoever did this," she said, gesturing at the mirror, "did it sometime between ten-thirty and two."

"Jorge could have—"

Catherine sighed. "You know better than that."

Tony's eyebrows drew together. "No, I don't. And neither do you. Any one of these jungle *muchachos* could have been persuaded to come in here for the right amount of money."

"These *young men*—" Catherine emphasized the words warningly "—have been with me since we opened up. They may not know my true identity but they're loyal, just the same. I couldn't suspect them any more than I could suspect you."

He continued to stare at her as she reached beneath the full weight of her hair and loosened her veil. She'd designed and sewn it herself, getting the idea from one of her early, less successful movies, a romantic adventure set amid the transplanted palm trees and rented camels of a Hollywood backlot. Someone in wardrobe had shown Catherine a belly dancer's costume, complete with face covering, and she had sewn the veil from memory, using a single square of opaque silk, with two small elastic loops stitched to the upper corners to fit securely over her ears. Once in place, it covered everything from her nose to her collarbone, obliterating her features—and her past—completely.

Tony watched her drag the supple material away from her face, a nerve working sporadically in his left temple. Suddenly self-conscious, he swiveled back to the mirror. "Then that leaves the guests," he conceded, rubbing the ball of his thumb along the curve of one crimson letter.

Catherine sighed, tossing the veil onto the bed. The concession had cost him nothing. He'd given in to her now, because she wanted him to, but later, in private, he'd conduct his own investigation of the staff. He'd probably do a check on himself if he thought it would help. Tony Garvas was, if nothing else, a thorough man.

Tony had worked for her since her early days in Hollywood. He'd been an ex-convict, thirty-five years old, just out of prison and eager for a job, when her uncle introduced them. She thought she'd been doing a community service when she hired him, but he soon proved indispensable as her chauffeur and bodyguard. It hadn't taken much to persuade him to accompany her down to Peru when she'd fled the country. They had worked side by side at the lodge ever since.

She often suspected his feelings for her went beyond the bounds of their platonic relationship, but if they did, he gave little indication and she never encouraged him. She didn't need a lover, she needed a friend and a confidant, and Tony was both. He had been indispensable to her in California, and he was invaluable to her now. She trusted his loyalty and his discretion. More than that, she trusted his instincts.

"You think one of the guests could be capable of doing something like this?" she asked, massaging the bridge of her nose.

Tony grunted. "This last bunch we brought up could be capable of anything. Mr. Hotshot Godot—" he spat out the name of the photojournalist staying in cabin number ten "—and that Wheeler woman—"

"Earle Godot was with me," Catherine interrupted. "I showed him some of the flora along the white-mud trail this morning. We weren't back until almost one."

"Did he eat lunch with the rest of you?"

She frowned. "I think he went to his cabin. Something about a headache."

"So he could have sneaked over here when you were in the dining room. Any one of the bunch could have come over while you were showing Jordan his cabin." His eyes narrowed. "And what about Jordan? I trust him least of all."

Buck Jordan? Catherine's thoughts shifted to the new guest in number three. The mysterious Mr. Jordan was an army officer, probably. An extremely attractive man, certainly. But an anonymous message-writer? Not likely.

"Buck just arrived," she said, shaking her head. "I doubt if he's even unpacked yet. He certainly hasn't had the opportunity to wander through this part of the compound."

"He's had plenty," Tony growled. "I found him and Mrs. Wheeler wandering around the back trails right after Carlos left him at the dock."

"Selena might have been showing him the area."

"That's what she said. Or she might have been sneaking him up to the cabin to do this."

Catherine squeezed her eyelids shut as the first wave of panic rushed in. She'd forgotten how consuming the old fears could be. They swept over her, as cold and unrelenting as the tide. With a superhuman effort, she forced them back. Still, her voice was less steady than she would have liked. "You're talking about some kind of conspiracy."

"Maybe." Tony folded his arms across his chest and planted his legs apart, unconsciously adopting a bodyguard stance. "If this message has something to do with your father and that business with Crane up in Los Angeles five years ago, then there could be more than one person behind it."

"Or it could have nothing to do with my past," Catherine said slowly, with more conviction than she was feeling, "in which case I could be jeopardizing my position by assuming it has." Her eyes snapped open and she stared at the mirror, as if through sheer concentration she could will the surface clean.

"It makes more sense to suspect someone's cracked our setup here. I think you should stay away from everyone for a few days. At least until I can do a little snooping."

"I can't do that," Catherine protested. "I'm running a lodge, remember? I can't just avoid my guests because we think someone might suspect something about my past. We don't know enough about this message, about who may be behind it, to start changing the way things work."

"I still don't like it," Tony said, his hair-trigger temper beginning to show. "And your uncle won't like it, either. He'll be on the next plane to Maldonado when he hears about this."

"Which is exactly why we're not telling him." Catherine turned on him, putting as much power behind her words as she could. "You know what his doctor said after his last heart attack. He's to stay in Los Angeles. He needs rest. He doesn't need a lot of unnecessary worry over something that might turn out to be a practical joke."

"This isn't a joke, and you know it."

"We'll see."

Tony dropped his arms to his side, his hands opening and closing into fists as he scowled at her. "Meanwhile, we just sit back and wait for this guy to make the next move."

"*If* he makes the next move." Catherine plucked several tissues from the box on the toilet tank and began wiping the mirror. "Meanwhile—" her voice held a warning note "—it's business as usual."

Tony hesitated, then gave an almost imperceptible nod. He was furious at her, she realized. No, not at her. At himself for having failed to convince her of the danger she was in.

In that way, he was a lot like Uncle Rudy. They were both protective of her, sometimes overly so. Her uncle's health had been declining for years, a fact he'd stubbornly overlooked while helping her recover from her breakdown after David Crane's death. When his weakness and shortness of breath had finally reached a point that even he couldn't ignore, Tony had stepped in to look after her.

Both men had her best interests at heart, she realized, but the protectiveness had begun to irritate her. Like the veil, and the masquerade she was playing at, Tony's almost obsessive need to shield her had become more crushing than comforting. She'd needed that care five years ago. But she'd been twenty-four years old then, a naive and frightened twenty-four, bewildered by her meteoric rise to fame, hounded by her public and the press, haunted by the death of her father. Then, she'd welcomed Uncle Rudy's help.

Now, almost thirty, she had begun to resent it.

With a flourish, she washed the last of the letters from the mirror. "There. You'd never know I had anything to hide."

Tony said nothing, his gaze fixed solemnly on her hands.

She looked down. Her fingers were streaked with red, as though she'd just run them across a newly opened wound. Slowly, wordlessly, without looking at him, she wiped them clean.

EVENING BROUGHT NO RELIEF from the heat. In fact, it felt more like a steam bath than it had earlier in the day, if that was possible, Buck thought as he closed the door to his cabin. He'd spent the entire afternoon in the sticky confines of his room, deliberately missing dinner so that he had some reason to visit the main lodge after the other guests had gone to bed. If he was surprised by anyone, cold chicken and coffee were as good an excuse as any to offer for his midnight rambling.

He eased himself down the stairs, automatically checking the compound for any signs of movement. Nothing. The torches that he had watched Enrique light earlier that evening had all been extinguished. And though the sky blazed with a billion stars, their radiance seemed to end where the jungle began. The clearing was as black as the bottom of a well.

Using the faint flicker of candlelight from the other cabins as a guide, Buck negotiated his way to the dark bulk that was the main lodge. By his calculations, the Wheelers were still awake, as was Reverend Woolsey. He had yet to meet Earle Godot, but from what Selena had told him over lunch, the young photographer was staying in cabin number ten.

He counted off. That one was dark. So were the rest of the staff cabins that ringed the clearing: the small one at the end for Tony, the larger cabin in the middle for Enrique, Jorge and the other staff. Catherine's cabin stood at the far end.

Catherine. He tasted her name like honey on his lips. He'd never met anyone as mesmerizing or as enigmatic. And his timing had never been more inconvenient. If he'd been anywhere else doing anything else, he might have been tempted to— He shrugged off the impulse as he skidded on a hummock of loose earth. He'd have to learn to keep his mind on his work, and that wouldn't be hard, considering the way he was going to be spending his evenings.

A light, moist film broke over his skin as he opened the door to the main lodge and slipped inside. He'd made a mental map of the dining room during lunch and he maneuvered past the enormous table in the middle of the room without needing to switch on his penlight.

The reservation desk was at the back of the room. He felt his way around the low counter, avoiding the dark shape on his left that he remembered as a revolving brochure rack and the murky bulk of a water dispenser on his right. Behind the counter there were three shelves stocked with pamphlets that described the region's flora and fauna, in- and outgoing mail, and embossed, leather-spined reservation books dating back to the year he assumed the lodge opened.

He counted his way to the third book, withdrew it and crouched, snapping on a small flashlight as he leafed through the pages.

"Damn." The light was dim but it showed enough. None of the recent handwritten entries, including Earle Godot's, matched the sample he'd been given in Washington. If his informant wasn't here, then where the hell was he?

A muffled sound from the second floor brought his head around. Dousing the light, he slipped the book back into its place and crept quietly toward the curving plank staircase that led to the upper level. On the top step he hesitated, his eyes narrowing at the flickering light that showed around the swinging doors to the lounge. Was this just another guest with a wayward appetite or was he about to meet the man who'd brought him almost seven thousand miles? He pushed the doors open.

Catherine sat alone at one of the small, ironwood tables that dotted the room, haloed by the golden glow from a single candle, the burnished sweep of her hair like flame in the flickering light. An account book and several piles of receipts were spread across the tabletop, but her mind was obviously far from the neat figures that marched across the pages. Half-turned away from him, she stared unseeingly out at the black void beyond the window.

Suddenly she swiveled in her seat, as though sensing his presence. For a moment they shared no words, just an unexpected physical awareness of each other that jolted Buck's senses. Then the naked emotion in her wide green eyes was replaced by a wariness that puzzled him, before that, too, was eclipsed by a distant, professional reserve that left him oddly shaken.

She broke the silence first. "First-night jitters?"

"First-night what?"

She gave a low, apologetic laugh. "It's a term we use around here. A lot of our guests find it a little difficult adjusting to the 'music of the night.'" She waved her hand at the almost physical membrane of insect noise pulsating from the jungle. "It took me a while to get used to it, too. Some nights I think I would have preferred a couple of lawn mowers or a blasting radio to all that out there."

Buck grinned, his stomach rumbling wickedly as he noticed the plate of orange sections and *gringo* bread beside her elbow. "I see I'm not the only one who missed dinner," he said, straddling the chair beside her. "May I?"

"Please."

She watched him tear into the chewy, unleavened bread with his strong white teeth, then follow it with several pieces of fruit. She'd been positively giddy when she saw him in the doorway, a ridiculous reaction considering they'd just met, but then she'd been experiencing a lot of ridiculous reactions since his arrival. She wasn't normally so...out of control. She knew nothing about the man, save for the aura of power and mystery that enveloped him, and though her brain told her he had nothing to do with the message she'd received, the sizzle of her nerves whenever he was around her seemed to imply that this man was dangerous.

He'd already finished the bread and was just about to pop another slice of orange into his mouth when he realized she was watching him. "Where are my manners? I'm devouring your supper."

"Go ahead. I think I might have overestimated my appetite," she replied, toying with the rim of the plate. "I can't seem to concentrate on any of this, either." She sighed, picking up a couple of receipts, then threw them down. "Accounting and I are old enemies."

"Me, too. I was always better at football than I was at math." Buck tilted one of the slips of paper toward the candle. "What's this?"

She glanced at the paper. "It's an order for fruits and vegetables from one of the markets in Cuzco. That's where we get most of our supplies. Carlos will bring the first load down the river in a couple of days. We're expecting a few more tourists next week. After that, our heavy season starts."

Buck rolled his eyes skyward, tugging mockingly at the collar of his shirt. "Then this is the off-season?"

"Afraid so. We've had rain the last few months. Most of the tourists stay away then, even those intrepid ones who like to think of themselves as real adventurers. By May, though, or early June, the weather's usually hot. It gets pretty humid then, too." She laughed at his woebegone expression. "Don't worry. In a few more days you'll be used to it."

"I'll take your word for it." Buck swung his leg over the back of the chair and walked over to a water dispenser near the window. "You said there would be a few more guests arriving soon," he said casually, working the dispenser.

His question had a loaded quality about it that puzzled her. "A few."

"Americans?"

She jerked violently as he came up behind her, his arm brushing the edge of her veil, but he merely set the glass of water down on the table.

"I'm sorry if I startled you," he murmured, hesitating for a moment beside her before he seemed to shake himself. "Americans?" he asked again quietly, resuming his seat. The question hung unanswered between them.

Why, Catherine wondered, was he so interested in how many guests were staying at the lodge? Or how many guests weren't staying there? An uneasy thrill of fear quickened her breathing before she realized he was probably making conversation. She was getting paranoid. The message on her mirror had affected her more than she'd imagined. "There'll be a few Americans," she said. "Would it make any difference if they were Japanese?"

He laughed easily. "No, ma'am."

She stared at him. There it was again, that damnable military politeness. She decided to broach the subject before her uncertainty drove her crazy. "Where are you stationed?" she asked.

Silence.

"Which military installation?" she clarified as he continued to stare at her. "You are in the army, aren't you? My— One of my relatives served for a while, too. I'd recognize the signs anywhere."

He raised one dark eyebrow in a quick salute to her, then tempered his intense expression with a lopsided grin. "I retired last month. I've been a civilian for fourteen days, nineteen hours and—" he checked his watch "—eight minutes, give or take a few seconds." At least he had been, he amended to himself, until he'd accepted this assignment. For some reason, the lie bit into him as he studied her eyes.

Ojos de gato. At least that's what the Spanish would call them. Cat's eyes. Untamed. Alluring. He wished he could see the rest of her face, no matter what kind of affliction she was hiding from the world. At least, then, he might be better able to judge her expression, to confirm the heated emotions he saw cascading through her. Now, he could only react, second-guessing what he thought he saw, what he wanted to see, until she chose to lower her gaze or look away. Like she did now.

A cold wind seemed to blow through him.

"I'm sorry." Her voice was like the flow of a mountain stream. "I didn't mean to pry. It must be my innkeeper instincts coming out. I like to get to know my guests." Her voice warmed and he knew that she was smiling at him.

"I guess I'm just not used to being a civilian yet. That's one of the reasons I took this trip," he ad-libbed, ignoring the sting of his conscience. "I'd hoped it would jump-start my system. You know, I still dream in khaki."

She laughed, relaxing against the back of her chair. "Then you should have gone to the beach instead of the jungle."

A small smile played around the corner of his mouth, gradually disappearing as they regarded each other silently across the tabletop.

They were dancing around each other again, not for information this time, or for confirmation, but for—what? Abruptly, Buck got to his feet before the slow, thick ache in his belly could give him the answer. He was on a job, dammit. He was still a soldier, even if the woman sitting across from him made him want to forget that fact.

"Thanks for the midnight snack. Next time—" he'd have to make sure there was never a next time "—I'll bring my own. Oh, by the way," he added, turning around just as he reached the swinging doors, "I think I'm bunking with a few unwanted guests."

She tilted her head to one side. "You've been hearing some rustling from the ceiling? Squeaking and scratching, too?"

"Uh-huh."

"Don't worry. It's only Romeo and Julian. They roost up under the eaves at night."

"Romeo and—Julian?"

Catherine leaned forward, her eyes glittering mischievously. "They're a couple of parrots who've adopted us. Enrique rescued them from a crate at the airport in Maldonado when they were just fledglings. They were part of an illegal shipment bound for a pet store in Texas. I guess we disappointed a few children, but at least these two lived. Most of the others in the crate had already suffocated by the time we released them."

"How long have you had them?"

"A couple of years. We'd hoped they'd return to the jungle, but I guess they've become too fond of Enrique's cooking. They're both males, by the way. We'd already named them by the time we learned about that, so we had to change their names to Romeo—"

"—and Julian."

"Right." Catherine's eyes turned challenging. "I hope they won't disturb you. They're a fun-loving pair, a little noisy in the mornings."

"Don't worry," he said, knocking open one of the doors with his shoulder. "I sleep like the dead."

HE TOOK THE BULLET low in his belly.

The impact drove him back and down, searing his insides as though a fire had ignited in his gut. Another bullet tore into the wall above his head and he jerked sideways, choking on a wave of agony.

The next bullet would kill him.

Clamping one arm across the oozing wound in his stomach, he began to inch his way backward toward the door, leaving a dark trail of blood behind him.

Buck bolted upright at the deafening shriek. He was halfway to the door before he realized where he was: the jungle, the lodge, the woman. It took another few seconds to identify the source of the raucous cawing outside his window.

Shakespeare's birds.

He swore softly and pushed the curtain aside. Two huge parrots wagged their kelly green heads at him from the other side of the screen before emitting another pair of earsplitting shrieks. Then, as if satisfied with themselves, they took wing, settling like multicolored sirens in the branches of a palm tree on the far side of the clearing.

They were a little noisy, she'd said. A little fun-loving. Hell, he'd been had.

And Catherine was probably loving every minute of it.

He grinned, picking up the shirt he had worn the day before, and began to wipe his face with it, stopping suddenly as he remembered.

He'd had the dream again.

He glanced down at the enormous scar that covered the left half of his stomach. Even after twenty years and several visits to the plastic surgeon, it was still puckered and ugly. And, in this heat, itchy as hell.

Occupational hazard, he supposed as he continued to wipe the sweat from his naked chest and arms before balling up his shirt and tossing it into a corner. No one said life in the military was going to be easy. His mutilated flesh was proof of that.

He methodically checked that his shoulder holster and revolver were still tucked behind the armoire where he'd hidden them the night before. Then he took a quick shower, dressed and wandered over to the main lodge. Reverend

Woolsey and the Wheelers were already seated at the big table when he walked in.

"Buck!" Reverend Woolsey waved him over. "Maybe you can settle something for us. Are there any native villages in the area?"

Buck stopped at the buffet to pour himself a cup of coffee, ignoring the rest of the food spread across the table. He'd never been a breakfast person. "We passed one village on the trip upriver yesterday," he told the Reverend as he sat down. "Small place, probably not more than thirty or forty people. They were mostly *mestizos* by the looks of them, not full-blooded Indians. Why?"

"Thought I saw someone last night," Frank Wheeler said around a mouthful of scrambled egg.

Buck recognized him from lunch the day before. He was a squat, powerfully built man with no neck and a fringe of iron gray hair that struggled, without much success, to cover his polished cranium.

"It was over by the edge of the clearing," Frank continued, rinsing the egg down with coffee. "The padre here says it could have been an animal."

"Possibly a jaguar," the Reverend suggested, thumbing through a pile of literature beside his plate, "or a peccary. Look, here's quite a good photo—"

"Could have been one of your half bloods, too," Frank said, ignoring the Reverend's glossy pullout, "come down to have a look-see."

"What time was this?" Buck asked. "I took a walk about eleven-thirty."

"And I was out about ten," the Reverend offered.

Buck winced. The compound sounded like it had been a regular freeway last night. He'd been lucky he hadn't been mowed down.

"Late. One, maybe closer to one-fifteen." Frank glanced at Selena for confirmation. "I came out for a smoke. Otherwise I wouldn't have seen a thing. I took a look around but it was too dark. Couldn't find much of anything this morning, either. One print. Could be a partial heel mark. Could be just about anything."

"Reverend, these peccaries you were talking about," Selena said, leaning in to inspect the Reverend's guidebook, "are they man-eaters?" She was a vision in chartreuse today, down to the pale green nail color on her fingernails.

The Reverend consulted his literature. "Infrequently, I believe."

"Then my money's on the Reverend's pigs." She bussed her husband's cheek affectionately, rubbing away the excess lipstick with her finger. "It's hard enough to get a good night's sleep around here as it is without worrying about prowlers and God knows what else. I thought we'd left all that behind us at home."

"Has anyone seen Catherine this morning?" Buck asked abruptly. The talk about prowlers was starting to make him nervous.

"She never takes her meals with us because of the—" the Reverend pantomimed in front of his face "—you know."

"Earle might know where she is." Selena nodded toward a pale, thin man who squinted myopically at them as he entered the room. "He's usually asking her something or other about the area. I've never seen a man with so many questions in all my life."

Reverend Woolsey beckoned Earle to join them. "Earle's a photojournalist," he said, making the introductions. "From Canada."

Earle nodded, combing a swath of lank blond hair out of his eyes. "Quebec, actually."

"I thought I heard a bit of an accent," Buck said dryly, shaking his hand.

"We're a regular United Nations." The Reverend beamed. "Earle's doing a photo essay on the Amazon. A last-frontier perspective, as I understand it."

Earle nodded, pulling a pair of wire-rimmed glasses from his shirt pocket and adjusting them on the end of his sharp nose. "I hope to have most of the lens work finished by early next month. That is, if Catherine can spare a little more time to show me around the area." He tapped the crystal face of his watch with one finger. "Actually, I'm supposed to meet her out at the lagoon this morning. I'm already late."

"I wouldn't mind seeing some of the country myself," Buck said, getting to his feet. What he really wanted to see was Catherine. After all this talk about prowlers, he had a gnawing urge to prove to himself that she was all right. "Care for some company?"

"Sure." Earle was already walking toward the door. "I'll just get my gear."

"Notice any unusual activity around the compound late last night, Godot?" Frank barked after him, ignoring the exasperated sound Selena made at the question.

Earle stopped, regarding him suspiciously. "Unusual? Activity? Last night?"

"Around the compound."

"Why, no," he said. "I was pretty tired yesterday. Went to bed right after supper. Overslept, in fact. That's why I'm running late now. I've probably missed all the best light." He disappeared through the door, Buck grimly in tow.

They stopped briefly at Earle's cabin to pick up a plethora of camera equipment, Earle waving off Buck's offer to help him carry it. Instead, he looped several cameras around his neck, wedged a tripod under one arm, a bag with miscellaneous fixtures under the other, and then led Buck toward a small path that ran behind the main lodge. The path continued past several small storage huts before it plunged into the jungle.

It was cooler beneath the trees. The little sunlight that pierced the thick, leafy canopy dappled the trail with strange configurations. They moved in and out of shadow, Earle in the lead, his head rolling from side to side as he examined every foot of the jungle they passed with fierce, professional concentration.

Buck followed him at a discreet distance, conducting his own survey of the area. It was entirely possible that his informant was staying somewhere out here, close enough to the lodge to keep Buck under surveillance, far enough away to keep his own presence hidden. He might even be the prowler Frank Wheeler thought he'd spotted last night. It was going to be nearly impossible to find him, Buck realized, his eyes sweeping up the trunk of one enormous tree, its upper branches supporting a second story of sinuous vines, mottled fungi and hanging vegetation. The jungle could swallow a man whole.

"Problems?"

Earle had stopped to rifle through his camera bag. "I've left a lens at the cabin," he said, looking back down the trail, his expression that of a man getting reacquainted with an old enemy. "I'll have to return for it. Will you tell Catherine I'll be late?"

Buck shrugged. "Sure."

"You can't miss the lagoon," Earle said. "Just don't leave the trail."

Buck eyed the living, breathing walls that rose around him as Earle walked away. What had Carlos called the jungle yesterday? *El infierno verde?* The green hell?

He glanced over his shoulder, then walked on into the belly of the beast.

Chapter Three

Earle was late.

Catherine dropped her knapsack on the narrow dock and scanned the peaceful waters of the lagoon, hoping that the rowboat at the far end of the lake contained the Canadian photographer. It didn't. Even at this distance, she recognized Enrique's wide-brimmed straw hat and, a second later, the cast of his fishing pole as he tried for the panfish that would become tonight's main course. Earle had kept her waiting again.

With an exasperated sigh, she dropped down beside her pack, resting her weight on her elbows as she stretched her long legs out over the end of the dock. Idly, she followed the flight of a lone black vulture, tipping her head back to bask in the sun's rays when the bird was finally out of sight. The lightweight opaque fabric of the veil molded itself to her nose, mouth and throat as she breathed, the musky perfume of the cloth mixing with the lush scent of the jungle.

She'd gotten used to the restrictions of the veil a long time ago. She hadn't had much choice, really. She'd absolutely refused to consider plastic surgery to alter her features when she'd gone into hiding, and the hot, wet climate of the Amazon made concealing her face behind a thick cover of cosmetics unthinkable. The veil was an alternative she could live with. Even the tourists seemed to like it. She knew many of them chose to patronize her lodge rather than any of the others in the area simply because they wanted to see the mysterious veiled lady. It added to her mystique. And it certainly added to her business.

She flexed one leg slowly, then the other, before drawing them up to her chin and wrapping her arms around them as she contemplated the far shore. There were other advantages to wearing the veil. Somehow, the impermanence of it kept her sane.

A familiar fist of regret began to beat in time with her heart. She was dead. She had seen to that. David Crane's accidental death, her flight from California, the fire that destroyed the canyon house had effectively erased her.

Catherine strove to suppress the old ache, to silence the bleak replay of remorse before it overtook her. She blinked away her morbid thoughts long enough to register Buck's lazy smile.

"Communing with the spirits?" His eyes moved with excruciating slowness over her, lingering on her hair, her eyes, the fall of the veil. He might as well have caressed her, his look was so intimate, so potent.

Catherine scrambled to her feet, accepting his outstretched hand before she had a chance to think better of it. His fingers were warm and strong, and she released them as soon as she could, though the feel of him seemed to seep right through to her bones. "I was waiting for Earle," she said, breathless. "I wanted to show him some of the hummingbirds in the area this morning."

"Earle had to go back to his cabin to pick up some camera equipment he forgot. He should be along in a little while. Will I do in the meantime?"

Catherine's heartbeat raced outrageously at the suggestion. "Why don't we skip the birds," she suggested, surprised that her voice could sound so normal. "Are you up for a trip on the lagoon?"

"Why not?" Buck bent down to examine the weathered old rowboat tied to the dock. "Is this thing seaworthy?"

"Absolutely." Catherine swung her knapsack into the boat and slid gracefully in after it.

After a moment's hesitation, Buck followed her, feigning a look of alarm as the boat rocked wildly. "This is one of the reasons I never joined the navy," he joked, clutching the side. He dropped the act, reaching over to take the oar from her. "I'll do the driving."

His playful mood was infectious. She leaned back, laughing. "I knew I should have checked my accident insurance this morning."

He flashed her a smile, looking boyish as two dimples cut into his cheeks. His eyes gleamed with mischief as he dipped the oars into the water. The lake was like a bed of smoky glass, and their passage barely scratched the surface. In the distance, Enrique still fished, pulling and casting his rod in soporific rhythm. Everything else around them seemed to be holding its breath, as though the world was waiting on them. In the expectant hush, Catherine fought the feeling that they were the last people on earth.

Suddenly, the bushes on the bank behind them exploded in a frenzy of green and brown as several awkward, lumpy birds took wing. They landed almost immediately in the branches of a low tree, blowing and hissing their displeasure at being disturbed.

"Hoatzins," Catherine explained, one finger drawing their long, frizzled crests in the air. "They're probably the most prehistoric-looking birds you'll ever see."

"I had a drill sergeant once who looked like that. I wonder if there's any relation?"

Laughter bubbled from her. "Don't you take anything seriously?"

The muscles in his forearms rippled as he swept the oars back. "Sure. Life, family, all the things people are supposed to." The oars reached smoothly toward her, then away. "I used to take my career seriously, too. Once upon a time." A muscle worked in his jaw as he bit back whatever else he had intended to say.

Catherine rested one palm lightly on the surface of the water as they glided on. "What did you do in the military?"

The oars faltered as Buck considered her question. It took him a moment to pick up the rhythm again. "I was an engineer." His mouth twisted around the word as though he hated what he was telling her.

"Did you enjoy it?"

"At first."

"And then?"

"Then it turned into a job." Buck let the oars drop, resting his hands high up on his thighs, his eyes narrowed against the glare of the sun. "I was pretty idealistic when I joined up. Just out of high school, still wet behind the ears. I think I'd have draped myself in the flag if they'd have let me." He turned over one of his hands, studying the lines that crisscrossed the palm. "My father was an army surgeon. I got more war stories from him than fairy tales when I was growing up. Maybe that's where I went wrong. I turned the army into a fantasy world, when it's no better than any other way of life. No better. Sometimes worse." The last words were edged with a bitterness he couldn't conceal.

"But you stuck it out."

"Sure. It was all I knew. Besides, I had a family to support."

The admission surprised her. "Had a family?"

"My wife and I divorced eight years ago. Hell of a thirtieth-birthday present. One day she decided she couldn't eat, drink and sleep the army anymore. Can't say I blamed her." Buck resumed his rowing. "My daughter lives in Nevada with her mother. I see her whenever I can and talk to her often."

"You must be very close," Catherine said wistfully. Marriage and children were two things she had crossed off her list long ago. "How old is she—your daughter?"

"She turned nine in January. The last time we spoke, she told me she wanted to be an astronaut when she grew up." His grin flashed. "Next month that will probably change to president." He regarded her intently. "Do you have any children?"

"No." She changed the subject before he could ask any more personal questions. "So what are your plans now that you've retired?"

He suddenly refused to meet her eyes. "This and that. I haven't really made up my mind yet." His infectious smile returned. "Does every guest get to cry on your shoulder, or am I just the lucky one?"

She skimmed her fingers across the water, arching her brow in mock disdain. "I counsel whomever's in the hot seat." She jerked a thumb over her shoulder at the shore. "Normally, it would be Earle."

He fell back, laughing. "I'm crushed."

Their eyes locked and, for a moment, they shared an emotion so powerful it left Catherine drained and aching for more. She looked away first, flustered, unsure of how to deal with the sensations Buck aroused in her, yet certain she had to deal with them in some way. The situation was impossible. She knew that; Buck didn't. It was up to her to put them back on a more formal footing, but her resolve faltered every time he looked at her.

"You like running the lodge, don't you?"

"I like people. This is one way I can still be a part of their lives."

"Because of your disability."

Obviously he assumed, like everybody else, that she was hiding terrible facial scars or the ravages of some disfiguring disease. Regretfully, she let the assumption pass. "Yes."

Buck reached up and ran his fingers lightly across the edge of the veil, stopping as she flinched. "Does it still hurt?" His voice was as gentle as a kiss.

Pain flared through her as she addressed the years-old ache that clutched her heart. "Sometimes." This had to stop. They were starting to tread on dangerous ground again. She tried wildly to think of some other topic of conversation, but he anticipated her and gave her a chance to catch her breath.

"How long have you operated the lodge?"

This was better. "Five years. My uncle Rudy and I opened up right after the craze for ecotourism started. People seem to want more than white sand and bikinis nowadays. We give them an alternative. Uncle Rudy's health started to fail a few years ago so now he's more like a silent partner."

"Why Peru?"

"My mother was born in Lima. She fell in love with my father when she was an exchange student in the United States." Warmth flooded through her as she remembered. Maria and Neil Taylor's love affair had been the topic of many long, delightful family conversations. "They married as soon as she graduated. My mother's father was American, too, so really I'm only a quarter Spanish. We still keep a home on the coast near Lima, though." She hadn't been there in years.

"Hello!"

They both jerked at the sound of the real world intruding on them.

"Earle." Catherine waved limply at the photographer, who was gesturing from the dock. Right now, giving Earle Godot another lesson in ornithology was the last thing on her mind.

Buck seemed to share her regret. "His pictures had better be worth it," he said, grunting as he began to pull powerfully for shore.

CATHERINE PUSHED BACK her supper tray, most of the food on it untouched. She despised eating alone in her cabin. It was really the only time she felt like a true pariah—banished to her room whenever the rest of the guests ate communally. Still, the limitations of the veil prevented her from joining them.

She picked up the soup spoon and forced herself to swallow several more mouthfuls of the broth before she gave up, dropping her spoon back into the bowl. Enrique was using too much coriander in the soup again. She'd have to speak to him about it in the morning. She covered the tray with her napkin, got up from the table and walked over to the bed. Sleep was what she really wanted, lots and lots of sleep.

Last night had been brutal. She'd tossed for more than an hour before finally getting up to go over to the main lodge to work on the accounts. Even then, the mind-numbing nature of the math hadn't relaxed her. She'd been wired, her mind returning again and again to the lipstick message left for her on her mirror. She'd half expected to see another just like it in the bathroom when she returned this afternoon from her walk with Earle, but, thankfully, the mirror had been clean.

She massaged her temples, slowly starting to unwind. She felt exhausted now, more than anything else. At least the debilitating fear she'd first experienced last night was gone. Buck probably had a lot to do with that. He had the disturbing ability to drive nearly every coherent thought out of her head. And that included the uneasiness she had about the message and the intentions of whoever might have sent it.

What was it about Buck that could affect her so profoundly? Was it his ready smile? Or the way he could make her laugh, no matter how hard she tried to stay serious? Or was it because, after five years of hiding behind a veil, he made her feel like a woman again?

A knock on the door made her jump.

"Just a minute," she called out, reaching for the veil she'd laid across the headboard.

"It's only me. Tony." The big man pushed open the door a few inches, his face grim. "I think you'd better come up to the lodge. We've got problems."

On the way, Tony briefed her, and by the time they reached the dining room, her guests had already assembled. All but Frank Wheeler. Selena broke off her agitated conversation with Buck as soon as the screen door slammed, half rising from her chair as Catherine approached her. Her face was pale beneath her tan.

"How long has he been gone?" Catherine asked, leading her back to the table. She motioned discreetly to Jorge, who was hovering in the background, and he disappeared into the kitchen, returning a moment later with a pot of hot coffee.

Selena waved away the cup Jorge offered her. "He said he was going out for a walk right after breakfast. That was hours ago. When he didn't come back, I thought he might have gone out to the lagoon. You know how that man loves to fish."

Catherine turned to question Enrique, but Buck forestalled her. "He says he hasn't seen him."

"Does anyone know if Frank took a flashlight with him?" Catherine asked, foreboding edging along her nerves as she glanced toward the windows. It had been dark for at least an hour. Sunset came early in the tropics, bringing about a terrifying change in the jungle. The familiar became unfamiliar, the innocent potentially lethal. She shuddered at the thought of Frank blundering blindly through an area like the swamp forest at this time of night. One wrong move could mean the difference between life and death.

"I was in the supply hut this afternoon," Reverend Woolsey spoke up from his seat at the end of the table. "I was thinking of taking an evening stroll myself and I wanted to stock up on a few things. None of the flashlights were gone then.''

"If Frank is out there, unequipped, then he'll probably have enough presence of mind to stay put," Buck said, pushing back his chair. "He doesn't seem to me to be the type of man to take a lot of unnecessary risks." Selena relaxed visibly at his words but the tight coil of concern in his own belly remained. Frank's choice of survival equipment, or lack thereof, wasn't the problem. It was the possibility that the retired cop had somehow stumbled onto Buck's informant out in the jungle that worried him. "If we formed teams we could probably cover the whole area in time—"

"—in time for Frank to enjoy one of Jorge's famous nightcaps before we all go to bed," Catherine said before he could voice what she was already thinking. He gave her a brief nod that showed her he was aware of what she was doing. There was no sense in alarming Selena any more than she already was.

"I've done some orienteering." Earle raised one finger. "I'll be glad to help."

Catherine nodded. "Good. We'll also need someone back at the lodge in case Frank comes in on his own."

"Selena and I will stay," the Reverend volunteered.

"I'll get some of the high-powered flashlights from the supply hut," Tony said, "and the walkie-talkies."

"It might be a good idea to round up a few first-aid kits, too," Buck suggested softly, taking Catherine's arm and drawing her aside so that Selena wouldn't overhear him. "Frank could be hurt."

"You're right," she murmured, momentarily distracted by the light blue flecks she'd discovered in his stone-gray eyes. He'd cut himself shaving, too, she noticed, as her hand came up of its own volition. Shocked, she stopped herself before she could press her fingers against the small cut on his chin. Instead, she smoothed the veil over her throat, the silky fabric poor consolation for what she imagined would be the bristly warmth of his face.

"Catherine?" Tony had been partway out the door before he reversed his course. "Is there something else?" His eyes jerked back and forth between them as he absorbed every detail.

He's in love with her, Buck realized. He wondered if Catherine knew. And if she did, if she cared for him, too. For some reason, the thought burned through him.

"First-aid kits," he repeated for Tony's benefit. "In case Frank's been hurt. He mentioned something this morning about seeing a prowler lurking around the compound last night. I don't think Selena's thought of it yet, but there could be a connection."

Catherine pulled away from him abruptly, fear surging through her. "A prowler? Why wasn't I told about this?" She threw a questioning glance at Tony. *I'm watching you.* Had her mysterious caller been outside her cabin last night while she slept?

"I didn't know anything about it, either." Tony exchanged a meaningful look with Catherine, shaking his head when she would have said something more. "Maybe we should talk about this later," he said in an undertone, his gaze flickering back to Buck.

Buck watched the exchange through narrowed eyes. What had just happened here? He was under the impression he had missed something vital.

"Jorge and I will check along the river if you and Godot want to hike out toward the lagoon," Tony said, looking to Catherine for confirmation as he broke them into teams. At her okay, he turned back to Buck. "Can you and Enrique handle the trail through the swamp forest?" Issued like that, it sounded like a challenge.

Buck didn't waste words. "Sure."

"Then get your gear. We'll meet back here in ten minutes."

They assembled again in half that time, each team equipped with flashlights, water bottles, first-aid kits and knapsacks.

"I want you to have one of the walkie-talkies," Catherine told Buck, showing him how to work the radio. "I'll take the other. We only have one set. Tony has a starter pistol he can use to signal us if he and Jorge find anything."

Tony shoved the pistol into his belt. "Remember," he said. "One shot means we've found nothing. Two means we've found Frank and we require assistance. Three means we've found Frank and we're returning to the lodge. Rendezvous back here in an hour, regardless."

It couldn't have been simpler than that.

Tony and Jorge had already left for the rough hike to the river, and Selena and the Reverend had disappeared into the main lodge, when Catherine decided to switch Buck and Enrique over to the lagoon trail. "It will be easier for you," she told Buck. "Earle and I can take the trail through the swamp. He's a little more used to the terrain around here."

Buck's smile was easy. "I'm sure my body will thank you in the morning."

"Do you have any other questions? It's not going to be easy out there this time of night."

"Worried about me?" He'd meant to reassure her, trying for the same light-hearted tone they'd used with each other since his arrival, but somehow the question simmered with more emotion than he'd expected.

"Just be careful." The expression in those emerald eyes was impossible to decipher. In the smoky glow from the lighted torches that lined the path, her veil seemed to shimmer with its own internal fire.

He cleared his throat, patting the walkie-talkie slung over his shoulder while he reined in his senses. "Don't worry. I'll keep in touch."

Catherine watched him set off across the compound, Enrique the smaller shadow behind him. Just before he reached the trees, he looked back, as though he was fortifying himself with one more glimpse of her before he plunged into the jungle.

She drew a steadying breath after he disappeared, unsure of what they had just shared. Whatever it was, it was dangerous, and, coming on top of Frank Wheeler's disappearance, very, very distracting.

She tried for a little professional distance, handing Earle the knapsack and keeping the walkie-talkie for herself. "Ready?" she asked, testing the strength of her flashlight. It burned strong and steady.

Earle slipped the pack over his scrawny shoulders and snapped on his own flashlight. "Ready."

Then there was only the jungle and the night.

They moved down the trail in single file, Catherine in front, Earle close behind. It was like walking into a tomb, Catherine thought, only in this tomb, the dead were waking and rustling all around them. She recognized most of the night sounds. In fact, she could probably identify each katydid and tree frog they passed. But the darkness blunted the familiar. She found herself questioning every whine, every whisper. A crash somewhere behind her brought her head around. What had that been?

Nervously, Earle shone his flashlight back down the trail. "Tree branch?"

"Probably."

He nodded, his eyes continuing to work their way around the comforting edges of the high-powered flashlight beam. "Pretty big tree." A light film of perspiration covered his face.

He'd been affected by the graveyard mood of the jungle, too, Catherine realized. If they continued to tiptoe through the trees like this, Frank might not be the only one needing to be rescued.

The crackle of the walkie-talkie made them both jump. "Catherine?" Buck's voice was like a lifeline.

She punched the talk button on the side of the radio. "Here. What have you found?"

"Just mud and spiders. We've come about a quarter mile. Still no sign of Frank."

"Nothing here, either."

"How's Earle holding up?"

She glanced behind her. His face still looked a little waxy. "Pretty good," she improvised, giving him the benefit of the doubt. She had the distinct impression that what Buck really wanted to ask was how she was doing.

A long silence washed through the receiver, then Buck's voice came again. "I'll keep you posted." He sounded reluctant to end the conversation. Finally he cut her loose. "Out."

It was like being thrown back into a drowning pool.

They resumed walking, the path gradually growing narrower, the soil wetter and more sticky. In some places, they waded through it, the oily gray muck pulling hungrily at their rubber boots. At least they'd worn boots, Catherine thought with disgust, wrenching one foot free with a sickening smack. She'd hate to have been caught out here with sneakers.

She swung her light to one side of the trail where the trees loomed like bleached bones from the black surface of a hundred stagnant pools. "Swamp," she said over her shoulder to Earle. "We've never been through this part of the jungle yet on any of our day trips. You'd probably get quite a few good pictures out of all this."

"Uh-huh." Earle sounded as enthusiastic as she felt.

They were reaching the top of a small hill when Catherine's flashlight suddenly flickered and went out.

"What's wrong?" Earle came up beside her, turning his own light on her malfunctioning one. "Batteries?"

"No. These things were all charged up last week. I think it might be a loose connection somewhere." Catherine squinted, slamming the flashlight a few times against her palm. Her timeworn remedy for fixing mechanical failures worked as it always had: nothing happened. The flashlight was dead. Suddenly, Earle's light seemed horribly inadequate.

"Do we turn back?"

Catherine considered, then shook her head, rattling the flashlight back and forth in a vain attempt to reestablish the connection. "Let's try to manage on yours." If that proved impossible, they'd have to return to the lodge.

They changed positions to accommodate the diminished light, starting down the hill just as the walkie-talkie came to life.

"Catherine, are you there?"

She pounced on it, motioning Earle to move ahead of her while she followed. Maybe this nightmare was ending. "What have you found?"

"Cat prints. Big ones. Enrique thinks they might be jaguar." Buck's disembodied voice wrapped around her, blunting the serious implication of his words.

Catherine's throat went dry. "My God. You don't think Frank—" The circle of light before her veered sharply and she almost lost her footing. "Take it easy, Earle," she whispered.

Earle whispered back out of the corner of his mouth. "I thought I saw something—over there—on the left."

They both stopped walking. Nothing showed now in the midnight void beside the trail. Earle slowly played his light over the trees in a wide arc. Just as the beam reached the bottom of the arc, something winked at them from the trees.

"There it is again!" Earle's voice raised an octave. "That flash! Did you see it?"

Catherine's senses tingled. "Get a little closer," she muttered, inching forward. "Slowly, Earle, slowly," she added as he lurched ahead.

They edged off the trail, Earle brandishing the flashlight like a weapon as they approached the source of the mysterious light.

"Buck, there's something strange—" Catherine began, groping for the walkie-talkie's transmit button. She flinched as a shot rang through the air, followed rapidly by a second, then a third.

Before she could say another word, the earth gave way.

"Buck!" She screamed his name once, dimly aware of Earle's high-pitched yelp, and then the tropical darkness flowed over her.

Chapter Four

"Catherine!" Buck jammed the walkie-talkie's transmit button down so hard he thought the case would crack. "Answer me, dammit! Catherine! Can you hear me?"

He heard what he thought was a faint cry through the receiver, then nothing. The silence shocked him with its finality. It was almost as though Catherine had never existed.

He whirled on Enrique. "How do we get over to the swamp trail from here?"

The young man's face was ashen in the glow from his flashlight. "We can't, Señor Buck, not from the lagoon. We must return to the main lodge first."

"Then we're going back to the main lodge—now!" Buck shouldered the radio and started back down the trail on a run, not bothering to check whether or not Enrique was following him. A hundred different images burned through him as he ran—gory, bloody images: Catherine stumbling innocently upon his informant in the jungle, Catherine struggling with the man before he whipped out a gun, or a knife, or a club, and—

His stride lengthened as his imagination leapt to even more grisly scenes, Catherine's horror and pain multiplying until he thought he would go mad.

"Which way?" Buck yelled as he came to a fork in the path. Without waiting for the cook's reply he took the more familiar right-hand trail, Enrique dropping farther and farther behind as his own speed increased.

Minutes later, the trail took a sharp bend and he blundered headlong into an enormous tree that had fallen across the path. He cursed as he got to his feet. He'd taken the wrong turn.

Chest heaving, he glared at the tree in disgust. *Slow down, mister,* he told himself grimly. *Think.* He would be no help at all to Catherine if he panicked.

By the time Enrique caught up with him, he had caught his breath and regained his senses. "I know, I know," he muttered, turning back. "Wrong path."

They plunged back the way they had come, following the bouncing balls of light thrown by their flashlights. It seemed an eternity before they reached the first fork in the trail. Several minutes later, they reached another. This time, Buck waited for Enrique to direct him.

"Left!" the cook gasped, his eyes rolling. "No, no—I mean right!" He sounded exhausted. Buck clapped him encouragingly on the shoulder before racing on.

By the time they burst into the compound, they were both bathed in sweat. Their sudden entry startled the group of people gathered around the steps to the main lodge. In the smoky light thrown by the torches, Buck vaguely registered Jorge, Tony, Reverend Woolsey and a very sheepish-looking Frank Wheeler with his short arms wrapped around his wife.

Tony frowned as they ran up to him. "Wheeler's all right. Didn't you hear the third shot?" He broke off as he caught a glimpse of Buck's face. "What's wrong?"

"Catherine," Buck said hoarsely. "At the last minute, she and Earle decided to check out the trail to the swamp forest while we took the one to the lagoon. I was talking to her on the radio when we were suddenly cut off. I think they could be in trouble."

Tony's eyes bulged. He whirled toward the path that led to the swamp forest, but before he could take more than a few lumbering steps, Catherine and Earle emerged like wraiths from the jungle.

Time stopped.

For a moment, all Buck could do was stare at her, his heart doing strange gymnastics in his chest. Then he leapt toward her, Tony a step behind him.

She was covered in mud. They both were. One sleeve of the cotton shirt she wore had been partially torn away, revealing a bloody scrape across her upper arm. A large bruise was already blackening on her temple.

Buck reached her first, drawing her gently to him. "What happened?"

Catherine grimaced, her head pounding from the contusion near her right eye. "We saw something flashing among the trees so we went off the main trail to take a look. One of the big trees had come down. We walked right into the hole it left when it fell." She shook her head in amazement, wincing at the effort. "I don't know how we missed it. It must have been at least three feet deep and triple that across."

Earle wiped his hand indelicately across his nose, trying to stem the weak end of a major nosebleed. His sodden shirtfront looked like it had absorbed most of the rest. He gratefully accepted the handkerchief Reverend Woolsey pulled from his pocket, clamping it to his face as he said, "I landed on da radio. Afder dad, we couldn'd dransmid."

"You scared the hell out of me," Buck muttered, feasting his eyes on Catherine. His hand came up to brush a lock of hair away from the scrape on her forehead. "You should have looked after this back on the trail." He glanced at Earle. "You had the first-aid kit, didn't you?"

Earle took a step backward. "She wouldn'd led me sdop," he whined nasally, still blotting his nose.

"I knew you'd be worried," Catherine murmured, giving in momentarily to his soothing touch. A quick glance at Tony's ferocious scowl was enough to bring her back to her senses. "I knew you'd all be worried," she amended hastily, addressing the rest of the group, "if we didn't show up. And I wanted to make sure that Frank was okay."

"Frankie's just fine," Selena assured her from the group's periphery. "He had a little run-in with the wildlife, that's all."

"I let the Reverend's peccaries get the best of me," Frank said, shaking his head. "I spotted a group of them right outside the compound after breakfast this morning and followed them for a good half mile down the river. I didn't know it then, but one of those jungle cats—"

"Jaguar." Reverend Woolsey supplied.

"One of your jaguars was getting an eyeful, too. We noticed each other about the same time. I took off, the cat took off, the pigs took off." Frank shrugged in embarrassment. "Finally found a safe spot halfway up a tree. But every time I tried to come down, the pigs came back. Ugliest-looking things I've ever seen. I figured I'd have to spend the night up there until these boys came by." He nodded toward Tony and Jorge.

"We practically had to pry him down," Tony growled, his black gaze measuring and remeasuring the distance between Buck and Catherine. Each time he came up with the same figure, his face seemed to grow darker.

"Thirty-five years on the force," Frank said, "and never took a bullet. Then I'm stopped cold by a coupla hams on the hoof."

"Let's finish this discussion in the morning," Buck said as Catherine swayed against him. "I think everyone's had just about enough excitement for tonight."

"Amen," the Reverend added. He turned to Earle, who was still clutching the bloody handkerchief to his face. "Need some help with that, son?"

"I should see that they're all settled," Catherine said weakly as the group began to break up.

"I think they'll manage without you for one night," Buck murmured, nodding toward the others. Frank and Selena had engaged Enrique and Jorge in an animated discussion on the steps to the main lodge, Frank pantomiming what was obviously his mad dash to safety. The Reverend was already leading Earle to his cabin. "Right now I want you to concentrate on two words: *bath* and *bed.*" Before Catherine could protest, he took her arm and began to lead her across the compound to her cabin.

"Now, just a minute," Tony began but she waved him away. They could talk in the morning. Right now, all she wanted to do was close her eyes and fall asleep.

At first, she wasn't sure that Tony had heard her, although after a moment's hesitation, he stepped back to let them pass. Even then, she could sense his anger and suspicion all the way to her room.

It took a moment for Buck to locate the candle on the bureau near the bed. It flared briefly when he finally put a match to it, then settled into a steady, golden flame. He returned for her then, easing her down on the alpaca spread. "Tell me where it hurts," he said softly.

"Everywhere," she groaned, mentally adding what she couldn't say to him. It hurt everywhere he didn't touch, every inch of her that he couldn't lay his hands on. She burned and froze in a thousand different places at once. "Ouch!" The bruise by her eye brought her back to reality.

"Do you have a first-aid kit here?"

"In the medicine chest."

He nodded, lighting another candle and disappearing with it into the other room. He was back instantly, his face grim. "What the hell's going on?"

Catherine snapped upright, her head spinning. He didn't have to say another word. She knew. The world rocked as she realized what had happened, what had stunned Buck. *He'd been here again. He'd left another message for her.*

She staggered to the bathroom, moaning when she saw the crimson letters scrawled across the mirror. This time he'd been more direct.

Will the dead stay dead?

The room pulsed. She would have collapsed if Buck hadn't been there beside her, catching her in his strong embrace as her legs suddenly gave out.

With a muffled oath, he swung her up and swiftly carried her back to the bed. She could barely breathe. She had no strength to fight the horror that clutched at her chest, no will to knock down the panic that filled her lungs. She'd been a fool yesterday when she thought she could shrug off the first message. Someone was out there waiting, watching. And what he knew, what he seemed intent on revealing, could destroy her.

"Stay there," Buck ordered. "Don't move. Don't even think. I'll be right back."

He strode out of the cabin, returning within minutes with a glass in one hand and a bottle of brandy in the other. "Drink this," he commanded, pouring out an inch of the amber liquid. He looked away while she brushed the veil aside and emptied the glass, gagging as the brandy hit her throat and stomach like a fist.

"More?"

"No, no." She sagged back against the pillow. "I'm all right." And she was, at least physically. Slowly, the room stopped spinning as the liquor worked its magic. Still, she kept her eyes clenched shut, afraid of what she'd see in Buck's face when she opened them, more afraid to face the truth in the bathroom mirror. *Will the dead stay dead?* What was she going to do about that?

The minutes dragged. Finally, Buck spoke, the quiet steel in his voice cutting through her mental defenses. "Catherine. Sit up. Please. We have to talk."

"Not now."

"Yes. Now."

Numbly, she obeyed him. Buck was right. She couldn't just pretend the message didn't exist. Neither could she pretend that Buck hadn't witnessed it, or her damning reaction to it. But she had no idea what she could tell him. The truth was out of the question.

"What's going on? Who wrote that? Why?"

"I don't know who wrote it," Catherine said slowly.

Buck's face darkened. "But you know why."

"Yes." The word was a whisper.

"Can you tell me?"

"No."

"Are you in danger? Can you tell me that much?"

Panic closed her throat for a moment. She finally succeeded in swallowing past it. "I don't know."

Buck drew an exasperated breath. Catherine looked as if she'd been whipped. The message on the mirror, coming on top of the escapade in the jungle, had drained her of every ounce of fire she possessed. He'd never seen a reaction like that to anything before. Whatever it meant, she was terrified to the point of paralysis.

He got off the bed and walked into the bathroom. Ignoring the enigmatic message on the mirror, he opened the medicine cabinet. The first-aid kit was on the bottom shelf. He took it out, then shook out a towel from the neat pile he found near the sink and moistened it with a little bottled water. What Catherine needed right now was some tender loving care. Maybe then she'd feel secure enough to confide in him.

Catherine watched him warily as he sat down beside her. He wasn't going to give up. She'd seen enough of him in action to know that Buck Jordan wasn't the type of man to admit defeat. The question was, what kind of opposition could she mount against him?

She flinched when he probed the gash on her shoulder, and his touch gentled. "This doesn't look too bad. I'll clean it and dress it. It probably won't even leave a scar. Just relax."

He waited until she had settled back against the pillow, her eyelids dropping closed, before he reached up and tore her shirt across the yoke, exposing the wound, the whole of her shoulder, and the graceful curve of her collarbone. Her skin was like cream.

"Just relax," he repeated as she quivered beneath his touch. He worked quickly, silently cursing the meager medical supplies he had to work with, the inadequate light and the tightness in his thighs that increased a hundredfold every time his fingers brushed her skin. In the golden glow from the candle, with the edge of her veil falling across her bare throat, she looked like forbidden fruit.

She drew back when he reached for her face, the fear flaring again in her eyes, but he merely explored the bruise near her temple, cleaning that, too, before snapping the first-aid kit shut. "How are you feeling now?"

"Better. A little tired."

He picked up the bottle of brandy and poured her another tall drink. "One more." He looked away again.

Catherine steeled herself for another bolt of fire. This time, it was easier to take than the first and she drained the glass. She sank back, exhausted, her blood humming.

"I want to help you."

There it was, his line of attack, when she least expected it. She said nothing, afraid if she opened her mouth she would give in to his demands. But right now, he was strength and she was weakness. There was nothing left in her to plumb. Maybe her survival depended on trusting him.

He seemed to recognize her weakening resolve. "Will you let me help you? Will you let someone else help you? Your family? I could call them."

She shook her head. "My parents died when I was a child. My grandparents are dead, too. All I have is my uncle Rudy."

"How can we contact him?"

"He's old. He's sick. This would kill him." Like it's killing me, she thought dully. "If he found out about the messages—"

"Messages?" His brows drew together. "There's been more than one?"

"I found the first one yesterday." She shuddered, thinking back to the scene with Tony in the bathroom. "It was written in lipstick, just like this one."

"What did it say?"

" 'I'm watching you.' "

He looked puzzled. "Are you sure it was intended for you?"

She laughed bitterly. "I'm sure."

"Does anyone else know you've received them?"

She hesitated. "Tony."

He glowered. "Do you trust him?"

She smiled to herself. "With my life." Something about the pained look that crossed his face at her words made her want to reassure him. "He's been with me a long time," she said. "He's like family."

Buck nodded. He'd have to be content with that, though her closeness to the surly manager rankled him. What was worse was knowing that Tony, of all people, was the one person at the lodge she felt she could trust with her secret. He ached to ask her what the messages meant but he had no intention of doing so. If she was hiding something, something about the lodge or about her past life in the States, then he had no right to insist that she tell him.

"Tony thinks one of the guests might be responsible."

"It's possible."

Catherine closed her eyes. The brandy was beginning to slow her words just as it had dulled the shock from the discovery in her bathroom. Or was it Buck who was having that effect on her? "One of them might have recognized me, might have known about the fire—" Her eyes popped open as she realized what she had just admitted to him.

He leaned over her, his hands pressing down into the bed on either side of her shoulders. "Do you trust me?" The unhurried timbre of his voice told her he knew he had the advantage. She was exhausted and beaten down. If he pressed her for information, she would have no choice but to capitulate.

She drank in the sight of him, his strong, quiet eyes, his dark hair and sensitive mouth. This close to him, the tiny scar on his lower lip was mesmerizing. "Yes, I trust you."

He smoothed down her eyelids. "Then go to sleep. We'll talk about this in the morning."

"Yes." She was dreaming before he withdrew his hand.

BUCK STOOD IN the darkness that enveloped Catherine's veranda for several minutes after leaving her, trying to talk himself out of his overwhelming compulsion to become involved in whatever was going on at the lodge. The lady had told him herself that she didn't want his help. Hell, he'd practically had to get her drunk before she revealed the little information that she had. And then the things she did say made no sense to him at all. Something about a fire? Something about one of the guests at the lodge recognizing her? He could fill a suitcase with what he didn't know. He could probably fill a boxcar with what he had no chance of finding out.

The situation was impossible.

For the umpteenth time that day, his senses throbbed with her image—the wide-set emerald eyes, the low, melodic voice. Fire and passion and pain. Pain more than anything else, he realized chillingly. Catherine was being eaten alive by something she would not, or could not, talk about. Something that had reached out of her past to leave ominous messages for her on her bathroom mirror. How much more would she endure before she turned to someone for help? What would it take before she accepted what he had offered her? Another message, more frightening this time? Another dark figure skulking around the compound, or creeping into her cabin, or worse?

Inwardly he groaned. His emotions were a mess, his priorities in even worse shape. He was in Peru to do a job, one job. No more, no less. Washington would put his butt in a sling if they found out his attention had wavered from the task at hand. Catherine's problem was her own. Maybe if he told himself that enough times, he'd start to believe it.

He dragged one hand across the back of his neck. What he needed right now was a cold shower and a stiff drink, not necessarily in that order. He was halfway down the steps when he saw one of the shadows that lined the boardwalk begin to glide toward the main lodge.

Buck rocked to a halt, every nerve twitching, his eyes locked on the black bulk that moved noiselessly, purposefully across the compound. The area was not as dark as it had been the night before. Someone, probably Tony, had left a few torches burning at strategic places near the jungle's edge to ward off another midnight visit by the Reverend's peccaries, although Buck was now convinced that the figure Frank Wheeler had seen was somehow connected to the messages on Catherine's mirror. The figure drifting across the compound moved close enough to one of the torches for Buck to fill in several details—the prowler was a man, a very nervous man, judging from the number of times he kept glancing over his shoulder. He seemed to be carrying something under his right arm.

Bending low, Buck moved swiftly down the steps, keeping the figure in sight as he ran across the patch of grass to the nearest cabin. Number ten. Earle Godot's. Buck's mind automatically recorded the information as he scanned the rest of the darkened cabins. Like Earle, everyone seemed to have gone to bed early. Everyone, that is, except the mysterious man ahead of him.

Buck rounded the front of the cabin, hugging the veranda as he closed the distance between himself and the prowler. As though he sensed he was being watched, the other man suddenly stopped and looked back. The black hole where his face should have been seemed to stare directly at Buck's hiding place. Buck flattened himself against the spindly wooden railing, cursing himself for being caught in such an awkward position, but the prowler seemed satisfied that he was alone. He resumed his steady pace toward the main lodge, cutting behind one of the empty cabins as he neared it.

There would never be a better chance than now to catch the dark figure. Buck sprinted across the grass, making for the front of the empty cabin. If he could beat the prowler to the veranda, he could take him down just as he rounded the side of the building. He registered the stealthy sound of footsteps as he neared the wall, counted three, then dove low and hard, catching the man at the knees and bringing him crashing down. They both fell heavily to the ground.

Buck rolled clear of the prowler before the other man could react, springing up to jam his knee in the man's kidneys while simultaneously jerking his head back. "Talk! Who are you and what do you want?"

"My neck, my neck! You're breaking my neck!"

"Reverend Woolsey?" Buck's soaring adrenaline took a sharp nosedive at the sound of the quavering voice. "What do you think you're doing out here at this time of night? I could have killed you!" He released the death hold he had on the Reverend and helped the man up. "I'm sorry. I saw someone walking across the compound and I thought— If I'd known it was you—" Buck winced as he pulled the man's shirt down over his lower back. The Reverend was bound to feel that one in the morning. "Are you all right?"

"I think so. That was quite a tackle, young man." Reverend Woolsey tried gamely to finger-comb his mane of white hair back into place but his hair, like his dignity, refused to comply. "I—humph—I seem to be a little winded by all of this."

Buck caught him as he swayed on his feet and steered him over to the steps. "Sit down for a few minutes. I'll get you a glass of water."

The Reverend waved him off. "No need, my boy. It will pass." He lifted one shoulder and then the other experimentally. "In fact, I'm starting to feel better already."

"What were you doing out here?" Buck demanded, noting with some relief that the Reverend's labored breathing was returning to normal. His foot hit something in the tall ferns next to the veranda and he bent down, groaning when he brought up one half of a broken dinner plate. "Don't tell me you were on your way to the kitchen again."

Reverend Woolsey nodded, sighing. "I feel foolish, especially after everything that's happened this evening. But I just couldn't seem to put Enrique's banana bread out of my mind."

"Would you do us both a favor, Reverend?" Buck asked, locating the other half of the plate and handing both pieces to Reverend Woolsey. "Next time you get the urge to raid the kitchen, would you bring a flashlight? I think it would be a lot easier on everybody's knees."

"Certainly, my boy, certainly." Reverend Woolsey pulled at his chin. "I'm not in any danger, am I? I mean, I'm out here almost every night. I don't know what I'd do if I suddenly came face-to-face with one of those animals." He glanced worriedly behind him as though expecting an imminent attack.

Buck clapped him on the shoulder. "You'll be fine." There were more monsters afoot in the jungle than the Reverend's peccaries. And Catherine was the one they seemed to be after.

"In that case..." The Reverend got to his feet slowly and started toward the main lodge. His appetite seemed to be the only thing that hadn't taken a beating that evening. He swung around again as a thought struck him. "How is Catherine? Recovered from her ordeal, I trust?"

"Just about."

"I'll check in on her in the morning," he said gently. "Good night."

Buck watched him melt into the darkness. A few minutes later he heard the squeak of the screen door to the dining room. Enrique's banana bread must be extraordinary if the Reverend could still eat after all this.

On impulse he jogged back to Catherine's cabin for a last look around. A preternatural hush had dropped over the compound. Even the ubiquitous insect noise seemed to have fallen silent. He draped himself over the deck chair beside Catherine's front door, prepared to wait out the Reverend's sojourn in the kitchen.

It took longer than he expected. Buck was fighting sleep by the time a shadowy figure left the dining room and walked across the compound to number twelve. The Reverend, Buck thought with weary resignation, judging by the way the figure was rubbing his neck.

He was sound asleep by the time the next shadow stirred and came away from the wall of the cabin next door.

Chapter Five

He took the bullet low in his belly.

The impact drove him back and down, searing his insides as though a fire had ignited in his gut. Another bullet tore into the wall above his head and he jerked sideways, choking on a wave of agony.

The next bullet would kill him.

Clamping one arm across the oozing wound in his stomach, he began to inch his way backward toward the door, leaving a black trail of blood behind him. The distance closed with excruciating slowness. Just as he reached the door, he glanced back. The gun materialized out of nowhere. He reared up, kicking at it with his last reserve of strength.

Buck lashed out, catching the woman who bent over him by the wrist and pulling her down on top of him before he realized where he was or what he was doing. By the time he recognized the emerald eyes and the delicate scent of her perfume, Catherine was already scrambling up out of the deck chair and the unexpected intimacy of the moment was lost. At least, that's what his mind told him. The hungry pull in his belly told him something altogether different.

"That must have been some dream!" Catherine's voice was a little unsteady as she straightened the edges of her veil.

Her movements were less graceful than usual, too, he noticed, watching her work the silk hem back into the collar of her shirt. Maybe he wasn't the only one affected by her tumble into his lap.

"I thought you were someone else." Buck looked around the sun-warmed compound to where Romeo and Julian squawked cheerfully from the branches of a nearby tree. "I thought I was somewhere else." Silently, he damned the dream. He should have known it would return, and return with a vengeance, once he agreed to take this assignment. "Don't tell me it's morning already?"

"You mean you've spent the whole night out here?"

He rolled out of the deck chair, groaning as his cramped muscles came to life. "I must have. I'm getting too old for this."

It was hardly an apt description, Catherine thought, taking a discreet but thorough inventory of him. His clothes were past redemption, indelibly creased by humidity and the obviously restless night he'd spent outside her door. The fine lines that radiated from the corners of his eyes were more pronounced as well, but he still exuded the same strength and vitality that had almost been her undoing the night before. And the effect his burgeoning beard had on her nerves was positively criminal. "You still haven't told me why you slept on my veranda."

"Just doing my duty, ma'am," Buck intoned gravely. "Actually, I spotted someone creeping between the cabins after I left you last night, so I did a little creeping of my own. I finally tackled him over by the main lodge. It turned out to be the Reverend on another cake run."

"No." She couldn't quite grasp what he was trying to say. "You can't mean—"

"I don't know who was more surprised," Buck said, rubbing the back of his neck reflectively, "him or me."

"No." Catherine tried desperately to swallow the gale of laughter that was building in her. "No."

"I think I left a little bit of both of us embedded in the grass."

It was no use. Catherine finally gave in to the absurdity of the situation, laughing until she collapsed in defeat against the door to the cabin. "Don't tell me my white knight has turned into a white elephant."

"Guilty as charged." Buck smiled at her. "That's better." He brought his hand up to brush a tendril of hair away from her forehead. The colorful bruise beside her eye had deepened to an ugly explosion of black and blue, but at least the haunted look in her eyes was gone this morning. "Did you sleep all right?"

"Like a baby." The words caught in her throat. "You should have taken some of your own medicine."

He laughed. "And miss out on all the excitement? Come to think of it, you're probably right. I should have never let you drink alone." Unexpectedly, his humorous tone died, along with the teasing glint in his eyes. "Can I make up for it this morning with a little conversation?"

Catherine went rigid. "That depends on the conversation."

They both knew what he was thinking. *Will the dead stay dead?* The words hovered between them as if they had been spoken aloud.

The inflexible lines of Catherine's slender body told Buck more eloquently than words just how nervous she was about sharing any more information with him. He was a fool to even ask, considering his own resolutions of the previous night. Why was helping her so important to him?

"We can talk about anything you want," he persisted. "Your choice. Or you can talk and I can listen."

Catherine's will wavered. She had erased all traces of the chilling message on her mirror as soon as she awoke, telling herself that she could deal with it alone. She had even composed a little speech to let Buck know that his offer to help her was appreciated but unnecessary. She couldn't think of a word now. Standing this close to him, seeing the look of concern on his face, had effectively wiped her mind clean.

"You can tell me as much or as little as you like. No pressure. No strings attached. I promise." Buck's voice was low and enticing. "Is it a deal?"

"Deal." The word was out of her mouth before she realized what she was saying. Before she could take it back, Buck had taken her hand in his, sealing their bargain with a warm, lingering touch that made her question who was in charge here—her head, or the traitorous pull of her emotions?

Reluctantly, Buck let her go. He'd convinced her. He could see that, although he didn't know for how long or for how much. The confusion in her eyes told him she was not certain why she had agreed to talk to him at all. He'd make sure he didn't betray her trust in him. Somehow, he sensed that trust was something Catherine had damned little of these days. A light breeze sprang up suddenly and he paused, sniffing suspiciously at his shirt. "Is that me or is the wind blowing from the swamp this morning?"

Catherine cleared her throat delicately. "The swamp's in the other direction."

"I was afraid of that." Buck rolled his eyes. "I think I'd better squeeze in a shower and a shave before we hit the dining room. Will you save me a spot?"

"I'll make sure the coffee's hot and black." Catherine's voice warmed as he bounded off the edge of the veranda.

"And while you're at it, save me a piece of Enrique's famous banana bread," he called back over his shoulder. "I hear it's incredible."

She watched Buck disappear into his own cabin, then made her way to the dining room, already starting to question her own judgment. Had she really agreed to let Buck help her? Or had the blow to her head totally addled her senses? It must have affected her nervous system, too, she mused. It had been years since she'd felt this much at peace.

Or this hungry. If confession was good for the soul, then trust was obviously good for the appetite, judging by the healthy rumblings emanating from her stomach.

She was mentally loading a breakfast tray when she reached the main lodge. She paused in the doorway to the dining room, frowning when she saw the bare buffet table. Breakfast should have been laid out an hour ago. Where on earth were Jorge and Enrique?

She jerked at the sound of a crash from the next room, then followed a string of mumbled curses into the kitchen. It had always been her favorite room in the lodge. Nearly as wide as the dining room, it had a generous linoleum counter that ran along three walls and a butcher's block table she often used for her impromptu late evening meals. Above the counter, tiers of shelving supported a comfortable hodge-podge of dishes, utensils and pots and pans. Two ancient refrigerators and a couple of stoves stood side by side on the fourth wall next to the door to the pantry. All four appliances ran on kerosene and all four had been pushed away from the wall.

"This one, too," Tony said disgustedly, emerging from behind one of the stoves. Enrique threw his hands into the air and let out another round of colorful Spanish words, stopping in embarrassment as soon as he spied Catherine.

"Not another breakdown." Catherine fought back a rush of annoyance. "I thought you said they were fixed." They'd had some trouble recently with the kerosene feed to the stoves, not too surprising considering the age of the appliances and the harsh jungle conditions under which they operated. Tony's recent overhaul of all four in preparation for their new guests should have assured them of worry-free performance through to the end of the high season.

"Enrique and I had these things working perfectly," Tony insisted. "Now none of them will fire up."

She gasped. "The refrigerators, too? How long have they been shut down?" In the tropical heat, food would start to spoil almost immediately.

"Long enough. The fuel lines plugged up last night. I'm going to have to replace them with new parts this time."

"How long will that take?"

"That's not the point!" Tony's voice cracked as he slammed a fist into the kitchen counter.

Enrique skittered back in alarm, his eyes bulging with shock.

"Outside," Catherine said firmly. "Now." The cool control in her voice cut through Tony's blind rage. He sucked in a lungful of air and stalked through the swinging doors into the dining room, Catherine close on his heels.

Tony spun around as soon as the swinging doors closed behind him. From the sporadic sounds coming from the kitchen, Enrique had started to unpack the refrigerators. "You're not actually thinking of swallowing this mess." Tony shook with the effort to keep his voice low and his temper under control. "Don't you find this a little suspicious? All four major appliances breaking down at the same time?"

She started. "You mean you think it was deliberate? Why would anyone want to tamper with a couple of old stoves?"

"Maybe someone's trying to tell you something."

"That's the most ridiculous—"

"What happened last night between you and Jordan? I spotted him in a deck chair outside your door this morning."

She sighed. There it was, the real reason for Tony's unlikely rage in the kitchen. He was still smarting over the scene in the compound last night. "Buck was just concerned about me after my fall."

He said nothing, still staring at her.

She took a deep breath. She'd have to tell him the rest of it sometime, although she would have preferred doing it when he was in a better mood. "I found another message on my mirror." Catherine repeated it, the words still having the power to fill her with fear. "Obviously someone's traced me to Catherine Tremaine. I assume he or she also knows I was Catherine Taylor."

His change in attitude was instantaneous. "Then we've got to work fast."

She raised an eyebrow at his urgent tone. "What do you suggest?"

"Close the lodge, at least for a couple of months. We can use the broken appliances as an excuse to clear everybody out."

"A couple of months?" Her mouth dropped open. "Tony, we're expecting five new guests next week. And seven more the week after that." She began to pace the floor, irked that he could so casually suggest closing the lodge. "Besides, I've already spoken to a few of our high-season staff in Maldonado. They're expecting to start work out here as soon as we need them. I can't just close everything."

"You'll have to, at least until things cool down."

She rounded on him. "And what if things don't cool down? What if this lunatic doesn't decide to leave me alone?"

"Then we close up for good."

Catherine gasped. "Are you out of your mind? Do you know how hard I've worked—how hard *we've* worked—to make a go of this place?" She pressed the heels of her hands against her eyes, numb at the prospect of giving up the only life she'd been able to build for herself since leaving California. There had been nothing but jungle here five years ago. The Phoenix Lodge had risen up out of the wilderness, just as the person of Catherine Monroe had risen up out of the ashes of her past. Running the lodge gave her some semblance of living, of being. At least here she could pretend she had hope, a future—without that, she'd be nothing at all.

Clumsily, Tony pulled her hands away from her face, his face reddening as he attempted to comfort her. "Sure, we've put a lot into the lodge. We can put a lot more into another lodge, if we have to. Or a hotel, or a club. Anything you want. But if someone's discovered your real identity, then we've got to cut and run."

"Absolutely not." Catherine jerked away from him. "If I leave now, what kind of guarantee do I have that this nut won't track me down wherever I go? What do I do then? Run again? And again? I've been doing that all my life." She swallowed convulsively, dangerously close to tears. "I can't live like that anymore. Some days I wake up and I don't even know who I am."

Tony reached up for her, then dropped his big hands miserably to his sides. "I'm afraid for you," he admitted thickly, stumbling over the words. "If I thought you were in danger—if I thought someone was out to hurt you—" his hands clenched "—I'd bust 'em wide open."

"Then help me stay and face whoever is doing this to me," Catherine whispered. "I couldn't do that five years ago. Maybe I should have. Maybe we'd both have a real life now if I'd been able to face who I am. Don't you see, Tony? This is our chance. Whoever this guy is, whatever he wants, I'm not running. This time it's going to be different. It has to be. Maybe the three of us can—"

"Three? You want me to let your uncle know?" He stopped at the look in her eyes. "You don't mean Rudy, do you?" he asked slowly, suspiciously.

"No." Catherine hesitated. "Buck was with me when I found the second message. He knows I'm hiding something."

Tony looked as if he'd been shot. "Jordan . . . knows?"

"Only about the lipstick messages. He's agreed not to ask any more questions. I think I can trust him." She marveled at how easy that was to say.

"You think—" Tony gaped at her. "That's just the trouble, Catherine. You're not thinking. You say Jordan was with you when you found the second note? How convenient! Maybe he actually wrote it!"

She caught him by the sleeve before he could stomp back into the kitchen. "I have to know I can count on you, Tony." She spoke urgently. "Trust me on this one, please."

Tony seemed to be weighing her argument. Finally, he sighed loudly. "You know I do. But him," he said, jerking his head toward the compound, "I'm going to watch."

She smiled, relieved. Tony could be volatile, a wild card sometimes. She was often amazed that she had any control over him at all. But they had come through too much together for her ever to doubt that he had her best intentions at heart, despite the ferocious scowl he now wore.

"How long did you say it would take to get parts for the appliances?"

His murderous look lessened. "Three days, maybe four. I'll have to make a trip into Cuzco for that. Maldonado's got nothing."

"I think we'll all have to make the trip," Catherine said. "It's either that or feed the guests canned beans and overripe fruit for the next few days. Will you pass the word on to Jorge and Enrique that we'll be leaving? I'll radio Carlos to let him know that we'll need his boat."

"Do you want to break the news to our guests or should I?" Tony still looked as though news wasn't the only thing he wanted to break.

Catherine squeezed his hand. "I can't let you have all the fun. I'll talk to them when they come in for breakfast."

CUZCO LAY LIKE A RUBY set in the emerald arms of the Andean mountains. Though it was situated only a half-hour plane flight from the frontier jungle town of Puerto Maldonado, it always felt to Catherine as though she had traveled several thousand miles across several hundred years to land in some magical, mythical kingdom.

Llamas jostled for space on the roads with mini-vans, ancient Incan stonework abutted colonial arcades, colorful ponchos clashed with T-shirts and blue jeans. And over everything lay a patina of grime and gilt.

Catherine woke early the morning after their arrival and took a quick shower. She'd arranged a major sight-seeing excursion for Buck, the Reverend and the Wheelers and she was anxious to get on with it. They had a lot of ground to cover.

Earle had elected to stay behind with Jorge and Enrique at the lodge, explaining that his tight schedule did not allow for any side trips. Reluctantly, she had left him there, a whisper of doubt going through her as she did so. If Earle was responsible for leaving the messages, she might be playing right into his hands by leaving him unattended at the lodge. Tony had obviously thought so, too, giving Enrique strict instructions to stay with Earle every moment they were gone.

It was all moot now. She finished toweling herself dry and dressed in a long-sleeved cotton shirt and matching cream-colored pants. At eleven thousand feet above sea level, Cuzco was much cooler than the jungle, though the high altitude produced its own set of problems. She'd cautioned the Wheelers and Reverend Woolsey to drink plenty of the local *mate de coca* until they were used to the thinner air. It was a piece of advice she'd have to take herself, she realized, as she checked her veil, locked the door to the hotel room and started slowly up a narrow flight of stairs to the Wheelers' room. Even that little exertion had her heart pumping.

"Don't bother knocking. I've already tried. There's nobody home."

Catherine whirled around, her hand still raised to the Wheelers' door. Buck rested casually against the opposite wall, lean and dangerous in the dim light thrown from the bare bulb in the ceiling. He was wearing a faded pair of jeans and a matching denim shirt with the sleeves rolled up above his muscular forearms.

"Were you waiting for them to get back?" she asked, taking another quick breath. The air seemed to have gotten much thinner in the time it had taken to register his presence. And a lot warmer. Where had she gotten the ridiculous idea that Cuzco would be cooler than the jungle?

He pushed himself away from the wall, advancing on her slowly. "Actually I was waiting for you."

Her palms grew moist as he stopped within inches of her, his gaze raking her eyes and her hair. If he would have touched her at that moment, she would have screamed with release.

He held her there with his presence for another agonizing second before he put a little more distance between them. "I figured you'd be up early to gather the troops together for a communal breakfast."

She swallowed, adopting the same casual tone with more than a little difficulty. "You were right. I thought you might like to try the new restaurant in the lobby."

"There's a better one in the main square."

She raised an eyebrow skeptically. "Really?" Where was all this leading?

"Checked it out myself earlier this morning." He took her elbow and began to steer her down the stairs. "Table for two right by the window. If we go now, we can still order the rolls they're so famous for."

"What about the Wheelers? And Reverend Woolsey?"

"Let them get their own buns."

She frowned. They'd already reached the heavy main doors that led to the street. "You know I don't eat in public—"

"Humor me. I need to talk to you. I can't do it with the others around." Buck dropped the lazy tone that had produced such a heat wave in her. His grim voice did just the opposite now, chilling her beyond measure. "You're in danger. I think someone may be trying to hurt you."

Catherine went limp. "What are you talking about?"

"Come on. I can explain it much better sitting down." Buck led her across the narrow street in front of the hotel and through the Plaza de Armas to a tiny, colonnaded café on the far side of the enormous main square.

The small restaurant was crowded with tourists, but he managed to snag a table against one of the windows that overlooked the square, dragging his chair close to hers to block out most of the curious looks the other patrons cast their way.

While they waited for Buck's coffee, he drew something from the pocket of his shirt. "I took a quick tour of the swamp trail yesterday while you were organizing this trip," he said. "I went all the way out to the fallen tree you mentioned. This was hammered into the tree beside it." He laid the small half-moon faceup on the table.

Catherine blinked. The object blinked back at her. "It's a hand mirror," she said tonelessly, reaching for it. She jerked back as blood bloomed instantly at the base of her thumb. "Ouch!"

"Careful," Buck said gently, taking her hand and pressing his napkin into the small cut. "The mirror looks like it's been broken from a larger piece."

"I don't understand."

"That's the source of your mysterious light," Buck explained, frowning. "It was set up at such a height and at such an angle that it would reflect whatever light hit its surface. I came back out to the site later in the day and tried it with a flashlight. Even a casual sweep of the beam reflected enough light to catch my attention. In the middle of the night, it must have looked like a beacon." The cut on her thumb had stopped bleeding. He continued to stare at it, his fingers lightly massaging the sensitive area of her inner wrist, before abruptly releasing her hand. "Somebody deliberately lured you off the trail."

"Why?" She shook her head in confusion. "So that we would fall into the depression left by that fallen tree? So that I would hurt my head and Earle would break his glasses? It doesn't make any sense."

Buck's coffee had arrived. He kept quiet until the waitress was out of earshot before he said, "There's more. The pit you fell into was at least three feet deep—"

"It was a big tree. Sometimes the root systems can be extensive."

"—but I think it was going to get a lot deeper. The roots left in the hole hadn't been snapped off, as they normally would be when a tree that size falls. They were sheared off." He let the implications of his words sink in. "By a shovel. I found a few spade marks in some soft dirt. Someone was digging a pretty big tiger trap out there in your swamp— only *you* were going to be the prize."

Her body went numb. "But—but how could he, or she, know I was going to be out there that night?" She struggled to throw up a dozen different roadblocks to Buck's logic. Anything was better than accepting the fact that someone was trying to physically harm her.

"He—or she—didn't. That's why the pit was still only half-finished. Whoever it was must have put up the mirror to see how closely it needed to be aligned, then forgot to take it down. Your coming out there that night was purely coincidental."

Each of his words was like a blow. "You mean he was waiting for me to take one of the guests on an evening outing? Then he planned to set up the mirror and—"

"Yes."

"Yes," Catherine echoed dully, turning to stare out the window. An Indian peddler in the main square was arguing with her hawk-nosed customer over the price of a beaded camera strap. Obviously the price was too high. The man walked away, the woman throwing what looked to be a few choice insults after him.

Catherine swiveled back to face Buck. "You said that you looked around the area where Earle and I fell. Did you find anything else besides the mirror?"

He hesitated before reaching into his pocket and fishing out something else. Keeping his fingers closed around it, he brought his hand close to her face. "Tell me what you think," he said, opening his fingers. A small, brown cocoon rested delicately on his palm.

Catherine frowned, bending forward for a closer look. What was that smell? Abruptly, her eyes widened with recognition. "Frank's—"

"Cigar. At least the end of it. I found it lying beside the path near the pit." He dropped the cigar fragment next to the mirror. "It makes sense, I guess. You told me the other night that Tony suspected one of the guests at the lodge was responsible for terrorizing you. Frank Wheeler seems a likely candidate, especially after finding this."

"He could have used one of Selena's lipsticks to write the messages in my bathroom," Catherine speculated reluctantly. She couldn't believe she was talking like this. Three days ago she would have rejected out of hand the idea that someone at the lodge was stalking her. Now she actually suspected one of her guests of being a crazed lunatic out to hurt her. Wake up, she wanted to tell herself. This is nothing but a dream.

The cut on her thumb began to throb and she tucked it protectively beneath the fingers of her hand. Some dream. It was more like a nightmare.

"Of course, we're forgetting the obvious." Buck took a mouthful of coffee.

"Which is?"

"That someone planted the cigar butt to throw us off the trail, to make us suspect Frank and Selena. Or Frank could have dropped the cigar himself on one of his innocent little fishing forays."

"In other words, I have to suspect everyone. A minister from Ohio, a French-Canadian photographer." Her voice turned ironic. "A police officer and his wife." One meek, one myopic, the others law-abiding citizens. The nightmare was rapidly turning into a circus.

"They all had the opportunity to leave the second message on your mirror," he theorized. "Things were in quite an uproar when Frank went missing. Anyone could have slipped away to your cabin while we were getting organized. It would have only taken a minute. Do you have any idea who might have been in a position to write the first message?"

She shook her head. "Tony and I have already gone through that. It could have been any one of them."

His gaze slipped a little. "I don't want to step on any toes, but if I had to suspect someone at the lodge, it would be Tony."

"Funny, he said the same thing about you."

Buck laughed. "I gather I'm not one of his favorite people."

"Not since he found out that you know about the messages I've received. We talked about it this morning before he went out to check on the replacement parts for the appliances."

"I think he took a disliking to me long before that." Buck covered her hand, his gentle touch punctuating his words. "I don't think he likes the way I look at you."

"Which way is that?" she asked, her voice falling on the last word. It was starting again. The breathlessness. The pounding heart. Was there no wind in this city? No fresh air? Every time Buck came close to her, she lost the ability to breathe.

"'Scuse me, missy. Are you one of the locals? An Incan princess, maybe?" A tourist at the next table suddenly leaned in on them, hoisting a camera. "D'ya think I can get a coupla shots? The kids are never gonna believe this."

"Ask if we can take his, too, Billy." His wife prodded him in the back. "The boyfriend."

"Blossom wants to know—"

"This is a private conversation," Buck growled over his shoulder.

"It will only take a minute."

"I said no." Buck's tone turned lethal, its effect on Billy immediate. He shrank back as though he'd just come into contact with a very poisonous, very deadly scorpion. "We were going to offer her some money," he protested although his wife now had her purse locked to her generous bosom.

"Let's get out of here," Buck said, giving Billy and his better half another scorching look. He slapped a handful of Peruvian *intis* down on the table to cover the bill, pocketed the mirror and cigar fragment, then stepped between Catherine and the tourists at the next table, shielding her with his body as they began to weave their way to the door. Halfway across the room, he hesitated, his attention drawn to something at the far end of the restaurant.

Catherine followed his gaze, expecting to see either the Wheelers or Reverend Woolsey at one of the tables, but no one in the noisy, jovial throng looked familiar. "What is it?"

"Nothing. Just someone I used to know." His eyes had taken on a remote quality she couldn't remember seeing before. "Do you think you can make it back to the hotel? I'll catch up with you in a few minutes."

Catherine nodded. "I'll meet you in the lobby." Curious, she lingered in the doorway for a few minutes more, watching as he approached a tall, red-haired man leaning against a wall near the door to the kitchen. The man said a few words to him, and Buck looked back, a slight frown on his face when he noticed that she was still there.

Embarrassed that she'd been caught spying, she turned for the door, colliding with a man who was inadvertently barring her exit. He flattened himself against the wall so that she could pass, and she recognized him as the hawk-nosed man she'd watched earlier in the square.

"Excuse me." His English was flawless, his manner impeccably polite, but there was something about the way his eyes bored into her as she pushed past him that made her uneasy. When she reached the sidewalk arcade that bordered the main square she glanced back over her shoulder, her discomfort mounting when she saw that he was still staring at her. She checked for him again a minute later, casually stopping to inspect the rainbow of textiles the street vendors had strewn on mats beneath the arcade. He was standing in front of an Indian shop several doors down, making a display of examining the pottery in the window. Somehow, she sensed his interest in the handicrafts was just as phony as hers was. He was following her. And she had absolutely no idea why.

For a moment she was tempted to return to the restaurant, but then she realized that that would mean going right past her pursuer and, for some reason, she dreaded getting that close to him again. Besides, there was no guarantee that Buck would still be there. But neither was she prepared to have the hawk-nosed man follow her right back to her hotel, if that was his intent. Forcing back a bolt of fear, she made herself go on, pausing to look at a sweater, a set of carved, wooden panpipes, a flapped woolen cap, all the while conscious of the man's stealthy progress.

When a mini-van roared up to the curb beside her, disgorging its load of chattering English tourists to the obvious delight of all the vendors in the arcade, she made her move, ducking into the unlighted interior of a small shop.

"Does this place have a back door?" she asked the old woman at the till. The shopkeeper motioned toward a small curtained opening in the far wall and Catherine darted through it, congratulating herself on her quick thinking when she emerged into the claustrophobic alleyway behind the store. She followed it gamely for several minutes, her apprehension gradually reasserting itself as she glanced up at the massive stones that made up the high walls on either side of her. The alley was more like a prison than a thoroughfare. She looked over her shoulder once more to reassure herself that she had given her shadow the slip and stumbled over a rough patch in the cobbled road.

Dear God. She forgot the rough road. She forgot the high walls. Her whole world suddenly shrank to the hawk-nosed man she'd spotted several yards behind her, and to the gun he had trained on her heart.

Chapter Six

Catherine's first impulse was to freeze, like a rabbit caught in the glare from a pair of headlights. Then she blinked. And bolted. A second later, she heard the big man behind her start to give chase.

It was like trying to outrace the devil, Catherine thought sickly. In a minute he had cut the distance between them to a half, and then to a third. She could almost feel his hot breath on her neck as she raced down the alleyway, the slap of his shoes like gunshots in her ears. At first, she ran serpentine, hoping wildly that he wouldn't be able to pull off a shot if she was dodging from side to side. She gave that up as soon as she realized she was wasting precious seconds. She risked a glance over her shoulder. For a big man, her pursuer moved fast. Her only hope lay in moving faster.

She lunged forward, panic lending her a burst of speed. Her pursuer stumbled as he tried to match her pace, and she slowly made up the distance she'd lost. But how long would that last? How long before her burning lungs gave out? How long before the stitch in her side slowly cut her in half? She had to get help and get it now.

She veered toward a small door set in the high wall, putting her shoulder to it frantically when she realized it was locked. Hawk-nose was only thirty yards behind her. Now twenty-five. Now twenty. Screaming her frustration, Catherine gave up, plunging back down the alley. She thought she glimpsed a curious face at one of the iron-grilled windows beside the door but she couldn't be sure and it was too late to run back and check.

Suddenly, a side street opened up on her left and she darted into it, realizing her mistake a fraction too late. The alley was connected to the street via a narrow flight of steps, and she crashed down them unceremoniously, landing heavily in a heap at the bottom.

Her right ankle twisted. She clamped her teeth around an agonized shriek, letting no more than a whisper of pain escape her lips. She'd broken the ankle, she knew it.

No, not broken, she decided as she staggered up, clutching the wall. But a bad sprain, anyway. Enough to slow her down. Enough to cut her chances against her pursuer to almost nothing.

She took a tentative step forward, then another, and another, falling into a half hop, half stumble down the street. It was empty, just as the alleyway had been. Had everyone in Cuzco vanished? She was beginning to feel like the last person on earth. She hobbled on grimly, cursing her throbbing foot. This was crazy. She would never outrun her pursuer like this. Even now she could hear him approaching from the alley. In a few seconds, he would round the corner and she would be his.

She strained toward another side street that suddenly materialized before her, reaching it just as Hawk-nose bounded out of the alley. *Help me,* she prayed silently as she pulled herself around the corner. *Don't let me die out here alone.*

As if in answer to her prayers, Cuzco came to life.

One minute she was totally isolated, the next she was bombarded by an ocean of humanity and a sea of aroma and color that made her wonder whether she was dreaming.

The market. Her mind clicked furiously as she waded into the bustling throng. She'd run right into one of Cuzco's sprawling outdoor markets. She swiveled around, spotting Hawk-nose just as he emerged from the side street.

He reacted more quickly than she had, stuffing the gun he carried into the waistband of his pants and pulling his shirt over it to conceal the bulge. His eyes met hers over the heads of the Indian merchants and he started toward her, his mouth twisting in a parody of speech—*I want to—*

She turned back frantically into the foray, missing the last words he tried to mouth at her. The man was a lunatic. Even here, he refused to give up the chase. At least he wouldn't try to shoot her, she thought thankfully, dodging a woman who balanced a tall tower of sweaters on her head. There were too many witnesses, too many bodies to intercept the bullets he, no doubt, still wanted to pump into her.

The market changed rapidly from a blessing to a curse as she pushed farther into it. The stalls were set no more than a few feet from one another and the empty spaces in between were crowded with large, heavy baskets and crates of surplus goods. The merchants, quickly recovering from the exotic picture she made, had obviously decided she was fair game, and no matter how hard she tried to shove past them, their sticky hands clung to her.

Catherine threw a quick glance over her shoulder. Hawk-nose was having the same problem she was, though his solution to it was much simpler: he barreled through the crowd, unmindful of how many feet he stepped on or how many outstretched hands he knocked aside. He was after blood.

Catherine spun around, recoiling at the meat cleaver that thudded into a haunch of beef inches from her nose. The stout woman behind the cleaver gave her a gap-toothed grin and drew her thick arm back for another blow.

This was madness. Suddenly, without warning, her ankle gave out. She cried out as she went down, then swallowed hard as she was buoyed back up to the surface of the crowd.

"Up you go." Buck's low, humor-filled voice was music to her ears as he set her back on her feet, his arms like two steel bands around her. "I thought I told you to go back to the hotel. I was on the other side of the square when I saw you dive into that little shop."

Catherine turned into him, pressing her face fiercely against the warm front pocket of his shirt. "There was a man following me."

Buck stiffened. "What man? Where?" His eyes narrowed as he scanned the shoppers around them. "Show me."

"There—" Catherine's voice died as she raised her hand to point out her pursuer. Hawk-nose was gone. "He was right there," she whispered, her eyes searching the crowd. "He followed me all the way from the restaurant. He had a gun. I thought he was going to kill me."

She trembled violently, and Buck caught her by the shoulders. "Don't worry. He's gone now. I want to get you back to the hotel."

Catherine stumbled as he began to lead her out of the market.

"What's wrong with your leg?"

"I fell down some stairs. I think I sprained my ankle."

"Then we'll make this quick and easy," he said, taking charge. Like a linebacker, he began to clear the way ahead of her, giving her his arm to lean against as he guided her through the maze of stalls and merchants. It took only a few more minutes before she was safely installed in her room.

Buck helped her into a chair, sliding a footstool beneath her injured leg. Then he knelt beside her and stripped off her shoe. The sight of her swollen, discolored ankle brought on a round of curses. "You ran down the street on this?" he demanded.

She winced. "It was either that or stick around to meet the goon who was chasing me."

"You said you thought he had a gun."

"He did have a gun!"

Buck put up one hand to calm her. "I'm not saying that he didn't. I'd just like to know why on earth he was after you." He shook his head over her ruined ankle. "I think you should see a doctor."

"No doctors!" Catherine shuddered. She had never gotten over her childhood distrust of the medical profession. "Can't you bandage it or something?"

"Or something. This is getting to be a habit," he muttered, going into the bathroom. He returned with a wet towel, giving her another dubious look as he wound it around her foot. "I'll see about getting you a support bandage after some of the swelling goes down."

"Thank you."

Buck sat back on his heels. "Did you recognize the man who was chasing you?"

"Not really."

One dark brow raised in question. "What does that mean?"

"I saw him outside the restaurant when we were talking. I'd never seen him before that."

"What did he look like? Maybe I'll remember him."

She thought back, shuddering. "Tall, heavy-set, black hair. I think he was Spanish. He had a hawk nose that made him look a little like a vulture."

Buck grunted. "Doesn't ring a bell. I was too busy trying to keep up with you to notice much else. You set a mean pace when you put your mind to it." His gaze turned speculative. "He obviously noticed you, though. He probably followed you all the way from the hotel."

Catherine tasted fear like a bitter pill on her tongue. "You mean I'm being watched here, too?"

"Seems possible. Whoever terrorized you back at the lodge might be trying to do the same thing in Cuzco." He straightened up and began to pace the room as he worked out a scenario. "Coincidence or not, we may have played right into Hawk-nose's hands by going over to the restaurant."

Catherine's eyes widened as she followed his line of reasoning. "If Reverend Woolsey and the Wheelers had been in their rooms—"

"Then you might have met them for breakfast instead of going out with me." Buck's pacing slowed to a thoughtful stroll. "Maybe one of them asked the other out for an early breakfast with the sole intention of leaving you alone today."

Catherine's skin crawled. "But what about you? Why didn't they lure you away, too?"

Buck bent down and lifted the towel off Catherine's foot, examining the swollen flesh. "I wasn't in my room. They might have just assumed I was already gone for the day." He risked a glance at her, wondering whether she'd ask about his absence that morning, or about the man she'd seen him talking to at the restaurant, but she was too absorbed in her own thoughts to pick up on it.

It was just as well, he thought wearily. He'd met briefly with his American contact, Jim Cochrane, in Cuzco that morning to try to get some more information from him about the whereabouts of his missing informant. He hadn't expected to see Jimmy again so soon. Obviously, Washington had some information they needed to pass on. He and Jimmy had arranged another meeting for that evening. If Catherine had been a little calmer, she might have started to ask her own questions and he would have had to lie to her. And lying to Catherine was one thing that was getting harder and harder to do.

Buck gently replaced the towel. "You know something."

"What?"

"You know something about these people," he repeated. "About why they're doing this to you. You have to tell me. I can't help you fight them any other way."

Her veil seemed to absorb all the color in her face. "I don't," she whispered.

"You do." Buck came down on his knees beside her, taking her by the shoulders. Her bones felt amazingly fragile beneath his fingers. "You may not know them, you may not know what they want out of all of this, but you do know why they're after you. 'Will the dead stay dead?'" he quoted from her bathroom mirror, his fingers tightening reassuringly as she jerked back. "You admitted to me in your cabin that night that you understood the message. Who died? Who might not stay dead? Were you involved? Was it someone you once knew?"

Catherine's eyes rolled shut. "I've never hurt anyone in my life," she said. It was a lie. She had hurt more people than she could count—the friends and co-workers she'd let mourn for her after Catherine Tremaine's "death"; the myriad of fans who had held candlelight vigils outside the burnt shell of the canyon house; and then there was David.

She choked at the memory. She had learned six months after the fire that Uncle Rudy had left David's body to burn when he'd torched the house. He had insisted that the investigators would need a body when they went through the ashes of the house, and David's had served that purpose. And she had said nothing, nothing when he had told her. He had been dead, after all. The memory was like a cinder in her mouth.

"Catherine?" Buck turned her face toward him. "Look at me." She had effectively shut him out. He never knew what she was thinking, what she was feeling, when she closed her eyes. The veil was like a wall between them.

Slowly, her eyelids raised. He sensed that the solution to more problems than he could imagine lay swimming just below the surface of her tears. "Don't cry. Please. I don't want to make you cry, but I have to know."

"I—I—" Catherine trembled violently, as the compulsion to confide fully in him roared through her. Two days ago, she had been willing to put her trust in him. But that was before the broken mirror in the swamp forest, before Hawk-nose in the alley, before the rebirth of all her fears. Two days knowing him, trusting him, could not compensate for a lifetime of running.

"I can't tell you," she said finally. Something inside her broke at the crushed look that came over Buck's face.

He drew away from her slowly, disappointment like a fist in his gut. She still didn't trust him, he realized. She still preferred to tackle this thing by herself. But the people who were terrorizing her were sick and they were very, very serious. She could be walking to her death.

His hands clenched. He had to get out of here. If he didn't, he'd lose what control he still had and force her to tell him what she was hiding. And force was the last thing he ever wanted to use on Catherine.

His fear for her and his disgust at himself turned his words into a growl. "I'll speak to someone at the main desk about sending up a bandage for your ankle. Meanwhile, if I were you, I'd keep off that foot." At least the sprain would keep her safely in the hotel, he rationalized as he turned and left the room.

She'd deserved that, Catherine berated herself angrily as the door closed behind him. What more had she expected? Buck had been amazingly patient so far. She'd been lucky to have him on her side. He'd been there when she needed someone after she'd discovered the second note and now, again, when he'd rescued her from the man in the market. But how long could she expect him to be her bodyguard without telling him who he was guarding or why? How long could she expect him to keep coming back when she kept pushing him away? If she had been Buck, she would have deserted herself a long time ago.

She sagged back on the bed, defeat claiming her. She was dead. Why not just admit it? She was facing a life sentence locked inside this empty, veiled shell, and nothing that Buck or her foolish heart could do would change that.

CUZCO DIDN'T SLEEP, Buck decided when he left the hotel later that evening. Either that, or the city ran in shifts, half the people living on the street during the day, the other half coming out in droves at midnight.

Dodging a tourist bus, he cut across the street and through the Plaza de Armas, heading for a narrow pedestrian alleyway on the northeast side of the square. Someone had strung up a loudspeaker system along a portion of the graceful colonial arcade that encircled the square, and the spirited Andean folk tunes that spilled from it followed him all the way up the alley.

He'd spent the entire day in his room, burning to go to Catherine but resigned to the fact that it would do no good. She was lost to him. At least, that's how it felt. The realization had gnawed at him for hours, until, finally, he had gone back to her room. But there'd been no answer when he pounded on her door, and he'd eventually left, frustrated. Even now, as he strode along the darkened streets through the old city, her eyes haunted him.

A small, neon sign on a building halfway up the street caught his attention and he loped toward it, recognizing the name of the bar from the brief conversation he'd had with his contact in the restaurant. Jimmy had said he'd find him at the back of the bar and, true to his word, the rawboned, red-haired ex-marine was right where he'd said he'd be, his back against the wall, one cowboy boot propped up on the chair beside him.

Buck took the empty chair across from him, scanning the room warily. In the murky light thrown by a few low-wattage light bulbs, the place looked almost deserted. He counted three conscious patrons scattered throughout the room and an undefined blob at a table near the window that was probably an unconscious fourth.

"Beer?" Jim Cochrane tipped back a bottle, his enormous Adam's apple working as he drained the last few inches of liquid.

"Why not."

"*¡Dos, aquí!*" Jim held up two fingers and motioned to the sleepy-eyed bartender behind the bar. "Any trouble finding the place?"

"No. I just followed the sound of your belches."

Jim snorted. "You don't sound so pretty yourself sometimes, buddy boy. Remember that little bar in Hamburg? We closed the place down, then opened it the next day and never even left our seats. I thought Herr Schmidt was going to lose it when he found us in the taproom."

"Yeah. I was a lot younger then." Buck waited for the bartender to slap down two bottles of beer before he continued. "What have you got for me?"

Jim leaned forward, shaking his head. "Not much. Washington got back to me just after we met this morning. As far as they know, the meeting's still on. They did get word that the informant was going to be a little late making the rendezvous. Sounds like he hit some kind of snag getting down here."

Buck frowned. "Sounds like something else is going on."

"You think our boy is playing games?"

"I don't know." Buck took a long swallow of beer. "It's not something I can put my finger on. I've got this gut feeling—"

"Go with the gut, boy." Jim nodded, encouragingly. "I've seen it get you out of a lot of tight spots before."

"The problem is, I don't know what it's trying to tell me. Something just doesn't add up—" He broke off, his eyes riveted on the woman he had just spotted leaving the bar.

From the back, she was like a willow, with a sweep of auburn hair that crackled like fire in the muted light. He was out of his chair and across the room before Jim could even react.

He whipped the woman around to look at him. "Cath—" Buck's throat closed. The eyes that met his were not emerald green, but midnight black.

"¿Señor?"

"I'm sorry. I thought—I thought you were someone else." Buck dropped his hand, backing away. This woman was nothing like Catherine. Was he starting to see her now, in every woman who came along?

"I could be anybody you want me to be, *señor*," the woman purred, interest animating her heavy face.

"Some other time." Buck made his way back to the table, the woman pouting with disappointment behind him.

"Looking for some female companionship, buddy boy?" Jim looked amused. "She's pretty, but let me warn you. They grow up real fast in some of the streets around here."

"Do me a favor," Buck said, suddenly coming to a decision. It was going to be impossible to get Catherine, and the danger she was in, out of his mind. Somehow, she was already part of him. He might as well accept that and worry about the consequences later. "Can you use your contacts back in the States to find out some background information on a couple of people for me?"

"Sure," Jim said, looking puzzled. "Does this have anything to do with the case?"

"No, it's a private matter." Buck borrowed a pen and a pad of paper from the man behind the bar and jotted down the names of the four guests staying at the lodge. His hand wavered as he hesitated over the fifth name and then, with a sinking feeling, he included it with the others he wanted Jim to investigate.

Jim's mouth moved silently as he read the list, frowning over the last name. "Catherine Monroe." He looked up at Buck. "Girl trouble? This doesn't have anything to do with the woman I saw you talking to this morning, does it?"

"Just find out whatever you can for me." Buck got up abruptly from the table. Suddenly the walls felt like they were closing in on him.

Jim threw up his hands in defense. "Just asking. You want me to get in touch with you as soon as I find out anything?"

"No, I'll contact you."

"Same as before?"

Buck nodded. "Thanks, Jimmy." He paused. "Say hello to Gloria and the kids for me, will you? Two little girls, right?"

Jim's freckled face creased into a huge grin. "Two girls and counting. Gloria's expecting again. I'm laying bets that it's a son this time."

"Congratulations. I've got a fiver that says it'll be another girl. I'm just sorry I won't be around to collect," Buck said as he pulled out a wad of *intis* to pay for the drinks.

Jim sighed good-naturedly. "Ah, well. Just as long as they're healthy and happy. That's what they say, isn't it?" He waved Buck's money away. "Keep it. My treat. Just remember you owe me a cold one the next time Washington puts us both back in the field."

"Right. Thanks."

"And, buddy boy..." Jim made a weapon out of his thumb and forefinger and cocked it in Buck's direction.

"What?"

"Watch your back."

It was his heart that needed watching, Buck thought grimly as he trudged back to the hotel. Somehow, the fine line between just wanting to help Catherine and wanting a whole lot more from her had started to dissolve. What was there about her that made his entire body ache whenever she wasn't around? What was there about a woman whose face he could never see and whose past he could never know that could tie his emotions into so many knots? It was like chasing a phantom.

She wouldn't be a phantom much longer, though. Not if Jimmy dug up some background on her. His footsteps dragged as he remembered the promise he had made to her back in the jungle. He'd told her he wouldn't pry, that he wouldn't make her tell him anything she didn't want to reveal. Tonight that promise had turned into just so much dust. A major-league headache settled in behind his eyes as he remembered the look of trust she had given him. He'd betrayed her, after all.

The loudspeaker in the main square was silent by the time he reached the Plaza de Armas. Instead, a blind musician with an unwieldy Andean harp had set up shop at the juncture of a small side street and the square. A crowd had gathered to listen to the haunting melodies he played, and Buck joined them. The music that drifted between his gnarled, stubby fingers only worsened the pain in Buck's head.

"What's he saying?" he asked a man next to him as the old musician began to sing.

"It is an old Quechuan folk song," the man explained. "This man, he sing about a woman. About her quiet eyes and her long, dark hair. About how she is stealing his heart from him."

The music played in Buck's head all the way back to the hotel. The tune had been impossibly forlorn, staying with him despite his best attempts to think of something else. If life imitated art, he thought as he threw himself down on the bed, then he was in for one hell of a ride.

A knock at the door brought him abruptly off the bed. "Who's there?"

"It's me."

He threw open the door. Catherine was waiting for him on the threshold, her body trembling slightly, but her voice calm and determined.

She took a deep breath, putting as much conviction behind the words as she could. "What do you want to know?"

Chapter Seven

For a moment, Buck had the horrible feeling that Catherine was talking about his meeting with Jim Cochrane, that somehow she had been in that dark, broken-down bar when he'd asked Jimmy to dig into her past.

Then he noticed the change in the way she held herself, the quiet determination in her eyes. Catherine had made a decision about something, and he was pretty sure he knew what it was.

"I hope I'm not bothering you," she said as she glanced around the room. She was relieved to see his bed hadn't been slept in, although the pillows were mashed against the headboard as though he'd lain there for hours, staring at the ceiling, unable to sleep. She dragged her gaze away before her imagination drew a more intimate picture of him. "It's after midnight. I didn't know whether you'd still be awake but I thought I'd take the chance and come up."

It wasn't the only chance she had decided to take tonight. She'd spent the day at war with herself. Half the time she'd wanted to dig a hole and crawl down into it, taking the secret of her past with her. The other half she had spent going over every word Buck had ever said to her, each look, every gentle touch. She was drowning in her past and there seemed to be nothing she could do to save herself. Maybe Buck was the answer.

"May I come in?"

"Please." Buck stood back, eyeing her ankle as she hobbled into the room. "Should you be walking on that?"

"It looks a lot worse than it is," she said, hesitating over which of the upholstered chairs to sit in. She finally chose the one farthest from the bed, conscious of the way he followed her progress all the way across the room. "Most of the swelling has already gone down. The bandage you sent up to my room helped."

"Glad to be of service."

She swallowed hard, noticing for the first time how dark the room was. There was only one lamp, and its soft glow barely reached into the corners. Across the room, Buck seemed painted in shadow. "I—I thought about what you said to me earlier. About your not being able to help me without knowing a little more about my past. You're right. I haven't been fair to you. I'll answer your questions now." She drew in a shaky breath. Her heart had started to pound as though she was running a race. Maybe she was. Maybe she was trying to outrun her own cowardice.

Buck stepped into the circle of light around her chair. "You don't have to do this."

"I do." Her chin shot out. She was determined to see this thing through, despite the tremors that shook her. "Where do you want me to start?"

He nodded, drawing up the other chair and reaching for her hand. "The messages you've received so far point to something that took place in your past. Do you have any idea what it could be?"

Catherine cleared her throat, concentrating on the warm, strong pressure of his fingers. "My house was destroyed by fire right before I left California five years ago. That's why I wear the veil."

His voice gentled. "You don't have to describe what happened to your face if it makes you uncomfortable."

He was still under the impression that she was scarred for life, Catherine realized. That, and her real identity, were parts of the story she could still not find the strength to tell him. "I left the country quite suddenly after the fire. I didn't tell anyone where I was going or what I was going to do. I just vanished. A lot of people—everyone I used to know, in fact—think I'm dead."

Buck's grip tightened on her hand. It was the only thing that betrayed his startled reaction. "Was anyone else hurt in the fire?"

"A man—a friend, a very good friend."

Buck said nothing.

"Actually, we were lovers. He died in the blaze. His name was David Crane."

Buck seemed to take a long time to digest her words. "Did his family and friends find out what happened to him?"

"No. I mean, I don't know. I just left him there." Catherine squeezed her eyes shut. She sounded like a monster. "I suffered a nervous breakdown right after the accident. Uncle Rudy brought me down here. I didn't really know what was going on around me for several months, and by the time I found out what had happened to David, it was too late. I know that's no excuse." She kept her eyes shut, afraid to see the contempt she felt for herself mirrored in Buck's face. The only thing that kept her speaking was the quiet strength of his hand. "I can imagine what you must be thinking about me."

"What am I thinking about you?"

"That I'm some kind of a—" Her voice broke over the words. "That I'm—"

"That you're a woman who has suffered a great deal. And you're still punishing yourself for things that were beyond your control," Buck said, bringing her fingers to his lips. "That's all."

She trembled at his soft kiss. If it was meant to comfort her, it was doing just the opposite, arousing feelings in her that were better left alone.

As though aware of her confusion, he let her hand go. "I think someone is trying to punish you for what happened."

"What do you mean?"

"The messages, the pit in the swamp forest, the man who chased you today—"

"And the appliances," Catherine added. "I told you they needed new parts. Tony thinks it was more than that. I didn't want the other guests to suspect that something was going on at the lodge."

"Then there may have been four incidents so far," Buck said. "Somehow they must all be connected to the fire. Either someone you used to know, or someone who used to know David Crane, has tracked you down."

Catherine's eyes widened. She'd been prepared for Buck's theory that someone at the lodge had stumbled onto her true identity. But it had never occurred to her that whoever was sending her the messages wanted to do more than just harass her. Could it be possible that someone was out to avenge David Crane's death? "What could this person be after? Blackmail? Revenge?"

"So far, the incidents seem to be designed to frighten you, though I think they're starting to escalate in intensity."

Catherine shivered. "You mean Hawk-nose."

Buck nodded. "We don't know whether he was actually trying to kill you, or just trying to terrorize you. Either way, you could be a target for blackmail or revenge or both. We'll know what as soon as we can identify who."

Catherine shook her head. "I've never met any of the guests at the lodge before. How could they be in on this?"

"It probably doesn't matter that you don't recognize them. One of them recognized you," Buck said. "He could have known of you from a friend or a business acquaintance. Or he could have known David. Maybe that's the link we need to concentrate on. What did David do for a living?"

Catherine hesitated. "He was a—writer." A screenwriter, she amended silently. At least, that's what he'd originally told her. It was only right before his death that he'd revealed that he actually wrote for one of the national tabloids. Could he have mentioned his sordid little exposé to his editor? Or to one of his other sleazy colleagues? She shuddered when she considered how many people could actually have known about her secret.

"Were you involved in the same line of work?"

She hesitated again. "In a roundabout way."

Buck studied her curiously. She was still holding something back. What else could there be in her past that was more damaging than the things she had already told him? "If there's something else I need to know—"

"No, there's nothing else." Catherine stared him straight in the eye, using a technique she'd learned from her days in front of the camera. She was someone else, anyone else, in a country far, far away. She was not in Cuzco. She was not Catherine Monroe. She was not lying to a man she had, only a few minutes before, ached to hold. Her gaze never wavered as she looked at him, but inside, her conscience—and her heart—cried out.

"All right." If Buck was less than satisfied with her answer, his face never showed it. "We're going to have to dig into the backgrounds of all the guests staying at the lodge. One of them has to have some connection to either you or David. I think it would be a good idea to ask a few questions about Tony, too, and the rest of the staff. They could just as easily be mixed up in this whole mess."

"I told you Tony couldn't possibly be involved," she insisted.

A storm brewed in his dark eyes. "Do you mind if I ask what Tony did for a living before he met you? I know you said that he worked for you while you were still in California. What about before that?''

She had to give him something. It might as well be the truth. ''He was in jail.''

Buck laughed bitterly. ''And you still insist this guy is Snow White?''

Catherine sat up, indignant. ''That was all over by the time I met him. Since then, he's been a loyal employee.''

''I'll bet,'' he said, changing the subject. ''If Tony's clean, and I can only take your word on that, then what about the others? Enrique and Jorge?''

Catherine shrugged, stung by the bitterness in his voice. ''I don't know. Tony suggested they might have accepted a bribe from someone to write the messages, but I don't think so. They've both been with me since I came to the lodge. I know their parents. I know their families. This kind of thing goes against everything they believe in.''

''Cancel the staff, then. That leaves Reverend Woolsey, Earle Godot and the Wheelers.''

''Yes.''

''What do you know about them?''

''Just what they've told me.'' She frowned as she tried to remember everything her guests had said over the past week. ''Earle is a photojournalist from Quebec.''

''Who's he working for? Or is he free-lance?''

''I don't know.''

''Does he have family in the United States? Has he ever lived there himself?'' His questions came like bullets.

''I don't know.''

One dark brow arched. ''Go on.''

Catherine continued, rattled by the businesslike edge to his voice. ''Reverend Woolsey is from Ohio. I think he's had a parish there for quite some time. His wife just died recently, I know that.'' Catherine looked up at Buck, thinking the woman's death might have great implications, but he stared silently at her. "As for the Wheelers, Frank is—was a police officer."

"Selena told me she'd met him in Vegas. Maybe that means he lived around the area."

"Maybe," she whispered. Buck seemed to be turning colder by the minute. "Do you think we should talk to them? Try to find out whether they knew me, or David, five years ago?"

"We can try. What do you have planned for them tomorrow?"

"I thought I'd take them on a tour of the city. I had to cancel today's activities after I hurt my ankle. Reverend Woolsey mentioned he'd like to see some of the old churches, and the Wheelers will probably come along, too. I think I can interest Selena in some of the jewelry in the local markets." Catherine paused, mentally planning the itinerary. "The hotel will furnish us with a mini-van if we want to take in some of the Incan ruins on the outskirts of the city. We could be out all day."

Buck looked down at her bandaged ankle. "Do you think you can manage all that now?"

She followed his gaze. "I suppose not." Silently, she cursed the stairs she had fallen down and the man who had pursued her. If it hadn't been for them ... Without warning, her venom turned inward. The condition of the road that morning had nothing to do with the position she was now in. This nightmare had started years ago.

"Then I'll lead the tour," Buck said quietly, cutting into her morbid thoughts. "I can probably pick up a map of the city in the lobby. In fact, this might work to our advantage. The others might open up about themselves a little more if we wander around on our own." His voice took on a bitter note he couldn't quite disguise. Abruptly, he left his chair, walking over to the window to stare out at the darkened streets. He didn't relish the idea of pumping the Wheelers and Reverend Woolsey for information under the guise of friendship. His mouth curled in self-derision. Then again, why not? He was already deceiving Catherine and the rest of the guests at the lodge about his real purpose for coming to Peru. The city tour was just another lie, and he was getting awfully good at lying. The constant subterfuge was starting to sicken him.

"Someone might be lying."

He stiffened. It was as if she'd read his thoughts. "What?"

"Someone might be lying," Catherine repeated. "Even if you get the others to talk about themselves, how can we be sure that they're telling us the truth? How will we know?"

"We won't." Buck kept his back to her, but his eyes met hers in the window as if he could not stop himself from seeking her out.

The disgust Catherine saw reflected there drove her backward. He knew she was keeping something from him, she realized. What else would have kindled the bleak emotion she saw in his eyes? Or maybe he was finally reacting to the information she had just given him about her past. A cold wind seemed to fill all the empty, aching places in her heart. What would she have seen in his face if she had told him the truth? What would she be if he ever learned the rest of the story?

Her shoulders sagged. She would be what she had always been. Catherine, alone. Inside her, the cold wind raged on relentlessly.

Buck finally averted his eyes from hers. "I don't think we'll have to worry much about false identities. If the message-writer had wanted to keep secret, he would have never made himself known to you in the first place. But if it makes you feel any better, we can do background checks on everybody staying at the lodge. I have a friend back home who does that kind of thing."

"You mean like a private investigator?"

Buck shrugged, still staring out the window. "Something like that."

The suggestion had been casual enough, yet Catherine sensed there was an underlying importance to it that eluded her. Was Buck testing her for some reason? She wished he would look at her. His broad back told her nothing.

"Should I call my friend?"

Catherine hesitated. It would certainly weed out any false information the guests might give them. On the other hand, it smacked of the same low tactics David had used on her. How could she stoop to his level? If a lifetime of running had taught her anything, it had taught her the importance of privacy. "No." They would have to find out what they could some other way.

Buck shook his head impatiently. So much for trying to get Catherine to condone his asking Jimmy for information. Hell, it had been a long shot, anyway. He had known she would refuse him before he even asked the question. And even if she had agreed to so underhanded a tactic, she would never have believed herself part of the investigation. He moved restlessly, guilt keeping his voice rough. "In that case, we're going to have to rely on trust."

"Trust," she repeated dully, as if there was no such thing.

"It's all we have."

Catherine's lips twitched at the faint condemnation in his tone. How long was he going to punish her for not confiding fully in him? How long was she going to have to address his back? For the rest of the evening? For the rest of the week? *Look at me!* she wanted to scream at him. *Look at me!*

He turned then, as though he had sensed her agitation, but his shuttered look ended any hopes she had of talking through their emotional stalemate. What would she have said to him, anyway, that would have made a difference? *Hello, I'm Catherine Taylor?* The ludicrous confession lodged in her throat. She could tell him nothing.

"I had better go," she said bluntly, ignoring the pain that shot through her ankle as she started for the door. "I'll see you in the morning."

She had her hand on the doorknob before his next words stopped her. "Does Tony know you're talking to me about all this?"

She hesitated. "No."

"Are you planning to tell him?" His voice was deadly with some hidden intent.

"Yes."

"What's he going to say when he finds out you've taken me into your confidence?"

Catherine's nerves tingled at the hitch in his voice. "He'll say whatever I tell him to say," she snapped, wrenching the door open.

In an instant he was beside her, slamming the door shut before she could leave. She wrenched it open again, and again he slammed it shut, barely missing her fingers.

She spun around, furious. "What do you want from me?"

Anger turned his gray eyes to black. "Nothing—everything!"

They faced off, neither willing to move, neither willing to bend, the inches between them electrically charged, as though touched by a hot wire. Catherine's breath came in quick, short gulps as she tried to stare Buck down, green eyes meeting gray until she thought she would burst from the contact. Time moved with a slow hand before she realized that suddenly, inexorably, their labored breathing had synchronized, deepened, taken on a sweet, aching thickness.

Trembling, battling the emotions he inspired in her, she moved back, but he moved with her, in some instinctive dance, until she was pressed against the door, his hard body lightly touching hers in all the wrong places. No, all the *right* places, her fevered senses relayed to her as his touch ignited a dozen different fires.

"Catherine..." Buck breathed out her name, running his hands along the delicious curves of her body. What had started as an apology ended as a plea as he moved against her, his hands on the full richness of her hips. His brain raced through an inventory of delight—the soft pressure of her breasts, the gentle rise of her belly and the warm promise below that.

Suddenly, he pushed himself away. "I don't know how to do this," he said thickly, running an unsteady hand through his hair. He read frustration in every line of Catherine's body. She had obviously felt the incongruity of their situation, too. They had strained together as though their sanity had depended upon it, yet at the same time, they had purposefully kept their faces apart.

Buck burned for the impossibility of her kiss. "How am I supposed to," he muttered, his eyes roaming the edges of her veil, "when I want to—"

She shook her head, her voice gone, her thoughts jumbled. The only thing she knew was the desperate need that he had kindled in her heart.

Slowly, hypnotically, he reached for her hand and brought it to his lips. Her fingers trembled over the small scar there and he drew one of them into the moist center of his mouth and then out, his tongue silken in its quest for her.

"We do it like this," he murmured, answering his own question as his mouth blazed a trail across her fingers. "And like this." He brought her other hand up to join the first, lightly raining kisses over the sensitive skin on the back of her hands, then turning them over to deepen his caress against her palms. "And like this."

Catherine swayed as his mouth moved to the inside of her wrists. They were barely touching, connected by the briefest, most innocent of caresses, but he was doing things to her bones, to her muscles, to the hot blood pumping through her veins, that were more shattering than the fevered, frustrated moments they had just shared. Her eyelids fluttered as his mouth moved higher, pushing aside the thin material of her sleeve to nibble on the smooth expanse of her forearm.

He backed away. She moved with him, as though bound by some invisible force. "More?" His whisper etched like fire into her flesh.

Oh, yes, more. The thought haunted her as she lost herself in his kisses. She could take more if she wanted. She could take all of him, every rigid, pulsating inch. The only thing that stood between them was the veil. And that was just a lie.

Her eyes snapped open. It was all just a lie—everything she was now feeling, everything she was making Buck feel. Their emotional relationship, whatever it was evolving into, had to end the minute she walked out that door. She wasn't free to give her heart, her soul, to any man.

Buck seemed to sense her withdrawal, raising his head to search her eyes. The look of anguish she knew must show there made him drop his hands and step away from her.

"I'm sorry," she whispered, an ache as old as time filling her.

One corner of his mouth turned up. "I'm not."

He reached for her again but she evaded his touch, groping for the door handle before she lost her resolve completely. "I should go back to my room. It's been a long day."

"And it's going to be an even longer night," Buck murmured in a voice so low she almost missed it. "Let me go with you."

Catherine avoided his disturbing gaze. "I think I can manage. My ankle's not that bad."

Buck's bedroom eyes were suddenly all business. "Actually, I was thinking more about the man who chased you this afternoon. We have no idea what he wanted or whether he'll show up again. I'd like to think the hotel was safe..."

His voice trailed off, but Catherine was able to fill in the words he didn't say. The hotel was probably safe *but they couldn't be sure.* They couldn't just ignore the incident that afternoon in the main square. For a moment, a remnant of the fear she'd felt when she first told him about her pursuer slithered along her nerves.

She jerked back from the doorway, the hallway beyond suddenly ominously dark. "Then you think he'll come back?" In the lamp-lit confines of Buck's room, she had managed to convince herself that Hawk-nose had crawled back under whatever rock he had come out from. Now reality was back and it was brutal. The thought that he could be out there, somewhere, waiting for her, filled her with dread. What if he had watched her limp her way down here tonight? What if he was, even now, waiting for her in her room? The air pulsed with a hundred different evils.

"Don't worry." Buck steadied her with a reassuring arm across her shoulder. "I don't think our man's the type to sneak into the hotel, especially when he knows that you could be with me, or one of the other guests. I think if you lock your door tonight and keep close to the well-traveled areas of the hotel tomorrow, you should be safe."

Catherine allowed him to lead her down the hallway to her own room. Despite his casual attitude, he insisted on checking out her room before he let her inside and then he pointed out the dead bolt on the inside of the door. "Remember, this isn't the jungle. I expect you to use this thing. And don't open the door to anyone until you know who it is."

She trembled slightly at the concern in his voice.

He smiled gently. "Get a good night's sleep. I'll see you tomorrow. Who knows, after my stint as tour guide, maybe this whole mess will be over."

"Maybe." And maybe not, Catherine thought as she slid the dead bolt into place after he'd left her. Finding out who was after her was only the beginning. Then would come why. She sank down wearily on the bed. And then who, again. But this time, that who would be Catherine Tremaine. And Catherine Taylor. What would she do then? She could hardly tell Buck the truth. Would he be content to walk away from all of this without learning the whole story? Her body tingled at the memory of his hands on her. Would she? She groaned softly, lowering her head into her hands, cursing her tragic past, the decisions she'd made that had brought her to this city, this room, this bed.

This man.

If she wasn't very, very careful, her heart would destroy her.

Chapter Eight

The foyer of El Inca Viejo was deserted when Catherine entered the restaurant the following evening. The maître d' was upon her almost immediately, his arms outstretched in welcome. "Miss Monroe! Always a pleasure! Ah!" He had noticed her pronounced limp. "You are not well."

"A sprain, Luis, that's all." She tugged self-consciously on her pant leg, wishing the telltale bandage wasn't so prominent. "I had a slight mishap near the marketplace yesterday."

He nodded sympathetically, as though he had heard it all before. "A nuisance, these streets." His small, manicured fingers danced lightly across his shirtfront. "Come, I will take you to your friends."

The table Luis led her to was partially screened from the restaurant proper by a tasteful selection of broad-leafed tropical plants in stout clay pots. Catherine saw Buck as they rounded the first graceful palm. He was seated at the table alone, casually elegant tonight, the denim of the day before replaced by a crewneck sweater and corduroy pants the same slate color as his eyes. He looked tired, as though the day out in the streets with the other guests had totally drained him. Or perhaps he had spent the same sleepless night she had, worrying about Hawk-nose and whoever had sent him. How often had his thoughts strayed to the scene in his hotel room? Had he relived each kiss, every caress, as she had? And had they filled him with the same wonderful, crazy, impossible feelings?

If he was surprised to see her, he hid it well, pulling out the empty chair next to his before Luis could get to it. His warm breath fanned her temple as she sat down. "I thought we'd agreed you wouldn't leave the hotel alone."

"I wasn't alone," Catherine murmured back, nodding her thanks to the diminutive maître d' as he exited with a flourish. "I was with Tony."

"Great." Buck retook his seat, obviously unhappy with her answer. "Where is the great white hunter?"

"He had to check in with the parts dealer down the street. He was able to purchase replacements quicker than he thought. They should be in place at the lodge by tomorrow night. That's why I'm here. I wanted to let everyone know that our flight back to Puerto Maldonado leaves in the morning." She took in the empty plates and crumpled napkins on the table. "Or am I too late?"

He shook his head. "Frank and the Reverend are getting better acquainted on the terrace. Selena left a few minutes ago to freshen up." The mischievous grin she'd come to cherish flashed across his face. "If I'm any judge of fashion, we should be here all night."

She couldn't help laughing. "Is it that bad?"

"Carmen Miranda wouldn't think so."

She laughed again, relaxing completely in his presence. What would it be like, she wondered, to have a normal relationship with a man like Buck Jordan? There would be nothing normal about it, she realized, her senses throbbing. He was quicksilver, disarming one minute, disturbing the next, and always, always, sexually potent, as though a fire raged just beneath his skin. Still, what would it be like to be able to share a meal with him? To have nothing more pressing to talk about than Selena Wheeler's latest fashion faux pas?

A trio of local musicians began to play at the other end of the restaurant, and she watched wistfully as several couples left their tables to dance, the pattern of the women's skirts forming a colorful kaleidoscope between the palm fronds. She would never know even that small pleasure with him.

"How's the ankle?" As though sensing her desolation, Buck brought her back from the carefree scene on the dance floor.

"Better." She rotated her foot gingerly. "It should be as good as new by the end of the week."

"Good." Buck brought one arm to rest along the back of Catherine's chair in a casual gesture that did things to her pulse that were anything but casual. "I'm glad you decided to come out. We have to talk."

Catherine braced herself for what she knew was coming. "You mean about your tour of the city."

"About the tour. About your returning to the lodge. About last night." He half turned toward her, his arm still on the back of her chair, and placed his other arm on the edge of the table so that she was caught in the warm hollow between them. "Mostly about last night. I stopped by your room before we came over to supper. You weren't there."

Her heartbeat picked up several more paces. "I told you I was with Tony."

One corner of his mouth turned up in an expression closer to a grimace than a grin. "Ah, back to the ubiquitous Tony. How is he?"

"He's fine." Catherine tore her attention away from the subtle movement of his lips. "He inquired about you, as well."

He laughed. "I'll bet he did. He was concerned about my health, no doubt. Or was he wondering just how much you'd seen of me since we arrived in Cuzco?"

Actually, he had been more interested in just how much distance lay between their two hotel rooms, Catherine remembered uneasily. Her earlier meeting with Tony had not gone well. He'd acted almost paranoid about her involvement with Buck, until she had told him about her run-in with Hawk-nose and described the cigar fragment and mirror Buck had discovered near the pit in the swamp forest. Then Tony had insisted that she abandon the lodge and her guests. This time he had been harder to dissuade, though in the end, her argument to stay had won out. But how long would her courage last? How long before she succumbed to the old urge to run?

She forced herself to look at him. "I don't want to talk about Tony."

"Neither do I." He traced the pale blue shadows beneath her eyes. "Did you get any sleep last night?"

"Yes. No."

He grinned at her. "Me neither." His fingers skimmed the skin of her temple, his thumb gentle and insistent on her brow. "Too much stimulation, I guess." His eyes probed hers, then dropped away, then reached back for her. "Or maybe not enough."

Her heart lurched at the silent questions he had dropped between them. "You mean the one episode with Hawk-nose in the marketplace didn't satisfy you?" she asked, her heartbeat thudding like a hammer in her chest.

"Don't."

"Don't what?"

"Don't pretend." He grasped her shoulders when she tried to turn away, forcing her to look at him. "Not in front of me. Not after last night. You're terrified of Hawk-nose and the messages you've been getting. I can understand that. You're terrified that someone has traced you back to the fire. I can understand that, too. But you don't have to be terrified of me. Catherine—" his grip on her shoulders tightened "—you don't have to be afraid of me."

But she did. Catherine trembled with the realization. In some ways, Buck and the emotions he ignited in her were more dangerous than anything she was now facing. She could deal with the messages. She could climb out of swamp forest pits and outrun hawk-nosed men and outwit anything else they could throw at her. But how could she cope with the physical yearnings he aroused? How could she accept the crazy dreams and desires he instilled in her? She was not a normal woman and this was not a normal situation. And *anything* that made her forget who she was and what she had come through was poison.

"People are looking," she improvised in panic, wishing someone—anyone—would interrupt their conversation.

"Let them look," Buck said firmly. "This is not finished, not by a long shot. I'll give you another twenty-four hours, but after that—" his voice dropped again to a low, silken threat "—we're going to talk. Not about Hawk-nose. Not about the messages. About us."

Buck leaned back in his chair and reached for his coffee cup. "As for my tour of the city," he said, grimacing as he drained the cup, "you could pretty much call it a bust."

Catherine swallowed hard, struggling to switch gears with him. "You mean you learned nothing?"

"Nothing that could stand up in a court of law. Frank never did show up. Selena said he was down with some kind of a gastrointestinal thing. She and the Reverend and I did a tour of the old city, Jordan-style." His quick grin hid a multitude of sins. "Then I brought them back to their rooms. No bombshells. No revelations. If our message-writer is one of the guests here in Cuzco, then he, or she, isn't talking. At least, not to me."

Catherine tilted her head to one side, considering. "Do you think Frank made up this story about being ill?"

"So he could slip out to meet up with Hawk-nose?" Buck shrugged. "I suppose it's possible. You didn't happen to see him wandering through the halls of the hotel when he claimed to be flat on his back?"

Catherine shook her head. "I was in my room for most of the day."

Buck fingered the handle of his coffee cup. "Long shot, I suppose. For all we know, he and Hawk-nose met up yesterday after the fiasco in the market. If Frank is our man, he might have already known that you were staying in today. In fact, he might have been planning..." his fingers stopped their restless movement as the implication of his words suddenly hit him.

"He might have been planning something for me at the hotel," Catherine whispered, each word like a knife thrust.

"Dammit!" Buck slammed his fist down on the table in self-disgust. "Why didn't I think of that this morning? If I'd have suspected he was setting up another 'accident' for you at the hotel, I would have never gone out with the others."

"But he didn't," Catherine said, wishing she could reassure him with a touch, a caress. She stared at the angry knot of his fist, imagining how it would feel to place her hand over his, to smooth out the long, lean fingers, to cradle his wrists and palms. In the end her rationale won out. She kept her hands locked in her lap.

"Maybe that means he's not the man we're looking for, after all. He had his chance and didn't act on it."

"Maybe." Buck's eyes narrowed as he glanced toward the glass doors to the balcony where Frank Wheeler and Reverend Woolsey were deep in conversation. "And maybe it means he's a lot smarter than we think."

Catherine followed his gaze. Wreathed in a cloud of cigar smoke, his craggy features creased into a look of utter bliss, Frank Wheeler seemed an unlikely suspect. She wondered what kind of cop he had been. Tough, no doubt. Tough but fair. The description materialized out of nowhere, but once it had, she couldn't shake it. "He doesn't look capable of hiring someone like that guy to follow me."

"None of them do," Buck said quietly, following her train of thought. "As far as appearances go, you have a bunch of saints staying out at the lodge with you. But you can't judge them by their looks alone.'' His tone turned urgent. ''You don't have that luxury.''

Outside, the conversation had taken a comical turn. Frank Wheeler choked out a cloud of smoke as the Reverend put the finishing touches on what looked like the joke of the century. ''At least the Reverend's having a good time,'' Catherine observed quietly.

Buck frowned. ''You wouldn't have thought so if you'd seen him earlier today. He seemed—strange.''

''Strange?''

''Maybe *confused* is a better word. He didn't say much at all during the tour, at least nothing I could make sense of. Half the time I don't think he even knew where he was. I asked him once or twice if he was feeling well, but he kept insisting we continue the tour.''

''You're right,'' Catherine agreed, ''that doesn't sound like the Reverend. Maybe the plane trip disoriented him. Or maybe the altitude was too much. I've seen it happen before. Did Selena notice anything wrong?''

Buck snorted. ''I don't know when she would have had the time. She talked practically nonstop for six hours. I could hardly get a word in edgewise.''

''It couldn't have been that bad.''

''You're right, I'm exaggerating. Her years as a Las Vegas show girl were entertaining.''

Catherine rolled her eyes. ''I'll bet.''

''But those Girl Scout stories,'' Buck said, shaking his head mournfully, ''and the jobs she held before she hit the kickline. Down-on-her-luck jewelry designer, down-on-her-luck actress, she even sold plastic kitchenware door-to-door before—'' He stopped at the horrified look on Catherine's face.

Something in the colorful list of Selena's previous occupations had stripped away Catherine's veneer of control. For a moment, Buck caught a glimpse of the pain and the fear that she tried so hard to keep hidden from him.

"What is it?" he demanded, reaching for her hands. "Do you think she might have known you, or known of you, through her work?" He pressed on when Catherine shook her head, tightening his grip on her fingers when she tried to pull away. "Show girl?" He began to list off the jobs, despising himself for badgering her, yet determined to learn what terrifying connection to Catherine lay buried in Selena's past. "Designer? Actress?"

Bingo. The shock that coursed through Catherine's body was just as great the second time around. "Actress." Buck examined the word as though it was set to explode. "Films, television, stage."

Catherine sat like a stone.

He tried another track. "I assume you weren't in the business yourself or you would have recognized Selena. She's a hard woman to forget."

Still nothing from her.

Buck pushed his hand through his hair in exasperation. "You mentioned last night that the man who died in the fire was a writer. Did he write any scripts?"

Finally, Catherine stirred. "He may have. I don't remember."

Buck frowned. He had begun to recognize when she skirted the truth. It was not so much the way she said the words but the involuntary tensing of her whole body, as though she expected a blow. "Not good enough."

She turned to look at him, her gaze never wavering, although the pale cast of her face told him just how much the sentence cost her. "I don't want to talk about it."

"You have to." He reached for her. "How many times do I have to tell you that this isn't a game? There are very real people out there determined to do very real damage to you. You can't just pretend this isn't happening."

She jerked away from him, her voice brittle. "Don't you think I know that? Don't you think I'd let you know more if I could? But there are others involved here—'' She turned away, refusing to finish the sentence.

"Others? You mean Tony? And your uncle? Just who are you trying to protect?"

Me! She wanted to hurl the word at him. *I'm protecting myself!* Instead, she said nothing, too close to tears to risk opening her mouth again. She hated losing her composure in front of him, hated the vulnerable way it made her feel. But more than that, she hated having to watch him struggle so valiantly to help her while she held the truth just out of his reach.

Buck wasn't ready to accept her silence. "What kind of hold do they have on you?" he demanded.

She took the coward's way out, skirting the truth. "Is it so hard for you to understand that I owe them? My uncle risked everything to bring me down here after the fire. He helped me purchase the lodge. He spent months away from his practice while we were setting up, and then, once we opened for business, he came down as often as he could to help. He'd still be here if his heart hadn't given out. I can never repay that."

Buck's face twisted with anguish. "You can. You already have. With five years of your life. And every minute—*every second*—that goes by, you pay a little more. How much are you willing to sacrifice to keep your secret? Your health? Your life?"

Catherine's eyes sparkled with unshed tears. "Everything."

"Dammit, Catherine." Buck bit back a torrent of frustrated curses, silently condemning the brass back in Washington, his missing informant, the heat, the food, the sleepless nights—everything and everyone but this woman whose intransigence, whose tears, could bring him to the brink of emotional ruin. "Listen to me," he said, reining in his temper. "Don't do this—"

"I have to," Catherine whispered. "You don't understand—"

"Then make me understand!" Buck's control snapped at the same time he spied Selena coming toward them. He restrained himself, barely. "She picked a fine time to make an appearance."

Catherine watched her approach in horrid fascination, trying to picture her on a soundstage, the set crew behind her. Tonight she was wearing a sarong, several sizes too small and several shades too loud. A number of hibiscus sprouted at regular intervals from her upswept hair. Was it possible they had performed together at one time? How could she have forgotten a woman as outlandishly vibrant as Selena Wheeler?

"And I thought the facilities out at the lodge were primitive," Selena said, sliding cheerfully into her seat. She gave Catherine's hand a quick squeeze. "Buck told us about your accident. I hope you gave that shoemaker a piece of your mind."

"The one who was supposed to fix your heel," Buck said casually at Catherine's puzzled expression, dropping a spoon into his coffee cup. "You're lucky you didn't break your neck when it came loose."

"Honey, you'll be up all night with that stuff," Selena warned him. "I don't think they've heard of decaf down here." Her attention shot back to Catherine. "Are you sure it's just a sprain? I'll be happy to take a look at it." She peered under the table. "I took a first-aid course a few years ago. They taught us to set every bone in the human body."

"I think all I need is a little rest," Catherine assured her.

"I could use a little shut-eye myself," Buck said, looking around for their waitress. He finally spotted her clearing a table and beckoned her over. "What time did you say our flight leaves in the morning?"

"Early. About 7:00 a.m."

Selena looked startled. "You mean we're going home already?"

Buck met Catherine's troubled gaze. "That's one way of putting it."

THE AIR HAD TAKEN on a frigid bite by the time they left the restaurant, although the sidewalks were as crowded as they had been earlier in the day. Catherine sidestepped a street vendor selling plastic-wrapped packages of disposable pens. The woman was replaced almost immediately by another waving toothbrushes. An army of her sisters seemed to wait in the shadows.

"Talk about pressure sales," Buck muttered, guiding her past another clutch of merchandise.

"It is bad," she agreed, "but for most of these people, this is the only way of life they know."

Near the hotel they stopped to let the Reverend purchase several intricately woven bookmarks for a few of his parishioners. As if sensing an avalanche of sales, the vendor began to pull out a dizzying array of handcrafted merchandise. Soon they were all bartering.

"Señorita—"

Catherine glanced down. The dark-eyed little boy in the striped T-shirt had materialized out of nowhere. He rattled off something too low for her to hear, then made a grab for her wristwatch. Before she could stop him, he had darted into the crowd, her watch held high in one hand.

"That was a gift," she cried out, springing after him. A sharp stab of pain in her ankle brought her up short. Still, she managed one more excruciating step before Buck intervened.

"Stay here," he ordered. Then he charged after the boy, and Frank followed a moment later.

It didn't go well from the start. He careened off an old woman with a tray full of passion fruit, then narrowly dodged two more, focused on the fleeing strip of white and red that was Catherine's thief. Every time the crowds thinned enough for him to make up any distance, the boy veered down another side street, his skinny legs pumping furiously.

Soon the kid left the main square altogether for a bewildering maze of narrow streets and deserted alleyways that had Buck reeling. After several minutes, he had to admit that he was lost. He had also begun to question his logic in starting the pursuit. In this altitude, in the middle of the night, no watch was worth it.

He slowed to a walk, admitting defeat. The boy was gone. Buck was turning to go back to the hotel when Frank stumbled around the corner.

"Did you see which way he went?" Buck asked, half-heartedly.

Frank shook his head, his breath coming in short bursts. His bout with stomach flu seemed to have left him in surprisingly good shape. "I lost sight of him right after we passed that last church. I thought you knew where you were going."

The blind leading the blind. Buck didn't know which of them looked more ridiculous. A flash of color in the side street off to his left brought his head around. In the watery light thrown by a nearby street lamp, it might have been anything.

"See him?" Frank inched forward.

"I don't know." Buck took a tentative step, his eyes narrowing. There it was again. He signaled Frank, his voice dropping as he peered through the gloom. "Go around to the other side. You can probably cut him off there."

Frank nodded and slipped away.

Buck walked on. It wasn't a side street at all, he soon realized, but an alley. A dead-end alley. He could just make out the high stone wall at the far end. In between him and the wall lay a no-man's-land of overturned crates, upended barrels and collapsed cardboard boxes. The boy could be anywhere.

He took another step forward. "I know you're here."

Silence.

His eyes roamed the mute buildings on either side of him. From what he could see, there was only one door that led out of the alley, set in a recessed well in the wall of the building on his right. It was padlocked shut. The boy couldn't have escaped him, then. He had to be here. Somewhere.

Buck refocused on a large, metal drum a few yards away. "I won't hurt you."

More silence. The unearthly quiet was beginning to unnerve him. Something drove his foot forward another step. It didn't feel right. He replayed the events of the last few minutes as his eyes roamed the midnight recesses of the alley. The watch. The chase. The kid's unerring sense of direction, as though he knew exactly where he was going.

Buck stopped, his senses tingling. It was a setup. Someone or something had deliberately lured him away from the others.

A single drop of sweat formed between his shoulder blades, inching its way down the ladder of his spine as he absorbed the small sounds of the night. A rattle to his left—a cat? A creak to his right—the building settling? In the distance, a car horn blared briefly. The smell of rotting garbage grew stronger.

Buck dropped into a crouch, his nerves screaming. Where the hell was Frank? He should have been back by now. A small, moist sound caught his attention. Definitely human, definitely coming from the wooden barrel to his right. He moved toward it. "Come out from behind there," he ordered. "Slowly. Keep your hands where I can see them."

Seconds crept by before the young boy Buck had chased across Cuzco emerged from behind the barrel. He was younger than Buck had originally assumed, probably no more than eight years old. Grime and poverty had worked years into his face. Catherine's watch dangled limply from one hand.

"Señor Buck?" His voice was a sly whine.

"You know who I am. What do you want?"

"I have a message from him."

"From who?"

The boy smiled. "From the man you came to Peru to meet."

Inwardly, Buck cursed. He should have known. Only his informant would use a child to pass along information. The scar tissue across his stomach began to itch. "What message? Where is he?"

"He is in a safe place. He will come to the jungle on the next boat."

"That's all?"

"That's all."

The boy began to ease toward the mouth of the alley, hugging the wall, his wary eyes never leaving Buck. "This is mine now," he said, waving Catherine's watch in the air. "He said I could keep it."

"Sure, keep it," Buck said grimly. Maybe the watch was the boy's payment for doing his informant's dirty work. Something still bothered him. "How did he know I would come after you?"

The boy looked back, knocking a tangle of black hair from his eyes with a grimy fist. "Easy, *señor*. He said you were a hero."

The word boiled in his gut long after the boy had disappeared.

"WE LOST HIM down one of the back streets," Buck informed the others when he and Frank rejoined them on the steps to the hotel.

"He had us beat from the start," Frank said. "The kids around here must be built like mountain goats."

"This one was, anyway," Buck muttered under his breath.

"Never mind," Catherine said. "I can replace the watch." She shot Buck a questioning look. He wasn't telling them the entire story, she was sure of it.

"Did anyone catch what the kid said before he got away?" Selena asked. "It all happened so quickly, I lost most of it."

"What do you mean?" Frank took a fresh cigar from his pocket, stripped off the cellophane and moistened the tip. "He didn't say anything."

"Oh, but he did," the Reverend piped up. "I recognized it immediately."

Frank bit and spat. "Some kind of Bible thing, padre?"

"Goodness, no. It's a common enough expression. 'Ask me no questions, I'll tell you no lies.' Only the lad got it wrong. He said, 'Ask me no questions, *tell me no lies—*'"

Selena's elbow caught him in the chest before he had a chance to say more. "Catherine, honey, are you all right?"

"Catherine!"

"Catch her!"

Buck leapt forward just as Catherine collapsed.

Chapter Nine

"He knows. The Reverend knows." Wearily, Catherine pushed the heavy weight of her hair back from her face. After the cool, thin air of Cuzco, the jungle seemed particularly hot and oppressive. Tony's cabin was already an oven and it was only eleven o'clock in the morning.

"He knows," Catherine repeated slowly. "Why else would he have chosen to misquote that particular expression? Tell me—"

"—no lies," Tony finished for her, giving the words a guttural twist. He hadn't moved from his place in the corner near the bathroom since Catherine had started to speak. Now he joined her at the table.

"Tell Me No Lies," she echoed, the sick feeling welling again in her stomach. *Lies* had been her second film, the one that *Performers* magazine had predicted would send brilliant new actress Catherine Tremaine right to the top. It hadn't been a particularly good script, but she'd taken it anyway, obsessed by the similarities between her character, a woman trying unsuccessfully to flee her tormented past, and herself. No wonder the Reverend had chosen the title of that particular film. He was warning her. *Her time was running out.*

"Any chance he might have been accurately quoting the kid?"

She'd briefly considered that possibility, too, before discarding the idea as preposterous. "Tony, he was only a boy. A street kid. He's probably never seen a motion picture in his life. Besides, no one but Selena and the Reverend heard him say a thing. And only the Reverend could quote it back to me."

"So you collapsed right in front of him." The words had an accusatory ring she didn't like.

"I told you I made up an excuse."

"Your ankle."

"Yes."

"And you think the old man bought that? You think any of them bought that?"

"Yes. Yes. I don't know." The words flew at him. Abruptly she left the table and hobbled to the window. Her nerves were shot. So were his, for that matter. Why else would she be yelling at him? Why else would he be so defensive? They hadn't had a civilized conversation since they'd left for Cuzco.

No, that wasn't right, her conscience reminded her. Their relationship had started to deteriorate long before that, with her discovery of the first note in her cabin. With her turning to Buck, instead of Tony, with each subsequent incident. No wonder he'd lashed out at her when she'd told him about the theft. By bringing in an outsider, she had jeopardized everything they had worked so hard to build.

Everything Tony had worked so hard to build. Once activated, her conscience proved relentless. Hadn't she always suspected that Tony's feelings for her were more than merely platonic? Buck was a rival, at least in Tony's mind. From now on, she'd be wise to remember that.

"This is getting us nowhere." She limped back to the table and eased herself into her chair. The bandage was beginning to irritate the tender flesh of her ankle. She rolled it off before addressing him. "I don't know if the others were suspicious of my collapsing on the steps. Maybe they all recognized the title of the film. Maybe they all guessed who I really am."

"Now maybe you'll start to listen to reason," Tony said.

Her eyes turned wary. "What do you mean?"

"I mean, first the messages on your bathroom mirror, then the incident at the pit." Tony's mouth twitched. "If we can believe Jordan's description of it."

"He showed me the mirror and the piece of cigar he found."

"I could show you a cup of coffee and Enrique's fishing pole and claim that I found them in the swamp forest. It wouldn't prove a thing." He stared at her intently. "Jordan could be manipulating this whole thing for his own gain. He and the boy could have planned the theft together, hoping you'd lose your composure in front of everybody. Maybe he expected you to confess right there and then."

Beneath the veil, her lips tightened. "Don't."

"At least let me finish before you go defending him," Tony thundered, shoving the table aside.

"All right, I'm listening." Catherine calmed him, though her own self-control was as shaky as his. In a minute, they'd be at each other's throats.

Tony nodded, barely mollified. "Think back to that first day. Jordan didn't show up for dinner. Where was he? His cabin, like he claims? Or was he out in the forest, getting the pit ready?"

"He engineered Frank's disappearance so that I would walk into his little trap when we organized the search?"

"Wheeler's disappearance could have been coincidence. Jordan said himself that the pit wasn't finished when you fell into it." He looked at her for confirmation, his color slowly returning to normal as he laid out his theory.

"True."

"He's with you when you find the second message. Did you come across it together?"

"I was on the bed. He went into the bathroom to get a first-aid kit and saw the message on the mirror."

His grin was triumphant. "He could have easily written the thing and then called you in to see it. The same goes for the appliances in the kitchen. Jordan claims he saw a prowler. Maybe *he* was the prowler. Maybe he tinkered with the fuel lines so he could get you to Cuzco."

"So Hawk-nose could chase me through the market. So I could fall down a flight of stairs and sprain my ankle. So a street urchin could rattle off the title from one of my own films."

Tony scowled at the sardonic note in her voice. "You're not taking this seriously."

She shook her head in disbelief. "Seriously? Tony, how can I? Everything you've said rests solely on coincidence or speculation, or both! We could draw up scenarios like this for everyone at the lodge and still not prove a thing!"

Tony kicked his chair back in anger, his voice rising again. "Then let's get out of here! Now! Today! I can get us seats on the next flight out of Maldonado. If we can't prove that Jordan is behind all of this, if we can't prove that anyone is behind it, then at least we can get you out before anything else happens to you. And to hell with the lodge and everyone else!"

She struggled to her feet, her voice as strident as his. "I've told you before that I'm not running! Not this time!"

"You'd be saving your life!"

"I'd be cutting my own throat! Again!"

A look of disbelief crossed his face. "It's Jordan, isn't it?"

Something huge and crushing came down over her heart. "What are you talking about?" Her pathetic attempt to bluff him, to get him to listen to reason, sounded weak, even to her ears.

Tony's massive frame trembled as he read the truth in her eyes. "It's been Jordan all along. He's the reason you don't want to leave." He drew back from her outstretched hand, turning for the door, as though fearing what her touch might do to him. "And to think that I dreamed about—" His mouth opened and closed soundlessly as he grabbed for the handle. "I thought that you and I—"

"Tony, please," Catherine pleaded, coming after him. "You're tired. I'm tired. Neither of us is thinking clearly right now. Don't say anything you might—" The rest of the sentence hung, unspoken, between them.

Catherine's spirits sagged. The truth was, she couldn't face this. Not now. Not ever. Tony's silent declaration of love, coming on top of the terrifying events of the past few days, was simply more than she could handle. It was like watching the firm foundation beneath her shift, take on a new and frightening shape. Her soul was not equipped for any more.

Tony's face was still creased into a snarl. "You know what the sad thing about all of this is?" he said, sending the door crashing into the wall. "Jordan's going to destroy you. And you're going to let him do it."

They both turned at the soft steps on the stairs. Buck stood in the doorway, studying them.

Catherine inhaled sharply. *How much had he heard?*

"Enrique sent me to get Tony," Buck said evenly, his words betraying nothing. "He needs some help with one of the stoves." He planted an open hand in the middle of Tony's chest as the big man tried to move past him. "What's been going on here?"

Tony knocked his hand away. "You seem to have all the answers lately. You figure it out."

Buck's voice dropped a degree, taking on the icy edge that Catherine remembered from the restaurant in Cuzco. "Oh, believe me. I will. And when I do, I bet I'll find you right in the middle of it. Meanwhile, I'd suggest you leave Catherine alone. After what happened in Cuzco, she doesn't need—"

"I don't need you to tell me what Catherine does or does not need." Tony took a menacing step forward, pig-eyed and unpredictable. "I've already given her the best piece of advice that I can and I'm sticking by it." One thick finger jabbed at Buck's chest. "Now let me give you a piece of advice, soldier boy. Stay out of this. You hear me? You stay out of this. And stay away from Catherine."

Buck stood his ground. "I don't frighten that easily."

Tony pushed past him, the bang of the door punctuating his words. "Maybe you should."

HE SHOULD HAVE HIT HIM when he had the chance.

Buck stripped off his sweat-drenched T-shirt and tossed it on the bed, still seething from his unsatisfactory exchange with Tony. His right hand tingled from the punch he should have thrown.

A hell of a lot of good that would have done, he thought, as his temper cooled. They would have beaten each other to a pulp, and Catherine would be no closer to finding out who was terrorizing her.

An image of Tony's prognathic jaw and squashed nose swam into his consciousness and his fingers tingled again. God, he'd like to be able to pin this whole thing on him. What on earth did Catherine see in the guy to keep him around for so long? She'd refused to talk to him after Tony stomped off to the kitchen. In fact, they'd only exchanged a few words since he'd caught her as she collapsed on the steps to their hotel in Cuzco. He sure as hell didn't buy her story about her ankle giving out again.

But she wasn't talking. About the collapse. About Tony. About anything. And Buck had the uncomfortable feeling that, this time, he wasn't going to be able to get her to change her mind.

Grimacing, he ran his hand down the front of his chest. If the heat was going to be this bad, he'd have to get used to the cold showers again. At least the rusty river water that dribbled from the shower head was better than swimming in his own clothes.

He picked up a towel from the end of the bed and started toward the bathroom, then suddenly remembered the revolver he'd hidden behind the armoire. He hadn't checked on it since Cuzco.

He wedged one arm behind the wardrobe, his fingers skimming the webbed belt. The holster was still there.

The gun was gone.

IT WAS LATE AFTERNOON when Catherine walked Carlos to the river. She waited on the dock while the old man climbed into his boat, returning his shy wave of farewell once he was underway. In a few minutes, the distance and the heat had reduced his boat to an intermittent glint on the surface of the water.

Then even that was gone, and there was only the brown sweep of the river before her and the moist weight of the jungle behind her. And the fear. The fear.

She lowered herself to the dock before her legs gave way altogether. Maybe Tony was right. Maybe she should leave Peru, now, while she still had the chance. In another day, it might be too late. She quivered as the familiar impulse to turn tail and flee overwhelmed her.

The urge was overcome, almost immediately, by her logical side, the same practical, no-nonsense veneer that had sustained her for the last five years. The Phoenix was her home, her hope. Her only hope. It was the one thing of worth she still had. Running was impossible.

Her breathing gradually slowed as her fragmented thoughts seemed to take up the challenge. She had a lodge to operate, guests to entertain, expectations to fulfill. Carlos's unexpected reappearance so soon after their trip back to the Phoenix was a case in point. After dropping them off that morning, he'd continued on his way with supplies for the nature lodge upstream. On his return trip, he'd stopped in with an invitation to supper from the lodge's owner. It was a common enough occurrence but it wasn't something she could just ignore while she indulged her fears. The present needed her.

But the past refused to die.

Without warning, her mind seesawed, conjuring up an image of the second message she had found on her mirror: *Will the dead stay dead?* Someone at the lodge didn't think so.

A board creaked behind her.

Catherine whirled around, but the dock and the stairs to the boardwalk were empty. Her gaze shifted to the trees but she could see nothing out of the ordinary in their green depths. Was she jumping at ghosts, mistaking the ordinary sounds of the dock settling for an attack by her unknown assailant? What was next, she wondered moodily. Flying saucers? Spacemen? It made about as much sense as suspecting doddering old Reverend Woolsey of some diabolical plan to expose her.

If not the Reverend, then who? She scrambled to her feet before the questions could begin their insidious replay. She had work to do. First on her list was to find and placate Tony after their last disastrous argument. Next, she would organize the outing to Quester's Inn. And then, if there was time, she would seek out Buck, make him see that his efforts to help her were fruitless. That the desire they drew from one another had no place in the real world.

They had no future together.

She had no past.

All she had was the lodge. And she would crush whatever was trying to claw its way back into her life before it crushed her.

"THERE'LL ONLY BE the four of us tonight," Catherine informed Jorge as she dumped her load of life preservers into the bottom of the motorboat. The larger, sleeker craft she usually used for group excursions bobbed, unattended, at the end of the torch-lit dock. "This one will be easier to maneuver, anyway, especially through that rough patch of water on this side of Wolf's lodge."

"I take it Wolf is our gracious host for the evening." Buck had joined them on the dock, coming up so quietly behind them that she spun in surprise at the sound of his voice.

"He and his wife will both be there." She tried for a neutral tone, but the words came out in a rush. It had been a mistake to look at him. One glance was enough to shred all her noble resolutions. The network of lines around his eyes were etched deeper tonight, the hollows in his cheeks more pronounced, as though he, like Catherine, had spent the afternoon in bitter contemplation. It gave him a rough, world-weary air, as though he was a man who had seen too much of the dark side of human nature. Too little tenderness. She had to fight to keep from reaching out to him.

"Wolfgang and Rosalee Speer own Quester's Inn," she said in answer to his question. "She's Quechuan, from one of the mountain villages near Cuzco. He left a lucrative career in industry several years ago to travel around the world. Halfway through his trip, he stumbled into this area of the Amazon, and the rest, as they say, is history." She risked another look at him. The top two buttons of his knit shirt were in the wrong holes. Without thinking, she stretched up to unbutton them.

Immediately, his hands closed around her wrists, yanking her against him. "What do you think you're doing?"

"Your buttons—" She scarcely managed the words. Out of the corner of her eye, she sensed Jorge staring from his seat in the boat, fascinated.

Buck barely acknowledged the audience. "Then by all means, be my guest." He kept her wrists imprisoned while she fumbled over the material, holding her for a few more seconds after the buttons were correctly realigned. When he finally released her, it felt as though she'd been cut adrift.

Jorge sighed. "Señor Wheeler will be sorry he missed the festivities," he said, his head disappearing beneath one of the wooden seats. A fat, hairy-legged spider shot over the side of the boat.

"A reoccurrence of his Cuzco problem," Catherine explained, sidestepping Jorge's housekeeping activities. "Selena's staying behind to look after him."

"Pity," Buck murmured. His attention glided back to Catherine. She was wearing a dress tonight, a filmy concoction in royal blue that molded itself to her body, accentuating her slim waist and the achingly full thrust of her breasts. It was the first time he had seen her without the totally serviceable costume of pants and cotton shirt she usually wore. He decided he liked the change, maybe a little too much. "Is that new?"

Her temples flooded with color. "It used to be."

"It's very nice."

Jorge sighed again. "Company coming." Almost instantly, Reverend Woolsey materialized at the top of the stairs, Earle bobbing like a pale specter behind him.

Catherine forced down her feelings of apprehension as the two men approached. The Reverend looked almost childlike tonight, his pink face wreathed in an eager smile. Earle was toting an impressive amount of photographic equipment.

"In case we run into anything worthwhile," he told her as he clambered aboard the boat.

They purred away from the dock a few minutes later.

"Magnificent!" Reverend Woolsey marveled, tipping his head back to gaze at the thick band of stars that flowed like a celestial river across the evening sky. "I've never seen it so bright."

"*Mayu*," Catherine informed him from her seat at the helm. "That's what the ancient Incas called the Milky Way. It means river. On a night like this, you can see why."

About a mile up the river, she fished a flashlight out from under the seat in front of her. "If we're lucky," she said, clicking on the beam and directing it toward shore, "we'll be able to—" Two bloodred eyes glittered back at her. "There! Did you see it?"

The Reverend leaned forward from his seat in the bow. "Alligator?"

"Close relative. Cayman. They feed along the riverbank at night."

Earle twisted around to look at her. "Feed on what?"

"Anything that moves."

Buck groaned. "I was afraid you'd say that."

Catherine prodded him playfully with the toe of her sandal and was rewarded with a gentle squeeze of his hand on her ankle. Earle, she noticed, had positioned himself squarely in the middle of the boat.

A young girl with a shy smile and a headful of dark curls met them when they docked. Immediately, she attached herself to Buck, who hoisted her onto his shoulders for the short walk up the sandy trail to Quester's Inn.

The inn was similar to the Phoenix, although built on a smaller scale. Torches burned at regular intervals along the edge of the clearing. The main building, Catherine informed them as they marched up the trail, housed Wolf, his wife and their daughter. Behind it, two squat, thatch-roofed dormitories kept Wolf's paying guests. Tonight, those guests, a couple of Australian bird-watchers and a retired pharmacist from France, were staying in a small tribal village about three hours upstream.

Wolfgang Speer met them on the stairs, a middle-aged Teutonic giant with bronze skin and thinning blond hair burned almost white by the sun. "I see you've met Isabella," he boomed, a slight accent betraying his German origins.

Buck lifted the girl off his shoulders and set her down. "I have one like her back home. She's beautiful."

Wolf planted a kiss on Isabella's upturned face, then smacked her lightly on the bottom as she scampered up the steps into the lodge. "So she is. Just like her mother. And wait until you see what Rosie has in store for you tonight!"

The feast Rosalee Speer had waiting for them in the cozy, lantern-lit dining room was sumptuous by jungle standards: *ceviche* accompanied by corn on the cob and deep-fried sweet potato. Next door in the kitchen, half a dozen other main dishes waited, steaming.

Catherine lingered in a no-man's-land between the two rooms, helping Rosalee serve and remove an interminable number of plates and bowls. She'd refused Wolf's offer to eat at a small table curtained off from the rest of the room, telling him that she'd already eaten back at the Phoenix. It was a little ritual they engaged in every time she accepted one of his dinner invitations. One day, she supposed, she'd have to take him up on his offer.

Assuming she was around for the next invitation. Her hand jerked, dumping the serving bowl of corn into Buck's lap.

Isabella crowed with delight. "Do it again, do it again!" She clapped her hand over her mouth at her father's warning look. "Again," she whispered through her pudgy fingers. "With the peanut sauce this time."

"Maybe tomorrow." Buck grinned at her, juggling several lukewarm cobs. He flicked a handful of butter back into the bowl. "I hope everyone was finished with this."

"I'm—I'm sorry," Catherine stammered, mortified at her clumsiness. "I must have been daydreaming. I'll get a wet cloth." She fled into the kitchen.

Buck was already standing. "I'll go with her."

"You'll have a devil of a time getting that stain out," Reverend Woolsey called after him. He lowered his voice confidentially as he looked around the table. "Butter, you know."

In the kitchen, Catherine moistened a towel she found hanging on a bar below the sink. "Your pants are probably ruined," she said, turning to find Buck right behind her. Involuntarily, she took a step backward, the heat spiraling into her cheeks. "If you'll send me the bill for a new pair," she continued, gesturing weakly at the spectacular stain that ran down both legs, "I'll gladly—" Her voice wound down as she dabbed the air experimentally with the towel. "Maybe you better do this."

Gently, he took the cloth from her fingers. "You can't go on like this. You know that."

She couldn't meet his eyes. "If you mean dumping vegetables all over my guests—"

"I mean pretending that nothing's going on back at the Phoenix. You're only lying to yourself. And to me. You can't just will this guy away."

Unwillingly, her gaze snapped back to his. "Can't I?" Her hands had started to shake. She put them behind her back, suddenly terrified he'd see them, terrified he'd start to suspect just how close she was to the edge. She could almost sense the jagged rocks waiting for her at the bottom of that long drop.

Rosalee chose that moment to poke her head around the door. "Everything okay in here?" She frowned at the wet towel Buck held in his hand. "You'll want to take those pants off before you do any of that. I think Wolf has an old pair in the bedroom that might fit." The door whisked shut.

With a last, weary glance at Catherine, Buck followed Rosalee out.

The jeans Rosalee pulled from the ancient steamer trunk in the back bedroom were a well-worn, bell-bottomed pair. She shook them out fondly and laid them across the bed. "Nineteen-seventy. Wolf was in America then, doing all that hippie stuff, although just between you and me, I think he was a little long in the tooth to be hanging around a bunch of flower children. By the time I met him, he'd gotten all that out of his system." She flicked a microscopic piece of lint from the frayed hems. "I hear these are back in style now."

"Only in California."

Her face relaxed into a broad grin. "California. Disneyland. Mickey Mouse. Wolf took us there for a visit when Isabella turned four." She pointed to one of the many framed photographs that lined the walls, and Buck stepped over to it obligingly.

Three faces. Three identical grins. In the background, the spires of Sleeping Beauty's castle shimmered brilliantly in the glare from a perfect California sun. "Looks like fun."

"We went up Space Mountain three times." Rosalee's childlike side was showing.

Buck glanced at the photograph next to it, again a photo of Wolf, Rosalee and their daughter, only this time backed by an impressively ornate oriental temple. "China?" he guessed.

"Japan," Rosalee corrected, looking over his shoulder. "Isabella was six then."

"Some birthday present."

"Wolf is a generous man. Sometimes I think too generous, but," she said, shrugging, "he is entitled. Fathers and daughters. That is a special kind of bond."

The next photo was slightly overexposed. Buck squinted a long time at the slender, gray ribbon in the background before something clicked in his mind. "Autobahn," he said quietly.

She beamed. "Yes. We were there in February. Wolf still owns some business interests in Frankfurt. That's partly why he does so much travelling. Do you know Germany?"

"Some. I was there in February, too." *Only it hadn't been to look after business interests*. He'd been there to investigate the Serpent's latest robbery, for all the good that had done. Their investigation had turned up a few small fry, but the ringleader had dropped back out of sight, the same way he'd always eluded capture. Europe. The Philippines. Japan. America. A list of bloodshed and evil dating back twenty years.

And they'd never even gotten close to catching him. It was as if he'd vanished, as if he'd assumed some other identity.

Buck's gaze flicked back along the row of prints.

Maybe he had.

"WHAT ABOUT IT, Reverend?" Wolf's rich baritone could be heard throughout the house. "Are you up for a little Amazonian adventure?"

The Reverend set his coffee cup on the shaky, little end table beside the couch. "Now that you mention it, I've always wanted to see how the noble savage lives."

"What's going on?" Buck asked Catherine as he sat down beside her on a rustic plank bench that served as the Speers' second couch. He squirmed uncomfortably. Wolf's jeans were a little closer fitting than he had anticipated. Or maybe Wolf had been thinner in those days. Thinner, and a lot busier.

"Earle wants to see the Indian tribe I described to you on the way here," Catherine explained.

"I've got plenty of room in the boat," Wolf boomed. "You three could stay overnight and go back with Carlos tomorrow afternoon. Catherine, too, if she wants," he added, with a friendly nod in her direction, "though she's seen it all before, of course. What do you say, Buck? Game for it?"

Buck hesitated. It was a tempting offer. But how much could he learn with the others around? If Speer was the Serpent, it would be a lot safer to confront him when they were alone. Besides, he had a few things he wanted to check out with Jimmy back in Cuzco before he made his move.

"I think I'll pass on that one," he said.

Earle scrambled to his feet. "I've got my camera case in the boat. I'll just run down and get it."

"You do that." Wolf nodded pleasantly, smiling at Buck. "Sure you won't change your mind? You don't know what you're missing. A chance to meet a real live savage."

Buck shook his head. If his hunch was correct, he'd already met one.

"ARE YOU DOING this for me?" Catherine asked when the glow from the torch at the end of the dock had finally dropped out of sight.

Buck was only a dark shape at the other end of the boat, silent, almost brooding. He hadn't spoken to her since they'd left the lodge.

When his answer finally came, it was heavy with reluctance. "No."

She didn't believe him. She couldn't believe him, not after the brief scene in Rosalee's kitchen. What else would have made him reject Wolfgang's offer? He was obviously still trying to protect her. She wondered if she should point out that the worst thing that could happen to her out here was a little seasickness.

The painful silence stretched into minutes, the minutes into an hour. The only sound was the steady roar of the motor as the boat streamed along, slicing through the river, the black wash like velvet behind them.

The welcoming sight of the boardwalk had just slid into view when the boat suddenly lurched in the water. The motor revved on, but all forward motion stopped.

"I don't believe this," Catherine muttered, shutting the motor off. She groped for the flashlight as Buck climbed over the seats to the stern.

"Prop?" he asked, kneeling beside her on the wooden seat.

"Afraid so."

Together they hoisted the motor out of the water.

"I must have hit a submerged rock," Catherine said, playing the flashlight beam over the propeller. "The impact probably broke the shear pin."

"Do you have a spare?"

She snapped open the motor hood and inspected its underside. "One. There's a pair of pliers by your foot."

Something swished into the water from the far shore as Buck began the repairs. He looked around. "Cayman?"

She shrugged, reaching down to feel her feet. "Probably." Her toes were wet. The flashlight beam cut a crazy arch across the night sky as she realized why.

Buck looked up. "Hey, I'm not done with that yet."

She was too startled by the sight of the water in the bottom of the boat to answer him. "There's a leak somewhere," she whispered, her head snapping up at the sound of another ominous splash from shore. "I think we're sinking."

Chapter Ten

"We're *what?*" Buck demanded, launching himself off the seat. The soles of his shoes were soaked through almost immediately. "How bad is it?" he asked, peering around her.

Catherine made another pass with the flashlight. "Bad." The level of the water seemed to inch up as they watched. "Very bad."

A splash from the far shoreline goaded him into motion. "I need five minutes," he said, grabbing the flashlight from her, "maybe more. Can you get rid of some of this water?"

She nodded. Five minutes. A lifetime.

"Then let's do it!"

Buck spun back to the motor, jamming the light beneath his arm as he attacked the job. The broken pin was already out. All he had to do was snap the new one into place. The pliers slipped. His right hand shot out, catching the shear pin a second before it became part of the river. *Damn.* His fingers felt as thick as sausages.

He glanced behind him. Catherine was still on her knees, scrabbling beneath one of the seats. "What's the holdup?" he yelled. "Bail!"

"There's no bucket!" she yelled back. She hurled a life preserver out of the way as she scrambled to the next seat. The bucket wasn't under that one, either. Or the next.

The water continued to rise.

"Bail, dammit!" Buck yelled.

"I'm trying!" she screamed back. She'd reached the prow of the boat. There was nowhere else to look except— She rammed her arm into the narrow cupboard that angled into the boat's prow. Empty. No, not quite. She yanked out a squashed baseball cap. It would have to do.

Frantically, she began to bail. After the first capful, she knew it was no use. There was just too much water. It was as though the bottom of the boat had given way completely and she was trying to drain the river. She hurled another capful overboard, grabbing for the corner of her veil as it slipped off one ear. She'd never designed it for anything as physical as this. This was crazy. She yanked the veil back into place, bringing up another capful of river water, and then another. Her body worked on, fueled by fear.

Something long and black scraped the side of the boat.

"Buck!" she screamed.

"That's it!" Buck slammed the hood of the motor into place and dropped the mechanism back into the water. Moments later, the motor roared to life and he twisted the throttle open.

They lurched forward, the water in the bottom of the boat creating a drag that Catherine thought they'd never overcome. Somehow, Buck brought them to shore, driving the boat onto a muddy beach about two hundred yards upstream from the dock. Together they stumbled over the side, collapsing in the cool, damp sand.

No one said a word. The silence was blessing enough. Above them, the Incas' *mayu* continued its starry sweep across the night sky.

Finally, Catherine moved. "I don't know how you managed those last couple of yards."

Buck groaned. "I don't know, either." He rolled over onto his back, digging the flashlight into the sand as a makeshift torch. "You were beautiful out there."

"I almost got us killed." She propped herself up on her elbow, swiping halfheartedly at a muddy clump on one sleeve. Her dress was ruined. And as for the impractically dainty sandals— She twisted around for a better look. They were probably ruined, too.

The veil slipped again without warning.

They grabbed for it together, Buck jackknifing into a sitting position and launching himself across her. Her hand closed over the top corner of the silk a split second before his did, and she fell back onto the sand, the full, muscular weight of his body pinning her down as together they pressed the veil against her face.

He'd seen nothing, her hammering senses told her as his eyes blazed into hers. Not one extra inch of skin. She'd been too quick for that, too conditioned by years of fear and mistrust to allow him even a glimpse of her face.

Yet the agony of wanting him flashed through her. If only she could replay those last few seconds—the whisper of silk against her skin as the veil came loose, the sudden, powerful thrust of his body against hers, their fingers reaching together for the hem of the veil—and missing it. *And missing it.*

If only she could rewrite the scene, he would be kissing her right now, his mouth hungry and savage against her flesh, her fingers frantic on the thin cotton of his shirt, the zipper of his jeans. The walls would come down in a torrent of passion. An explosion of letting go.

And she would be free.

She almost wept when he looped the veil back into place and rolled away from her.

"I saw you fumbling with it on the boat," he said, brushing his hand across his hair and raising one shoulder in a gesture of defeat.

She struggled upright against a wave of depression, the sight of his own frustration adding to her anguish. "I mustn't have secured it properly."

He shrugged again, and her eyes were drawn to the flat plane of his midriff. His shirt had been torn cleanly across his navel, probably by an exposed nail head on the boat.

"I don't suppose—" She choked on the next word, horror coursing through her as she caught sight of the twisted flesh of his stomach. "You're hurt!"

He caught her hand as she tried to get a closer look. "Old wound," he said, glancing down at the scar tissue.

She expelled her breath shakily. "What happened?"

"Old story."

"I'm a good listener."

He laughed bitterly. "Not that good." His expression softened as he fingered a strand of her hair. "How about you? Still in one piece?"

"I think so." Apart from the ache in her heart, she was fine. "Though it felt like I moved the whole river. When I couldn't find the bucket, I thought— Well, you know what I thought." She shifted her hips to one side and pulled out the baseball cap, rubbing one finger over the stylized letters that made up the logo. "I guess thanks are in order—to whomever."

"Expos," he said quietly, taking the cap from her. "Based out of Montreal. Tell me it's yours."

"It's not," she whispered, reading his mind.

"Tony a fan? Enrique? Jorge?"

She moistened her lips. "I don't think so."

He hurled the cap across the sand. "Earle. That son of a bitch."

She scrambled after him as he strode to the boat. "You think he took the bailing bucket? Why? What could he have possibly hoped to gain from that? He didn't know we'd start to sink on the way home."

"I'm not so sure of that," he grunted. "Help me turn the boat." With her beside him, he managed to flip the craft over. Then he went back for the flashlight.

"What are we looking for?" she asked as he began to examine the hull.

"Holes. Like this one." He pointed to a small, neat puncture in the wood. "And this one." The flashlight beam picked out another. Together, they found thirty more.

"This must have taken him hours," Buck said, bending down for a closer look. "I wonder how he managed to camouflage the plugs? Some kind of paint, probably."

"You still think Earle—?"

"Who else? He was the only one who had the time to tackle a job like this. Everyone else was in Cuzco."

Her eyes widened as she tried to take in all he was saying. Earle was responsible for everything that had been happening to her. Earle. Mild-mannered, nearsighted Earle. Her first impulse was to laugh it all away. But some deeper part of her believed Buck. It would explain Earle's sudden desire to spend the night at Quester's Inn. Maybe it would explain the Reverend's puzzling quote in Cuzco, too.

"Do you think he and the Reverend could be working together?" she asked.

"Maybe. Reverend Woolsey could be the brains while Earle supplies the muscle."

She shook her head at the image that conjured up. Still, she couldn't deny the evidence before them.

Buck ran a finger along the inside of one of the holes in the hull. "Look here. He drilled the holes, then packed them with a mixture of mud and straw. The movement of the boat must have loosened the mixture enough to let in a little water. When we stopped to change the shear pin, the mud gave way altogether. We're lucky the boat didn't fill faster than it did or we'd be out there right now." He nodded toward the river.

"He tried to kill us." She gagged at a new thought. "No, not us. Me. He wanted me."

He drew her to him gently. "Who knows what he wanted."

"He wanted to kill me!" And suddenly it was there again: the fear—the blind, paralyzing fear. She backed away from him, shaking. "It was an accident that we found out about it tonight. If Frank hadn't been ill, we'd have used the bigger boat. No one would have been the wiser until the day I took this one out alone!"

Alone. Some prism in her mind caught the word and threw it back at her, doubling it, magnifying it until she could barely breathe. "He won't stop, will he?" she moaned, barely recognizing the sound of her own voice. "He won't stop until he makes me pay!"

"For what?"

"For my sins." For the lies. For the cover-up. For a lifetime of hiding. She shook uncontrollably and put her hands out as if to ward of an invisible evil. The next thing she knew she was stumbling down the beach.

"Catherine!" Buck shouted, stunned by her reaction. It took him a second or two to recover before he raced after her. He had never seen her like this before, so afraid, so totally out of control.

Though she had the jump on him, she was handicapped by her injured ankle. He caught up to her just before she reached the jungle and pulled her down with him onto the soft, spongy mat of vegetation beneath the trees. She fought him every inch of the way.

"Catherine, stop it!" Buck shouted, forcing her arms back behind her head, pinning her legs down with his, terrified that she would hurt herself before he had a chance to talk her down from whatever ledge she imagined herself on. "It's Buck."

She only twisted harder as he tried to get through to her.

"It's Buck," he repeated. "I'm not the enemy."

Slowly, the panic subsided. "Buck." She shuddered, clinging to him. "Buck."

"I'm here." He held her until the violent shaking stopped. "This can't go on."

"No."

"It will destroy you."

"Yes." She pressed her face against his shoulder.

He had left the flashlight back at the boat. He wished he had it with him now. Anything would be better than the inky void beneath the trees. In the dark, Catherine seemed to be made of shadows, as insubstantial as a ghost. He fought the irrational feeling that he could pass his hand right through her if he tried. In their struggle, her veil had come loose again. He could almost imagine the fragile loveliness of her face. He thrust the thought aside, gently replacing the strip of cloth across her nose and mouth.

The feel of the veil against her skin dragged Catherine back to reality. She struggled to sit upright, shakily looping the end of the veil around her ear, trying to think of some explanation for her behavior. Everything but the truth seemed horribly inadequate. And she couldn't give him that. Despite the pain in her heart, she couldn't give him that.

He seemed to be waiting for her to say something.

"I'm sorry," she finally managed, knowing it was the one thing he did not want to hear.

He exhaled heavily, his hand moving up to his face. She heard the rasp of his beard as he rubbed his jaw. "Whenever you're ready," he said softly. "I'll be waiting."

I won't force you. She read his thoughts like they were her own. And still, something kept her from speaking her heart to him. She felt like weeping.

They trudged back to the lodge in silence.

Buck stopped at the edge of the clearing. "Did you leave a candle burning in your cabin?"

"No."

"There's one burning there now."

She peered across the compound. He was right. She could just make out the slight waver of light against the curtains. "That's impossible," she protested. "You know I'd never—"

The flashlight he was carrying winked out, and he pushed her behind him. "Stay here."

She grabbed his arm. "You're not going in there alone. I'm coming with you."

"The hell you are."

"The hell I am." A little of the old spark flared in her.

Even in the dark, Buck recognized that streak of stubbornness. She was probably thrusting her chin out at him right now. A part of him rejoiced that she had fought back that attack of panic on the beach, while another part wished that she had stayed afraid, at least until he'd had a chance to check out her cabin.

"All right," he grunted finally. They could debate this all night and still come up with no satisfactory solution. "But stay behind me."

"Right behind you," came her determined whisper.

If the situation hadn't been so hopeless, he'd have laughed.

They crept silently to the veranda, keeping clear of the murky light cast by a few sputtering torches. The cabin was deathly still. Whoever was inside was doing a pretty good job of keeping quiet. Buck eased up the steps and tried the door. Still no sound from inside. Behind him, the compound shimmered, slumbering.

"Stay here," he mouthed to her as he crept inside. "I mean it."

For once, she obeyed him.

Her room was empty. Buck examined the stub of wax on the small table near the door. Whoever had lit the candle had left it burning for quite a while. If his intent had been to start a fire, he'd almost succeeded. Or maybe he'd intended something else. Something more insidious.

Buck glanced over his shoulder.

The bathroom.

Still holding the nub of candle, he moved forward, already knowing what lay behind that door. The bloodred letters on the mirror jumped out at him before he'd taken more than a step inside.

A sound brought his head around. Catherine. She'd guessed, too.

"Go back," he said as he tried to shield her from the message on the mirror.

"No. I have to see this." She pushed past him. The words on the mirror seemed to pulse with a life of their own.

IS IT SAFE?

She crumpled to the floor, wide-eyed with fear.

SHE SLEPT, FINALLY.

Buck stood on the other side of the makeshift blanket partition he'd rigged up in his cabin and listened to Catherine's breathing until the shallow, shaky breaths fell into a regular pattern. It wasn't a sound sleep. She kept crying out, as though whatever she was trying to escape still hunted her, even in her dreams.

Still, she was asleep. It was more than he could have hoped for an hour ago.

He lowered himself into the canvas deck chair he'd dragged in from the porch and massaged his temples tiredly. It was going to be a long night, and he had no intention of sleeping. Not while that maniac was loose out there. Not while Catherine tossed and turned fitfully only a few feet away from him.

She groaned again, and the iron band of tension around his head tightened. God, he wanted to go to her, to touch her, to try to give her whatever strength she needed to fight this thing. But she was fighting him, too. And he was losing.

It had been almost impossible to convince her that she should spend the night in his cabin. She had been almost hysterical. At one point, he'd even considered waking Tony. His head flopped back against the canvas. *Wouldn't that have been the kicker, going to Tony for help.* Finally her nervous energy, or whatever was driving her these days, simply ran out, and she'd allowed him to lead her across the compound to his room. How long she stayed here was anybody's guess. He didn't think even she knew what she was going to do next.

His eyelids suddenly sagged. He forced them open, his eyes automatically hunting for the thin curtain that separated him from the woman on the bed. It might have been a brick wall, for all the comfort it gave him. A brick wall cutting him off, forever, from the woman he had fallen in love with.

Love.

Cold comfort, indeed, in the middle of this green hell.

THE WOMAN IN THE MIRROR was a wreck.

Catherine stood with her back pressed against the door of the shower stall, too afraid to move forward, too afraid to turn back. The image that wavered between the letters of last night's message appalled her.

This was Catherine What's-Her-Name? Her muddled thoughts strove to fill in the blank, but all she could come up with was Catherine. Catherine. As incomplete as the veiled specter that danced before her.

Her vision blurred as the events of the last twenty-four hours skipped through her consciousness. She'd been alone in Buck's cabin when she'd awakened, dazed and uncertain, still caught in the grip of some broken, unholy nightmare. The seeds of that dream had propelled her, against her will, across the compound to her own cabin. But once here, all strength had deserted her. Even her thoughts were not her own anymore.

Tentatively, she reached for the crimson letters on the mirror. Her reflection did the same, the hand trembling violently as it approached her. She stepped back. The hand withdrew. She swallowed hard, forcing her tears down. The effort brought on a new bout of trembling. She was going to pieces, and there was nothing she could do to stop it.

They'll go away if you don't let them see you. Some long-forgotten snippet of conversation floated tantalizingly through her mind. *If you don't let them see you.* For a moment, she seemed to float along with it.

Then her gaze flickered back to her tortured reflection and she lurched forward, galvanized by the desperate plea she saw in those eyes. There was a box of tissues on the edge of the sink. She ripped out a fistful and began to scrub wildly at the letters on the mirror.

They wouldn't come off.

She scrubbed harder, telling herself that the lipstick had dried overnight, that the tissues were poorly made, that her own muscles were refusing to obey her. But the message remained. It was as though it had been written in... Her mind refused to finish the thought as she began scraping at the crimson words with her fingernails, beating the mirror with her fists, attacking her own reflection.

Is. It. Safe?

Her hands seemed to float in front of her face, bloodred, boneless. They were covered with David's blood. Her blood. Her senses swam. Surely that was wrong. Her hands had been clean for five years, hadn't they? Between her splayed fingers, the message on the mirror mocked her sad descent into that private, shadowed world where nothing, not even sanity, could find its way in.

Safe? Was she safe? She would never be safe. Never.

"Please," she moaned, backing away from the mirror. But it was already too late. He'd gotten what he wanted. The message-writer. The pit-digger. The boat-sinker. The face-less man who chased her in her dreams. Buck was so sure that it was Earle, but she knew differently.

It was David. Somehow, David had come back to haunt her. It wasn't enough that she was already dead. He meant to bury her.

She would not let him. She clung to that thought, lashing out furiously at the mirror. Image after image from her past burst into focus as she fought for control of her life. A picnic with her parents that had ended with a rain shower and ice cream. A particularly grueling scene in one of her movies that she'd aced in only two takes. The first time she'd seen the Phoenix, bathed in the glow of the rising sun. And Buck—his image dominated all the others.

Her fingers tangled in the veil. She ripped it from her face, attacking the message with it until the words were gone, until she was sated and sobbing with relief.

She raised her head. For the first time in five years, she could look at herself in a mirror without flinching. She looked terrible. Her lips curved into a watery smile that strengthened even as she stared at it. But she was free. She was Catherine Taylor.

And soon the rest of the world would know it, too.

"SEÑOR WHEELER IS IN the dining room," Enrique said helpfully, his attention returning to the green pepper he was dicing. The contents of several cast-iron pots bubbled cheerfully on the stove behind him. Tonight was vegetarian night at the Phoenix and Enrique took his vegetables very seriously.

Catherine counted to five slowly. "That's what you've been saying," she finally managed, suppressing a shudder as her fingers encountered the edge of her veil. "But I'm looking for Señor Jordan."

He pointed with his chin. "In the dining room, too."

Her excitement died, along with the explanation she had carefully prepared for Buck. If only she hadn't taken the time to shower— She banished the thought, telling herself that this was only a minor delay. Her story could wait until Buck was alone. After all he'd done for her, he deserved to hear it first.

"Señor Reverend Woolsey is with them," Enrique added, sniffing experimentally at a large onion.

Catherine's stomach lurched. "You mean they're back from Wolf's already?"

He nodded. "*Sí.* Carlos brought them by half an hour ago. About two o'clock," he added at her blank expression.

She nodded weakly. Two o'clock. Between waking in Buck's cabin at eleven and showering in her own about two, she'd lost nearly three hours. Her spine stiffened. Three hours of her life gone. That was something that would never happen again.

"What about Earle?" she demanded.

Enrique's response didn't surprise her. "I have not seen him."

Probably under a rock somewhere, she fumed as she stomped out of the kitchen. All the way back to her cabin, she played a mental tape of what she planned to do to Earle Godot when she finally found him. The scene was still rolling when she clicked the cabin door shut behind her. The image melted, replaced by the eerie sounds of Morse code.

Someone was using the radio.

Her heart slammed into her ribs as the blips swamped her senses. She picked up a fragment: *-S-T-H-E-F-*. It made no sense at all. Obligingly, the word was repeated. *A-R-M-S-T-H-E-F-T*. It was followed by her father's name, and then by her own.

Rage followed hard on the heels of despair as she charged blindly forward. The thought that she could be walking into real trouble made no impression on the fury that engulfed her. Earlier, she had decided not to run. Now she had decided to fight.

The man at the radio turned in alarm as she burst through the door. Their eyes met for one agonizing second.

"You," she whispered.

Chapter Eleven

Buck stepped away from the table, his eyes dark with shock. Behind him, the radio continued to spew out its damning coded sequence. "Catherine—"

She lurched for the door, too numbed by his betrayal to answer.

He reached it first, blocking her way before she'd taken more than a few steps. "Catherine, wait—"

"I'll scream," she choked out, trying to move around him.

He moved with her, his body tense and angry, his face twisted into a grim parody of the man she thought she knew. "No you won't. You'll walk to the corner and sit down until I've finished transmitting. Stay quiet until I have a chance to explain."

"I have all the explanation I need," she shot back, taking refuge in a sudden, unexpected bolt of fury. He followed her gaze as she glared at the radio. "You won't get away with it, you know."

The false bravado in her voice did not fool him. "Sit down, Catherine or I'll—"

"Or you'll what?"

A look of regret passed over his face. "Do us both a favor and sit down."

Something in the weary resignation of his voice silenced her. She moved to the corner and slid to the ground, her legs drawn up in a half crouch, still tensed for action.

Buck quietly acknowledged her dogged determination. "You never give up, do you?" he murmured as he returned to the radio. He glanced at her frequently as he finished copying Jimmy Cochrane's message, then transmitted some information of his own before he shut the radio down.

The silence was far worse than the code had been, falling like an accusation between them.

Buck finally gave up waiting for her to speak. "You probably have a lot of questions."

"And I suppose you have all the answers."

"Most of them." He stood up. "We'll be more comfortable if we talk in the other room."

"Another order, Herr General?" The sarcasm didn't suit her, but it was all she had left.

His mouth twitched. "A request."

She ignored his outstretched hand as she got to her feet. It was harder to ignore the fleeting look of pain that crossed his face as she inched around him. For a split second, her anger deserted her, replaced by such an overwhelming feeling of loss that she thought she would gag. A few hours ago, Buck had unknowingly saved her from herself. Now he had cut her loose again into the bleak torrent of her past. Betrayer and savior. He was both. She did not know what was worse: losing the freedom she thought she had gained or losing the man she thought she could trust.

She avoided looking at Buck as she stalked into the next room, her anger reasserting itself as she turned to confront him. "All right. I'm listening."

Buck sighed. "You're going to make this hard for me, aren't you?" He didn't wait for her reply. "My name is—"

"Don't tell me. It's Bond. James Bond. Or maybe I should say Benedict Arnold."

The small smile that began to touch his lips faded. "This thing with the radio has nothing to do with you."

She forced out a laugh. "I find you in my cabin, using my radio—" *digging into my past,* she wanted to scream at him "—and you say it has nothing to do with me? What kind of a fool do you think I am?"

The biggest fool there is, she thought. The kind who stakes everything she has on a man. The kind who should never listen to her heart.

Buck swallowed her sarcasm with effort. "My name is Buck Jordan," he began again. "I'm an officer in the United States Army."

"Corps of Engineers," she supplied with derision, thinking back to the day they had spent on the lagoon. Her senses worked overtime, supplying her with more details than she cared to remember: the way the sun had bronzed his skin, the way his little-boy smile had pulled at her emotions. The memories made his betrayal of her all the more painful.

"I work for a special-investigations unit of the military police."

Her throat went dry. It was worse than she thought. He was probing into her father's death.

"And...?" The word left her like a rusty note.

"And I'm here in Peru to meet with an informant who has information vital to our country's military security." Inwardly, Buck winced. He did sound like James Bond, for God's sake. No wonder she wore such a look of hostile skepticism.

"I'm here to get a name," he said quietly. "Have you ever heard of the Serpent?"

For a moment, confusion replaced the hostility. "No."

"In a few days, if all goes well, the whole world will know him." He tapped the papers he had brought with him from the radio room. "The Serpent is an illegal arms dealer. For the past twenty years, he's been selling stolen American

arms and ammunition to militant organizations and para-
military groups all over the world. We received word several months ago that one of his former henchmen was
willing to cut a deal with the military. He agreed to give us
the name and location of the Serpent in exchange for protection from his former boss and immunity from prosecu-
tion. It's as simple as that.''

"Why should I believe you?"

"Because it's the truth."

She wanted to believe him. God, she *needed* to believe
him. But there were still too many unanswered questions for
her to accept what he was saying. "Then why the radio?
Why the continued charade? Why don't you just get your
name and go?"

Buck grimaced. "Complications. I was supposed to meet
the informant here at the lodge a week ago. He never
showed. Since then, I've been trying to find out what went
wrong. I talked to an American contact when we were in
Cuzco and he assured me that the rendezvous was still on.
Since then, no informant, no name, nothing."

"I'm so happy we could oblige you with a free trip to the
city," Catherine said, her sarcasm resurfacing. She stopped,
stunned by what she saw in his face. "We did oblige you,
didn't we," she said in disbelief. "The plugged fuel
lines—"

Buck coughed awkwardly, lowering his head and rubbing the back of his neck. He looked like a schoolboy who
had been caught cutting classes. "Now that you mention it,
Uncle Sam does owe you for that. Tinkering with the appliances was the only way I could think of to get back to Cuzco
without arousing any suspicion. I overheard Enrique and
Reverend Woolsey at lunch the day I arrived talking about
the problems you'd been having with the stoves. I figured I
could make it work to my advantage, especially after my
informant refused to show his face. I thought if I turned up
in Cuzco, in person, I could rattle a few cages in Washing-

ton. They need me on this job. And so far, all I've been getting is double-talk. If I walk, and I'm damn close to doing that," he muttered under his breath, "Washington's got nothing."

"Why?" Catherine asked. His story had the ring of truth, and that made her all the more suspicious. "What makes you so indispensable?"

He focused on a spot on the wall above her bed. "The informant told my superiors he would deal only with me. That's why I came out of retirement. He and I go back a long way."

"How long?"

He still refused to look at her. "Twenty years. We became buddies right after basic training. I'd just been posted to a base in Washington state. He was a weapons tech there. Somehow he got involved with the Serpent. One night on a security patrol, I surprised him and several of the Serpent's men robbing the ammunition depot. And there was nothing I could do to stop them." His hand moved to his chest and the faint ridge of scar tissue palpable beneath his shirt. "Nothing."

Catherine's skin crawled. The story was hauntingly familiar. "What base was it?" she heard herself ask. She knew the answer before he opened his mouth.

"Camp Bradley."

Her father's base.

She swayed in shock. Buck and her father had both been stationed at the same base. They'd both been caught up in the same arms robbery. She doubled over as the memory of that night and all the cold nights after it swept through her.

"Catherine!" Buck snapped out of his bitter reverie and reached for her.

She jerked free of his grasp. "No!"

"You believe me, don't you," he demanded, forcing her to look at him. "You believe me because you know something about that night! What do you know? Tell me!"

She moaned, too terrified to finally say the words.

"Tell me!"

"No. Please, no."

He was losing her. He could see that in the frantic, wide-eyed way she backed away from him. He had to get through to her, *now*, before she retreated completely behind that wall of secrecy she'd erected for herself. Desperately he played his last hand. "I asked my contact to run a background check on you while I was in Cuzco."

The look of betrayal in her eyes was almost more than he could bear. "You did *what?*"

"I thought I was doing you a favor. Hell, I thought I was doing both of us a favor. I couldn't go on watching you suffer." He approached her slowly, still afraid that she would bolt. "I radioed him as soon as we returned to the lodge. I canceled the request. I couldn't let something like that come between us."

Her eyelids fluttered as she absorbed this new piece of information.

He drew his hands along her shoulders. "Catherine, what would Jim have told me if he'd done the check?"

Catherine swayed slightly. He was giving her a choice. He was telling her the decision was ultimately hers. She could lie now and spend the rest of her life running, or she could give up. No, it was no longer a question of giving up. She had given up years ago. Now the question was whether she had enough trust in him, enough trust in herself, to resume living.

It took all the courage she had to look into his eyes. "He would have told you that I don't exist."

His hands fell to his sides. "What?"

"That I've never existed, until now." Her voice dropped to a whisper as she fumbled beneath her hair for the loops that held the veil in place. Barely breathing, she pulled the veil away from her face and waited for his response.

A minute dragged by. And then another. And still Buck refused to say a word. The temperature outside climbed another degree. The air in the cabin slowly thickened with the heat.

Finally he said, "Catherine Tremaine."

Catherine's shoulders sagged with release.

Buck shook his head in disbelief. He'd braced himself for the unexpected, but he hadn't been prepared for this. Not this. There was no mistaking the high cheekbones, the delicate nose and the full mouth. The woman before him was the much-sought-after actress of stage and screen, breathtakingly lovely, highly talented and, according to all reports, very much deceased.

"You're Catherine Tremaine," he repeated softly. Apparently reports of her death had been greatly exaggerated.

"I was. Once." She'd never felt more exposed in her life. "And before that, I was Catherine Taylor," she said, stripping away another layer of lies, "Neil Taylor's daughter."

He sucked in his breath. "Neil Taylor was in charge of the ammunition depot at Camp Bradley."

"Yes."

"Did you also know that he was one of the Serpent's men?"

A single tear glided silently down her cheek. "Why do you think I ran? I've been hiding from that fact all my life."

"Come here."

He gathered her in his arms and held her while she wept. She was as fragile as he remembered from the hotel room in Cuzco, as fragile and as lovely. Although he tried to avoid looking at her, his gaze kept returning to her face. It was as though he were getting his first glimpse of paradise after resigning himself to the view from a window. A shuttered, curtained window.

He felt a poignant loss when she finally drew back.

"I haven't done that in a long time," she said, hiccuping. Morosely, she rubbed at the wet stain on his shirt. "I've made a mess of your shirt."

"Don't worry. It's drip-dry. So am I."

She gave him a watery grin.

"Do you want to talk about it?"

Her relief was replaced by the hollow ache she had come to accept as a natural extension of herself, as though grief could be worn like an arm or a leg. She pushed a tangle of hair away from her face. She didn't need another arm or leg. And she certainly didn't need the deadweight of guilt she'd been carrying around for twenty years.

"You know about the shooting," she said slowly.

"I know your father was killed during the robbery. That's what started the investigation into your father's involvement in the theft. I think the story was picked up by every news hound in the country."

"In the world," she said, sinking down onto the bed. "A friend of my father's took me in right after he di—right after the shooting. The phone rang every night for weeks. We found footprints in the flower beds, in the driveway." Her fingers fluttered over the alpaca spread. "One morning even the trash cans were gone. I don't know what they hoped to find. That I was a chip off the old block, I guess. Some kind of card-carrying terrorist, just like my father. Peddling secrets with my skipping rope." She squeezed her eyes shut against the old anger, the old shame.

Unwanted memories sprang up like weeds—an image of herself as a child, her tearstained face pressed against the window as she peered at the crowds outside the house. *"What do they want? Why won't they leave me alone?"*

"Come away from the windows, Catherine. They'll go away if you don't let them see you."

An errant tear slid down her cheek. "I stayed in my room for weeks."

The mattress depressed as he sat down beside her. "Someone should have looked after you," he said fiercely, protectively, as he reached for her hands. "You would have been—what?—nine, ten years old? Those vultures wanted a story, and with your father dead, you were it. The military didn't let out the full details of the investigation for several months."

"By then I was in California," Catherine said. "My uncle Rudy left his medical practice in Lima as soon as he heard the news and came for me. He changed my name soon after he arrived."

"Catherine Tremaine."

She nodded. "That was long before drama school. Before the fame."

"*Rumors, The Medusa,*" Buck said, thinking back to the films he had seen. His wife had been a big Catherine Tremaine fan right before the divorce. "*A Woman For the Taking.*"

"*In the Making,*" she corrected absently.

"Sorry, I didn't get out much in those days."

"It doesn't really matter. All that ended the night of the fire."

He frowned as he tried to follow her story. "Why would you go into hiding over something like that? Big stars face tragedies all the time. You would have been page-one material for a couple of days. 'Movie Star's Home Gutted By Blaze!'" he said, improvising a newspaper headline. "But after that, things would have died down. Even David's death could have been made to seem all part of the disaster."

"The fire wasn't the disaster. The fire was the cover-up."

His frown deepened. "I don't understand."

She stood up and began to pace the room, too agitated to sit still while she described her relationship with David Crane and the events leading up to her nervous breakdown. By the time she had come to the part about David's double life as a tabloid journalist, he was pacing with her.

"So you decided to fake your own death."

"That was Uncle Rudy's idea. He knew the press wouldn't leave me alone, not after seeing what they did to Daddy. He thought the best way to protect me was to make me disappear again. Permanently, this time."

"Exit Catherine Tremaine, enter Catherine Monroe."

Miserably, Catherine nodded, pausing in midstride to scoop up the veil from the floor. She crushed the light-weight material between her fingers, hating the gauzy clutch of the fabric. How had she managed to wear it next to her face for so long? The weight, the color, the cut—everything about it made her throat constrict.

Buck gently extricated the cloth from her hands. "I think we're going to want to use that again."

"You're joking." The grim set to his mouth told her he was not. "But I thought Earle— Why can't we just confront him about the messages and the boat? Why do I have to wear this—this *thing* again?" It had almost cost her her sanity to remove it. It might just drive her mad to have to put it back on.

"Because Earle is not the one we're after."

Somewhere inside her, the nightmare of fear and confusion she thought she'd escaped began to rewind. "I—I don't understand," she stammered. "The hat, the boat—who else could it be?"

"Sit down," Buck said gently, leading her to the edge of the bed. He sat down beside her, propping his elbows on his knees as he began to page through the notes he'd taken from Jimmy's transmission. "My contact in Cuzco was able to do a little snooping into the background of the other guests. Not much, but enough to clear Earle of trying to kill you last night."

Catherine shook her head in disbelief. "Don't tell me he's just a small-time photojournalist." For twenty-four hours, Earle Godot had been the devil. Something in her refused to give that up.

"Oh, he's a little more than just a snap-happy photo-bug," Buck said, twisting his head to look at her. "Mr. Godot owns a piece of the magazine he's working for, a very large and expensive piece. In fact, the man's mortgaged up to his—" he cleared his throat, searching for a safer noun "—up to his wide-angle lens." His heart constricted at the involuntary smile that played across her face. God, he could sit and look at her mouth all day. Instead, he looked back at his notes, forcing himself to concentrate. "Everything he owns is riding on the first couple of issues."

"Why does that make him innocent? If anything, it seals our case against him. A feature article on Catherine Tremaine would be his meal ticket."

"An article on Catherine Tremaine, owner of the Phoenix Lodge, might sell a few magazines, you're right. But an article on Catherine Tremaine, cayman's breakfast, wouldn't be worth the paper it was written on."

Her shoulder sagged. "In other words, I'm worth more to him alive than dead. There'd be no reason for him to sabotage the boat."

He nodded.

Catherine sank down onto the bed, her arms out-stretched above her head, a bone-numbing weariness settling over her. They were right back were they started from, which was exactly nowhere. They had too many suspects, too many clues and not enough motive to pin terrorism and attempted murder on anyone. "What about Frank and Selena?" She forced the words past her lips, covering all the guests more out of habit than a real desire to go on with the discussion. "What did your contact tell you about them?"

Buck exhaled loudly. "Frank and Selena Wheeler. Recently married. Sixty-five years old and fortyish." He tapped the papers with his forefinger at Catherine's exasperated groan. "That's what it says here. Jimmy must have liked that one." He squinted at his hasty scrawl. "Selena's a former show girl and actress and Frank's a retired police officer, LAPD." His voice dropped a notch as he glanced at her. "Any chance he might have been there the night of the fire?"

She sat up, drawing her knees to her chest. "I don't know. By that time, I was in no condition to take note of anything."

Buck nodded. "On the odd chance that you and Selena did a film together, or that Frank was involved in the investigation of the fire, it still doesn't mean that one, or both of them, planted the messages and rigged the boat. If they wanted to blackmail you, there'd be easier and less life-threatening ways to do it."

"You think their motive could be blackmail?"

"What else?"

It was a question she couldn't answer. "What about Reverend Woolsey?"

"John Woolsey," Buck muttered. "No surprises there. He's exactly what he claims to be—a clergyman. His wife Marjorie died several months ago. He took a leave of absence soon after. A daughter lives in Illinois. A son is somewhere out west."

"That's all?"

"His parish wants him back. I guess no one can deliver a sermon quite like the Reverend."

Catherine dropped her feet to the floor, deep in thought. "We're missing something—something crucial. One of the guests has to have something in his or her background that we're just not seeing."

"If we knew how he discovered your true identity then we might be able to figure out who he is." Buck looked at her curiously. "Any ideas on that one?"

Catherine frowned. "No. Uncle Rudy was pretty thorough when he erased my past. Tony is the only other person who knows who I am, and he would never betray me."

"Then until we nail this guy, I want you to wear the veil," Buck said firmly. "If this lunatic is operating a few cards short of a deck, then there's no telling how he might react if you revealed your identity now. His entire scheme hinges on your efforts to stay hidden. If you ruined things for him, he might go over the edge."

Fear flickered through her. "You're saying he's mad."

"He's out to hurt you. That's mad enough for me." He touched her face gently, still not used to seeing her like this, loving the play of emotions that animated her mouth, her eyes. His thumb moved with tantalizing slowness over the small beauty mark that rested just above her top lip. He could explore her face for a lifetime and never tire of it. "There's something else."

Suddenly Catherine feared what he was about to tell her. "What is it?"

"I brought a gun to the Phoenix. It's missing."

Her breath lodged in her throat. "You think *he* might have taken it."

"I think it's possible." His eyes turned hard. "I don't want you out alone at night. If it's possible, keep someone with you during the day as well."

"You really think he'll try to kill me?" The last words fell to a whisper.

In the tormented silence that followed her question, the muffled click outside the window sounded like a gunshot. They both froze, their eyes automatically locking. Buck recovered first, lunging for the door. She raced after him, snatching up the veil as she ran. By the time she reached the veranda, whoever had been lurking outside the cabin had vanished.

"Did you see him?" she gasped, holding the veil over her mouth and nose as she scanned the compound. Her eyes fell on the brilliant blue feather Buck had in his hand. "One of the birds?"

"Probably." He didn't look convinced. "Go back inside. I'll have another look around."

By the time he'd rejoined her, shaking his head in frustration, she was beginning to believe she had imagined the whole thing.

"Nothing. The entire compound's dead."

She glanced at her watch. "It *is* siesta time."

"Tell that to Heckle and Jeckle."

She took the feather from him, turning it over in her hand. They'd obviously overreacted. What else could it be? From all indications, the man they were after liked to operate after dark, when his chances of being caught were less likely. The last place they should have expected to find him was on her own veranda in the middle of the day.

"Some detectives we are," she said bitterly. "We can't even locate a pair of overweight, overindulged parrots."

"Sorry, ma'am." Buck adopted an exaggerated Southern drawl. "Not my area of expertise."

"Parrots?"

"Or porches."

She smiled in spite of herself, stabbing him with the feather. "You're a big help."

He caught her hand, the tender light of humor in his eyes rapidly changing to desire. "And you're beautiful."

"No one's said that to me in a long time," she said, shivering uncontrollably as he drew her forward into the muscular shelter of his arms.

The feather drifted silently to the floor.

His first kiss was like a question, the briefest joining of lips, as though he expected her to vanish the moment his mouth touched hers. Then he kissed her again, really kissed her, this time driven by a need that was beyond wondering, beyond fear. She could feel it, too, the letting go. There was no veil between them now, no secrets, no hidden shame. There was only the need and the hunger and the sweet, hot pull of their senses as they explored each other's mouths and bodies.

She moaned, tipping her head back as his tongue began to take her throat in long, slow strokes. This was pain—exquisite, scorching, relentless. Their bodies broke, then came together, then broke again as they teased the passion, long denied, from one another.

"I could get used to this," Buck groaned as he dragged his mouth back to hers. "And this." He dropped his head to the open collar of her blouse, nipping at the buttons to get to the sensitive skin beneath. "And this." His body surged against her, demanding a response and finding it as her hips met the heated thrust of his.

"Everyone's asleep," Catherine whispered, her body lighted with indescribable flame. They moved together again in a kind of sinuous dance, touching and teasing in a ritual as old as time. "We have the whole afternoon." She barely recognized the breathless invitation in her own voice, barely registered his husky response as he drew her down onto the bed, his hands quick and hungry on the thin barrier of clothing that separated them.

The fabric fell away like a fleeting thought, his shirt and pants soon joining hers in a jumble on the alpaca spread. Her filmy underthings followed a heartbeat later.

"Let me do that," she breathed when he yanked at the last piece of clothing between them. She knelt beside him, sliding her fingers into the elastic waistband of his briefs. He was lean, hard muscle beneath, damp with the potent fever of tropical heat and desire.

He pressed her back against the bed when her mouth sought out the thickened ridges of scar tissue on his stomach. "Catherine." Her name was a rough command. "Catherine, when this is all over—"

She shook her head, not wanting to hear, not wanting to think, wanting only to submerge herself in the pure pleasure of loving him. Unbidden, a sliver of apprehension sliced through her when he raised himself over her. For a moment, she caught her breath at the enormity of her actions. *When this was all over.* But then he was filling her, and she was past all thought, all caution, bound to him by the overwhelming agony of desire. Of consummation. Of release.

She cried out when the hot, white light of fulfillment took them both.

They lay entwined for a long time afterwards, her head nestled on his shoulder, their heartbeats slowing in concert. Outside the window, the sun burned on into the rich, thick hush of late afternoon.

Finally, Buck stirred. "I think things just got a lot more complicated."

She stiffened slightly, dread cutting through her at the implications of his words. "What do you mean?"

He pulled back so he could see her face. "Just that I think I'm falling in love with you and— Whoa—wait a minute." He grabbed her by the shoulders as she rolled away from him. "I could have sworn you were starting to feel the same way."

"I—" She tried to swallow the lie. "It's not that I don't, it's just—" There. It had come out, anyway. A backhanded admission that she felt the same way he did, when she didn't. When she couldn't. She fumbled for something else, glancing at him quickly, then averting her gaze before he could see the agony she knew must show in her eyes.

How could she tell him that she didn't love him? How could she admit that lovemaking and being in love were not the same thing? Buck had brought her back to life, it was true. He challenged her senses and stirred her emotions in ways she had never imagined. But love? Love meant always and forever. Love meant no regrets and happily-ever-after. And right now, with a madman on the loose, with death hanging like a sword over her head, with a lamentable past and a questionable future, she couldn't be sure of anything, least of all falling in love. She might never find the courage to give him those three words.

He was still studying her. "You're worried about the messages," he supplied, finally.

"Yes. I can't think of anything else right now." She brought the words out in a rush, angry with him for giving her such an easy way out, furious with herself for taking it.

He looked at her for a long time before gently drawing her back into his arms. "Don't worry," he murmured as he began to stroke her hair. "This thing can't last forever. And after it's over, we'll have all the time in the world."

Her glance fell on the discarded parrot's feather as he spoke. "All the time in the world," she repeated as she slowly relaxed against him.

In her heart, she wished it was true.

Chapter Twelve

He took the bullet low in his belly.

The impact drove him back and down, searing his insides as though a fire had ignited in his gut. Another bullet tore into the wall above his head and he jerked sideways, choking on a wave of agony.

The next bullet would kill him.

Clamping one arm across the oozing wound in his stomach, he began to inch his way backward toward the door, leaving a black trail of blood behind him.

The distance closed with excruciating slowness. Just as he reached the door, he glanced back. The gun materialized out of nowhere. He reared up, kicking at it with his last reserve of strength.

The oath told him he had hit someone. Maybe he had bought himself a little time. He scrabbled for the door handle, touched it and fell back, groaning. He was reaching for it again when the familiar voice behind him cut him down.

Buck woke, choking.

He drew in a lungful of thick, moist night air, shuddering himself fully awake while the dream slowly evaporated. How many times was that now? Two? Three? His nights in the jungle were becoming increasingly impossible. If he ever came face-to-face with his informant, he wouldn't know what was real and what wasn't.

He swung his feet over the side of the bed and groped for the candle on the bedside table, padding toward the bathroom as soon as the flame caught.

In the mirror above the sink, his bloodshot eyes stared back at him. Day-old beard glittered in the tepid light from the candle. He moved the sputtering flame closer to the glass, running his hand thoughtfully across his jaw. Maybe a shave would make him feel a little more human.

Hell, why not a top hat and tails, as well? He grimaced at his reflection. It was two o'clock in the morning, if his battered travel alarm could be trusted. A little late to be so concerned about personal grooming, especially since he knew the real reason for his sudden interest in a clean shave.

He was afraid to go back to sleep. Afraid that, if he slept, he'd find himself back at Camp Bradley. Afraid that his informant would be waiting for him with a gun, the way he'd waited for him twenty years ago.

That fear, and the need to conquer it, were the only things that kept him from procrastinating further in front of the mirror. Clenching his teeth, he picked up the candle and plodded grimly back to bed.

He was going to beat this thing if it took all night to do it.

HE TOOK THE BULLET low in his belly.

The impact drove him back and down, searing his insides—

This time he caught himself before the dream wound out to its inevitable, bloody conclusion. He groaned, glancing at his clock. Two-twenty. That shave was looking better and better.

He rolled onto his feet, fumbling for his pants, as more of the dream came back to him. This time something had been different. This time, he'd have sworn that Catherine was the one behind the gun.

He didn't need Freud to interpret that one for him.

He yawned, drawing back the curtain to look over the compound. It glowed with an eerie incandescence, the vibrant greens of the jungle anemic and bloated in the flickering light. Jorge was still leaving a couple of torches burning all night. Buck didn't know whether that would do any good or not. Despite the strides that Catherine had made in putting her past behind her, there was still a major hurdle that she seemed incapable of crossing, a hurdle of her own making. The compound could blaze with a thousand lights and she'd still run, never feeling safe enough to entrust her life, or her love, to any man.

Catherine was still hiding, from Catherine this time.

The thought kicked at him.

He glanced toward her cabin. A light burned faintly at the window. That wasn't surprising, considering how troubled she'd been when he'd left her. She'd probably slept as little as he had. He opened the door and started across the compound, not knowing what else he could say to help her, but knowing he had to try.

"AN OMELET FOR ZEE LADY," Buck said half an hour later, embellishing his culinary skills with a sinfully accurate French accent as he set the plate down on the butcher-block table. He ogled Catherine broadly from the stove while he slid another helping onto his own plate.

Catherine laughed helplessly. "You've missed your calling," she teased him as she speared a slice of fresh tomato with her fork.

"You mean chef extraordinaire?"

"More like impersonator par excellence. With a routine like that, you could give Inspector Clouseau a run for his money."

The spatula dropped back into the skillet with a clatter. "No, thanks. If your experience in Hollywood is anything to go by—" He let the sentence hang, unfinished. He'd promised not to talk about Catherine's past tonight. Only then had she agreed to accompany him to the kitchen for a late-night snack. But the conversation ever since had been banal at best as they skirted the real issues. Her life with her father. The hideous events with David Crane in California. Their lovemaking that afternoon. That was the real topic Catherine wanted to avoid. He knew it. She knew it. Everything else was smoke and mirrors.

He grimaced as he took the stool next to hers, his hand automatically moving to the left side of his chest.

She looked up from her omelet. "Does it still hurt?"

"What, this?" The directness of her question surprised him. But then, everything about the lady was a surprise. He pounced on her willingness to talk. At least it was an opening, a beginning. "No, it doesn't. I think it's more subconscious than anything else. I guess I just got used to protecting the area and never outgrew the need."

Catherine nodded, shoving a half-eaten slice of tomato around her plate, another question hovering unspoken on her lips. She had a million things she wanted to say to him. A million things she needed him to answer, all tied to the time they'd spent together in her cabin. She stole a glance at him, wondering if he burned with the same unrelenting hunger. One afternoon of love would never be enough. *But it would have to be enough.* How could she possibly give him any more of herself, of her heart, right now?

How could she possibly deny him?

She hooked her feet around the legs of the stool, suddenly miserable, conscious of the few inches that separated them. The warmth from his body drew her like a moth to flame. If she put out her hand, if she reached out to touch him, to kiss him— She did neither, forcing herself to take another bite of omelet, hiding behind another question. "Your scar. Do you mind if I ask—"

"How it happened?" Buck stared down at the egg cooling on his plate. "Actually, it's a legacy from that night at Camp Bradley." He picked up his fork and began to eat, stopping after a few mouthfuls. "I told you earlier that I'd surprised my friend robbing the ammunition depot. Well, he surprised me, too."

She sat, stunned by the revelation. "You mean he shot you?"

His mouth twisted. "Just the once. I guess I should be happy about that. They actually gave me a medal for it when the investigation was all over. Bravery above and beyond the call of duty, or something like that. I didn't pay much attention at the time." He picked up his fork again and stared grimly at his plate. "And all I had to do was lie there and bleed."

She swallowed hard at the cutting edge in his voice. "Yet you agreed to come down here and meet with him."

"I owe him."

"He tried to kill you."

"He also saved my life." He turned to look at her, his gaze flat and unwavering. "He called a doctor before he and the other goons left the base. That call was the only thing that saved my life. I can't forget that." His gaze turned ugly, introspective. "Believe me, I've tried."

"So you're ready to forgive him."

"Forgive him?" He barked out a laugh. "I'd just as soon stick a knife between his ribs."

She shook her head, confused. "Then why did you agree to act as the military's liaison?"

"Because they needed somebody." He sighed heavily, pushing his plate back. "Because he refused to deal with anybody else. And because, despite everything that happened, I guess a part of me still believes in the system."

"The military?"

"A man's honor."

He got up abruptly and went to the stove. "More coffee?" He refilled both their cups without waiting for her reply and returned to the table. They'd finished drinking most of the strong, bitter brew before she spoke again.

"So what happens now? You've told me you expected to meet with this man right after you arrived at the lodge. Where is he?"

Buck shrugged. "Cuzco, as far as I can tell."

"He refuses to join you here?"

"*Refuse* is not the right word." His eyes turned speculative. "He's got the whole thing orchestrated for his own means. I thought it was a setup at first. It had even crossed my mind that he might be trying to finish what he started all those years ago, but I don't think so anymore. I think he wants me here for a reason."

She felt the blood drain from her face. "Me?"

His smile flashed briefly. "He's good, but not that good. No, I think he wanted me to meet Speer before he made the rendezvous."

"Speer? Wolfgang Speer?"

"The one and only."

She shook her head. "Why would your informant want you to meet Wolfgang Speer?"

"To lay a little groundwork." He sat forward as she continued to shake her head in confusion. "Catherine, Wolfgang Speer is the Serpent."

Her jaw dropped. "You can't be serious." He was more than serious, she thought, searching his face. He was positively grim. "Wolfgang Speer has been an institution in the Amazon for at least ten years," she said, trying to drum up some kind of defense. Wolf had always treated her with the utmost respect and concern. He couldn't possibly be the man Buck was after. "He's admired by the townspeople, trusted by the native tribes, adored by his guests. His lodge is more popular than mine."

"His history also reads like a terrorist's travelogue," Buck informed her. "Southeast Asia. The Middle East. Central America. His so-called travels, including his recent trip to Germany, coincide with most of the dates of the major arms robberies. Granted," he said, looking reflective, "some of

the dates don't match, but that doesn't mean he didn't coordinate the robberies from the jungle. He's been *where* it
went down *when* it went down for nearly twenty years. And
with a radio system like the one you have, he can monitor
political and military developments and oversee illegal
weapons sales whenever and wherever he wants. All he
needs are a few well-placed military types to coordinate the
arms robberies for him and to transport the goods to a secure distribution center.'' He rubbed his side gingerly. ''And
we both know how skillful he is at recruiting men like
those.''

Men like those. Men like Buck's informant and her father. Catherine shook her head wearily. She'd played
guessing games with herself for years, trying to figure out
her father's reason for betraying her and his country. Had
it been for the money? Or the power? Or had Neil Taylor
simply given up after the long, drawn-out death of his wife?
Whatever the reason, it had died on the blood-spattered as-
phalt with him twenty years ago.

''Are you going to eat those eggs?''

She looked down at the half-eaten food on her plate, her
stomach rolling at the sight of the clotted lumps of cheese
that lurked in the pale flesh of the omelet. ''I think I've lost
my appetite.''

''Maybe this wasn't such a good idea after all.''

''Are you going to arrest him?''

He frowned, jumping subjects with her. ''That depends.''

''On collecting enough concrete proof to put him away?''

''No, that would take too long. We'd be starting from
scratch. By the time we gathered up everything we needed,
Speer could be gone. That's where my informant was supposed to come in. He's the only one who can positively
identify the Serpent. Our original plan was to notify the
Peruvian government of the Serpent's location as soon as we
had the ID. The current president has no more love for this

guy than we do. He'd probably cut through the bureaucratic red tape himself to get rid of him if it meant drying up the arms supplies to the guerrilla groups operating in this country. Everything hinges on that ID.''

Suddenly Buck stopped speaking, swiveling his body toward the door to the dining room. ''Are you expecting someone?''

She turned with him, tensing. ''No.''

He gestured at the veil beside her plate and she grabbed it, covering her face just as Reverend Woolsey walked through the door.

He blinked at them. His face had the soft, rumpled look of someone who had just awakened. ''I thought I saw a light on in here.''

Catherine relaxed slightly. She should have expected a visit from him sometime tonight. His midnight forays to the kitchen had become legendary. Enrique had even taken to leaving small plates of food wrapped up and ready for him in the refrigerator.

''More fruit and fried yucca?'' she asked, recalling the night she'd made him a light snack.

He seemed pleased that she had remembered. ''No need to go to all that trouble, my dear,'' he said, looking with interest at their cold omelets. ''I'll have whatever you're having.''

''There's still some left in the pan,'' Catherine volunteered, self-consciously clearing the table on her way to the stove. It was a little too late now to hide the fact that she had eaten a meal in full view of Buck. She wondered if the Reverend would manufacture an explanation for her uncharacteristic lack of modesty. Or would he just assume she had absorbed the food through her veil like some kind of amoeba?

She coughed back a laugh, avoiding Buck's puzzled look as she set a generous helping of eggs and fruit before the Reverend. The events of the day were finally starting to get to her—that and the lack of sleep. In a few more minutes, even the specter of the Serpent would seem like one big joke.

"Did you enjoy your visit with Wolf?" Buck asked casually.

The Reverend looked up from his plate, his eyes gleaming. "Undoubtedly the highlight of my trip to the Amazon. The man is amazing, truly amazing. Like our own inestimable hostess," he said, smiling benevolently at Catherine. "Wolf is a fountain of information about the area. And the native tribe he took us to see was fascinating." He tapped his fork against his bottom lip thoughtfully. "They've seen white people before, of course, but even then, they seem to treat him like a god. He has that manner about him," he added, rather apologetically, as though he had trodden on larger, more celestial toes. "You both saw it."

"The last of the true Renaissance men," Catherine said.

Buck quirked an eyebrow at her over the Reverend's head. "More like 'have gun will travel,'" he muttered dryly.

"Yes, yes," the Reverend said, oblivious to Buck's sarcasm. "Marjorie would have loved it. My late wife," he added, sighing.

Catherine nodded, as though hearing the name for the first time. "She liked to travel?"

"Very much." His fork clattered to the table, forgotten. "We spent some time in Brazil when we were first married. Ministering, you know. Marjorie was in her element there. We'd planned on returning to South America for years after that, but things didn't work out. This trip was to have been our chance to turn back the clock." His eyes misted.

"Did your children—" Catherine stumbled at the warning look on Buck's face. "Do you have any children?"

"A daughter, Elizabeth." The old man's smile returned briefly. "Beautiful girl. She and her husband had their first child right after Marjorie passed away. My son, John, was killed in an accident a couple of years ago." His eyes had turned misty again. He pulled his handkerchief from his pocket to dab at them.

A small vial entangled in the folds of the white cloth spun to the floor. Catherine picked it up for him, catching sight of the label before he took it from her fingers. Her omelet suddenly threatened to make an unscheduled, unsightly reappearance.

"I'm currently under a doctor's care," the Reverend informed her, pocketing the pills.

"Of course," she mumbled, too shocked by what she'd seen to attempt anything else. For the next few minutes she was incapable of saying much more, relying on Buck to carry the conversation while her thoughts jumped frantically, returning again and again to the label on the vial. By the time the Reverend had said good-night, Buck was looking at her as if she was crazy.

He turned to her as soon as they were alone. "What the hell was that all about?"

"Didn't you hear it?" she demanded, ripping off the veil. The cloth had begun to suffocate her. "He admitted he had a son who died several years ago."

"You think David Crane could be John Woolsey's son?"

"Why not? It could fit." She forced herself to think clearly, trying to tie up all the loose ends. "If David was the Reverend's son, his wife's recent death might have compounded his loss. Maybe Marjorie's death pushed him far enough over the edge to finally come after me."

"He's punishing you for the deaths of both."

"Yes."

Buck looked unconvinced. "You're reaching."

"What about the medication?"

"Heart pills," Buck speculated. "High-blood-pressure pills. Maybe he's hypoglycemic."

"I recognized the label," she said, gripping the edge of the table.

He crossed over to her. "Take it easy."

"He's on an antidepressant. A powerful antidepressant. That's why he's so hungry all the time. Increased appetite is one of the side effects, especially if the dosage is too high." She sifted through her consciousness for more, the memories tormenting her as she dragged them from the past. "Insomnia, forgetfulness, confusion. He was probably suffering from adverse effects the day he took the tour through Cuzco."

"How do you know all this?"

She laughed bitterly. "I was on the same medication following the fire." Her voice broke as she remembered those shadow-filled days. The blackouts. The delusions. And all of them a by-product of the depression and the medication.

Buck took her gently by the shoulders. "You're sure?"

"I'm sure."

She shivered, letting him draw her into his thoughtful embrace. Was it possible? Had they found their madman?

SLEEP ELUDED HER. And when it finally did come, hours later, it made a mocking appearance. Her dreams kept catching fire. No matter how hard she tried to stop the flames, change the patterns, the result was always the same: Buck, the lodge, the veiled woman, all burned.

Catherine finally staggered out of bed at dawn, dressing in the same clothes she'd worn the day before, too discouraged to select anything new from the armoire. A pile of week-old receipts and invoices on the corner of her desk eventually drew her to them. Even math was better than contemplating the fury of emotions in her head.

She'd added the same column of figures six times, coming up with six different totals before she gave up, scattering the papers with an exasperated sweep of her hand. The pen and account book followed them to the floor.

She was doing it again. Using her work to distance herself from the truth. Glumly, she followed the flight of a pair of brilliantly colored macaws across the pale blue sky outside her window. In an hour, the sun would be high. In another, the air would be too thick to breathe. By then, her guests would be awake, if they weren't already stirring. Catherine Monroe would have met them as they left their cabins. The woman she had become couldn't think of a single reason to step through that door.

Catherine Monroe. Catherine Tremaine. Catherine Taylor. Who was she?

An image of Buck as he had left her last night filled her head. The strong, firm mouth. The dark eyes. That ridiculously short haircut. If he was with her right now, he'd probably say something completely off-the-wall to make her take her mind off her situation. *Their* situation. Or else he'd kiss her. For a moment, she breathed in the scent of his mouth. Why was it so hard to let him come close to her?

Why was it so hard to let herself go?

I love you. Those three words could not erase the past. How could they possibly build a future?

The door to number ten flew open and Earle bounced out, already fitting a lens to his camera. He'd taken several shots by the time he disappeared into the main lodge. She watched disinterestedly as Tony collided with him coming through the door. They exchanged a few words, probably unpleasant, before Tony began to stalk toward her cabin.

She'd never really noticed his grim gait before. Her depression mounted the closer he came. By the time he knocked on her door, she was totally miserable.

"I'm taking the Reverend and the Wheelers along the white-mud trail this morning," he informed her stiffly, obviously still smarting from their last encounter. "Do you want to join us?"

"It will have to wait."

Immediately he was suspicious. "What do you mean?"

"Something happened yesterday—" Another knock on the door broke into her recount of the previous day's events.

Tony glanced out the window. "It's Jordan," he hissed. "I'll get rid of him."

"Let him in," she said wearily, steeling herself for the inevitable confrontation between the two men.

"But your face—"

"He's seen my face."

"What? He knows—everything?"

In reply, she pulled the door open. Instantly Tony was beside her, shielding her from Buck's gaze as though he couldn't quite believe what she had told him.

"He knows," she repeated gently, stepping around him. "Buck, come in."

For a moment, she thought he'd have to fight a duel before Tony would let him pass. Then, like a reluctant tank, Tony moved aside, his face that of a man who has seen the ultimate betrayal.

No one spoke.

Finally Catherine cleared her throat. "I told Buck my real name yesterday," she said, throwing him a quick glance, hoping he'd see the wisdom in keeping his own part in it a secret. "He'd already guessed that I was hiding something. I just couldn't keep up the charade any longer." She looked at Tony, willing him to accept her decision. It was all the apology she was prepared to make.

He kept silent, burning Buck with his stare.

Catherine took a deep breath and continued, her voice growing stronger as she recounted their meeting with Reverend Woolsey and their theory that he was the man responsible for terrorizing her. She omitted everything about the Serpent and her discovery of Buck using the radio. The story was simply not hers to tell, and though she trusted Tony with her life, she did not feel as secure trusting him with Buck's mission, especially knowing the animosity between the two men.

By the time she had finished, Tony was breathing heavily. "So, you've got it all figured out," he spat at Buck. He hadn't looked at Catherine since she'd started to speak.

Buck refused to be intimidated. "We think so."

Tony glanced back at Catherine. "You are going to tell your uncle about this latest development, aren't you? Or is he expendable, too?"

She flushed at the contempt in his voice. "I planned to radio him this afternoon. If he's willing—" She was cut off by a blood-curdling scream from the compound.

Chapter Thirteen

Buck reacted first, reaching the door to the cabin in two powerful strides. "Veil!" he yelled over his shoulder to Catherine, and she dived for the protection of the thin cloth as he yanked open the door.

The ludicrous scene that met his eyes on the front porch stopped him cold. Selena and Romeo—or was it Julian?—were engaged in some kind of interspecies face-off next to the stairs. Either that or Selena had become completely unhinged.

"Take one more step, buster, and I'll have you for supper!" Selena warned, her back to the door, oblivious of the audience she'd attracted. The parrot screeched enthusiastically as she threatened it with something that looked like a cross between a martial-arts maneuver and an aerobics routine.

"What the hell!" Tony slapped the doorjamb in disgust.

Selena whipped around. "You!" she said scornfully, as though Tony and the parrot had been cut from the same predatory cloth. "I might have known it. That thing scared the life out of me."

Catherine smothered her desire to laugh behind an apologetic cough. "Romeo was probably just curious," she said as the bird launched itself toward less-populated sanctuary in the canopy of a nearby tree. "I've seen the Reverend feeding him in the mornings. He must have thought you had some bread with you."

"Honey, where I come from, the only thing wearing feathers is me. I don't like birds enough to feed 'em. As long as that one keeps his distance—" her withering glance seemed to take in Tony as well as the parrot "—we'll do fine." She clattered noisily down the stairs and plucked a compact camera from the bottom step. "Well, what do you know. It isn't even damaged. I was sure I heard a pop when I dropped it."

"Taking up photography?" Buck asked, recognizing the camera. "Earle's, isn't it?"

She nodded, handing it over. "He left it on the dining room table after breakfast this morning. I thought I'd return it to him. I was on my way over to his cabin when— *boom*." She made it sound like a missile attack.

"There's a problem with the release lever," Buck said as he examined it. His voice trailed off as Catherine bent closer.

Their eyes locked for a moment and then she pointed to a small device on the back of the camera. "You mean this?"

The length of veil along the curve of her cheek was uneven where she'd twisted it in her hurry to follow him out onto the porch. He reached up, his expression carefully neutral, and smoothed it down, then turned his attention back to the camera.

"The film's probably been exposed—" He stopped, staring. The film chamber was empty.

"That can't be right," Catherine protested, taking the camera from him. "I watched him with it this morning. He took several pictures of the compound when he left his room."

"He snapped one of me over breakfast," Selena said. "With my mouth full." Judging by her tone, she felt that was grounds enough to convict the man.

Catherine's look of incomprehension suddenly cleared. "He must have taken the film with him."

"And leave the camera?" Buck shook his head. "I don't think so." He turned to Selena. "Where's Earle now?"

She pointed to the edge of the compound. "He and Frank went out to look at the herb garden. I was under the impression that he wanted to take a few parting shots of all of us today, for his magazine. That's why I thought he needed his camera."

Buck eyed Tony. "Do you think you can keep him busy for a little while?"

He considered Buck warily. "You gonna do what I think you're gonna do?"

"If you'll help me."

Tony's gaze flickered to Catherine. "I'll help her."

Buck nodded tightly. It was probably as good an answer as he was ever going to get from him. "Then I'll need about fifteen minutes," he said, starting down the stairs.

Catherine grabbed his arm. "Where are you going?"

"Earle's cabin. Where else?"

AT FIRST GLANCE, Earle's room was as empty as his camera had been.

"He's gone," Catherine said in disbelief as she took in the neatly made bed and crisply folded towels. If she hadn't known differently, she would have assumed that number ten had been vacant for weeks.

"Not gone, just incredibly neat." Buck grimaced as he poked beneath the bed. A tastefully patterned carpetbag shot to the far wall, followed by a soft-sided suitcase.

"What are we looking for?" she asked as he unzipped the larger bag and shook out half a dozen cotton shirts and several pairs of pants.

"Anything that doesn't fit, no pun intended."

She stepped back as a cascade of shorts and socks joined the rest of Earle's attire on the alpaca spread. He'd been living out of his suitcase ever since he arrived, she realized, shuddering.

Buck read her mind. "Maybe he's attached to his luggage," he said, tossing the bag to the floor in disgust.

Or maybe he was expecting to make a quick exit, Catherine thought dully, just as soon as he got what he came for. Nausea burned briefly at the back of her throat as the realization pounded itself home.

"So we were right about him," she murmured as Buck took a short tour of the bathroom.

"Looks like it." He emerged, shaking his head. "Nothing in there. He must keep his passport and papers on him." His attention shifted to the armoire on the far wall. "Here's where he keeps the rest of his gear," he said, throwing open the doors. A quick inventory of Earle's camera equipment told them what they wanted to know: there was not a single roll of film anywhere.

"He's been taking photos for weeks," Catherine said weakly. How many shots had the man pretended to take? Hundreds? Most of them had been in the jungle. Her knees gave a wobbly twist as she remembered the countless hours she had spent with him on the trails, pointing out an exotic flower or unusual plant, waiting patiently while he lined up the shot.

While he pretended to line up the shot.

Buck picked up a paperback book on Amazonian wildlife, flipped through it idly and tossed it onto the bed. "What I want to know is what he was after. Blackmail seems as good a motive as any, but why didn't he just come out and ask you for money? Why bother with something as cryptic as the messages on your mirror? And why the attempts on your life? It doesn't make any sense."

What made even less sense, he thought uncomfortably, was the fact that his search had not turned up the gun that was missing from his cabin. Had Earle stashed it somewhere in the jungle? Or was he working from some secret agenda they did not yet understand?

The cabin door swung open and they both jumped. It was Tony.

Buck fought back an exasperated snarl. "What's happening?"

"Wheeler said Godot left him a couple of minutes ago." Tony kicked the door closed behind him, eyeing the mess on the bed with distaste. "I thought he might have come back here. Find anything?"

"Enough to hang Earle Godot as an impostor," Buck ground out. "Not enough to find out why."

"I can find out why," Tony muttered, cracking all the joints in his fingers.

"We just want to talk with him, Tony," Catherine said. "We don't want to hurt him."

"She's right." Buck stepped in firmly. "The last thing we need right now is for you to go off half-cocked."

Tony turned his flat gaze in Buck's direction. "I'm getting a little tired of hearing from you."

Buck braced himself for a showdown.

The door suddenly opened again.

Earle.

Catherine doubted if his startled gaze even registered her presence or Buck's. He certainly didn't notice the stew of clothing on the bed. All he seemed to see was Tony, but that was enough. He blinked once, then ran for the stairs. Roaring, Tony lunged after him.

"Don't hurt him!" Catherine screamed, springing forward. Her right ankle chose that moment to give out, and she landed awkwardly on her knees, crying out as the pain radiated along the length of her leg. The whole cabin shook as the door crashed shut.

"You okay?" Buck yelled.

She struggled to her feet. "Don't worry about me!" she gasped. "It's Tony! He's going to hurt him!"

Or kill him, Buck thought as he wrenched open the door and barreled down the stairs. He'd seen enough back-alley fights and barroom brawls during his early years with the military police to recognize a murderous rage when he saw one. The only question was, what was he going to have to do to Tony to stop him?

He never got the chance to find out. By the time he reached the boardwalk, it was all over. He found Earle slumped in an exhausted heap on the wide, wooden planks. Except for the thin stream of blood that ran from his nose, he might have just finished running a fifty-yard dash instead of fleeing for his life. Tony lingered, like Goliath, a few feet away.

"Got him," he said gruffly, shoving his shirttail back into the waistband of his pants. He wasn't even breathing hard.

"I can see that," Buck said, trying to make some sense out of what he had just witnessed. Obviously he'd underestimated Catherine's influence on Tony. And that was all it had been, he realized as he watched the big man's gaze flicker toward Earle's cabin and the woman who waited anxiously for them on the veranda. If it had been anyone but Catherine, Earle would be dead right now. Catherine probably knew it, too.

"Help me get him back to his cabin," Buck said, nodding toward Earle. "I think Catherine has a few questions she'd like to ask him." He knew *he* did.

"Uh-uh," Earle said, finally showing a little life. He glared at Tony, managing to look pathetic and offended at the same time. "I'm not saying a word if he's going to be there."

Buck crouched beside him. "You're hardly in a position to give orders," he said quietly. "We already know what you're hiding."

"Not a word. I'll only talk to Catherine." He pouted, looking Buck over. "And I guess you can be there, but not *him.*" He clamped his hand over his dripping nose as if to emphasize that fact.

Buck looked up at Tony. "Okay with you?" It was going to have to be if they wanted to get to the bottom of this.

Tony seemed to realize it, too. "Make him talk," he ordered, hauling Earle to his feet. "And remember—" his eyes glittered dangerously "—I'll want a report."

"Oh, you'll get it," Buck said, gritting his teeth. That, and a one-two combination if his patience wore any thinner. He took Earle's other arm. "All right. Let's go."

They practically dragged him back to the cabin.

It was like witnessing an execution, Catherine thought uneasily as she sat down in one of the chairs that Buck had pulled up to the table. Earle occupied the other one, still sniffling, steadfastly refusing to meet her eyes. The wretched expression on his face condemned him more eloquently than any words possibly could.

"Talk to us," Buck said softly from the corner. He had positioned himself behind and to the left of Earle. Now he pushed himself away from the wall and walked toward him.

Earle blinked myopically, his eyes shifting first one way and then the other. He'd never replaced his glasses since his fall into the pit in the swamp forest. Without them, he seemed oddly fragile and defenseless. "What do you want to know?" he asked.

"Everything," Buck said. He hooked a camera from the pile of clothing on the bed and brought it over to the table. "Starting with this. You're not here to shoot nature shots, are you?"

Earle cleared his throat. "I'm a professional photographer, if that's what you mean." He sighed deeply, avoiding Catherine's gaze. "But I—I finished my shoot a couple of weeks ago in Iquitos. I was on my way home to Montreal when I met a man who said he had another job for me."

Catherine's nerves buzzed. "What man?" she asked, sitting forward in her chair.

Earle shook his head. "I don't know. I never saw him. We did all our talking by phone." He looked up hopefully, as if that frank admission would somehow win his reprieve.

"Go on," Buck said abruptly.

Earle's narrow shoulders sagged. "I thought it was another photography assignment. I figured I could use the money."

"To help float the magazine."

Earle sat up, obviously startled. "How did you—?" He glanced quickly between them, then fell back in his chair, shrugging, as if nothing else could surprise him. "Yes."

Catherine moistened her lips. "What was the assignment?"

"I was to leave several secret messages for the owner of the Phoenix Lodge," he answered dully. "I still had my equipment with me, so I pretended I was on a shoot. My cabin was paid for, all part of the deal, and I was told I'd receive the rest of my money when the job was completed. I thought, why not?" A pleading look came over his face. "It was just a gag, anyway, wasn't it? Some kind of practical joke? I thought everyone here was in on it."

"Right," Buck muttered. "Nothing but a great big joke." He fished the broken bit of mirror he'd discovered at the swamp forest out of his pocket and flashed it in front of Earle's face. "Recognize this?"

The detour he'd made to Catherine's cabin after he caught up with Tony and Earle paid off in spades. Earle practically shot off his chair. "It's a hand mirror," he squeaked, groping for the edge of the table.

"Guess again."

He shied violently when Buck dropped the mirror onto the table, his eyes jumping to Buck's free hand as though he expected a blow from that side. "It's just a hand mirror," he insisted, his voice stronger now.

He's lying, Buck thought, studying Earle's face. He had to be. If Earle admitted that he had dug the pit and planted the mirror, then he'd have to admit that he knew his so-called assignment was more than just a friendly prank. And that could lead to some very uncomfortable questions from the local authorities. Or worse, from Tony. No wonder the skinny little photographer was sticking to his story. He was hoping to get out of this whole mess with his skin—at least, what there was left of it—intact.

"What about this?" Buck asked. The grimy baseball cap he dropped casually onto the table looked like a relic from better times.

"I gave that to Jorge," Earle said defiantly. "He mentioned that his nephew collects caps."

"His collection just got smaller," Buck said. "We found this stuffed into a cupboard on the boat we took down to Wolf's. Any idea how it got there?"

"None."

"I suppose you have no idea how the hole in the hull got there, either?"

"Holes."

"What?"

Earle's eyes opened very wide. "Jorge must have told me there was more than one hole," he said, backtracking furiously. "I figured you had hit some rocks in the water—"

"Was that your plan? That we'd hit some rocks?"

Earle goggled, comprehension finally dawning. "Listen, you're not going to blame this on me! I had nothing to do with the damage to the boat! Or with that piece of mirror! Or with anything else, for that matter! All I did was write a couple of weird messages. That's all." He struggled to his feet. "I'm getting out of here."

"Sit down."

"I'm not—"

"I said, sit down." The hint of violence in Buck's voice was enough to knock Earle back into his chair.

"Three messages," he whined. "That's all the man told me to write. Three messages."

His nose began to bleed again. Catherine found an unopened box of tissues in the bathroom and brought them out to him. "Is there anything else you can tell us about the man who paid you to leave the messages?" she asked. It was the only real lead they had.

Earle's head flopped back. "I only spoke to him a couple of times on the phone," he said, his voice muffled by the thick wad of tissues. "Like I told you, I don't know what he looks like. I don't even know his name."

"Who did the contacting?" Buck asked.

"He did."

"You have no idea how to reach him?"

Earle swallowed noisily. "He left me a phone number to call in case of emergency. But it's not his," he added hastily when Buck leaned in. "I think it's an answering service of some kind. I was to leave my name and number and wait until he got back to me."

Buck began to prowl the room, his adrenaline surging. "At least it's something. Can you remember anything else? It doesn't matter how insignificant."

"No. Yes."

Buck spun around. "Which is it?"

Earle raised his head cautiously, the blood-drenched tissues still clamped to his face. "I thought I heard a woman in the background during one of the calls. And a baby crying."

Catherine and Buck exchanged glances. "Mean anything to you?" he asked softly.

She shook her head. "Nothing."

"The woman said something to him," Earle continued, his face fierce with concentration. "She called him—" he hesitated, fumbling for a name "—I think she called him . . . Kev."

Catherine frowned. "That's not a Spanish name. Do you recognize it?"

For a moment, Buck's shock made it impossible for him to answer her. *Kev. Kevin.* The memory of the night he was shot forced him to accept the next logical step in the progression. The man who had hired Earle Godot was the same man who had left Buck for dead twenty years ago. The same man he had crossed two continents to locate. His informant, Kevin Howard.

"I'LL RADIO YOU as soon as I find out what's going on," Buck said, making sure Earle was safely seated in the rear of the motorboat before he turned to Catherine.

She nodded, fidgeting with the buckle on one of the life preservers. "You're sure I can't go with you?" A distant part of her was aware that Tony had slid into the boat after Earle, but for the moment, she didn't care. All the way down to the dock, she'd fought the irrational conviction that this was goodbye, that somehow, someway, fate was working against them, conspiring to keep them apart.

Buck took the life preserver from her unresisting fingers. "Until we find out why Kevin Howard sent you the messages, I don't want you anywhere near Cuzco. You'll be safer here."

It made perfect sense, she had to admit, but it didn't make her feel any better. She shivered, despite the broiling temperature, fearing some evil she could not name.

"Let's get this show on the road," Tony ordered abruptly.

"Duty calls," Buck muttered, glancing over his shoulder. His voice lowered another notch. "How did you explain this to Tony?"

"He thinks you're sending Earle home. I told him he'd get the rest of the story when he got back from Maldonado."

"And he accepted that?" His hand came up. "Of course he did. He's a pushover, at least where you're concerned."

She sighed. "He only wants to help. Try not to antagonize him on the trip down the river."

A smile came and went so fast on his face that she almost missed it. "Don't worry. I'll keep things light and easy. I thought he was going to bust my chops the last time we went head to head." He ran a hand over his chin, his grin flashing again. "And I kind of like them the way they are."

"So do I." Her fingers brushed his forehead. "Your hair's starting to grow out," she observed quietly.

He caught her hand, his mind filling in the features that her veil hid from him: the delicate nose, the high cheeks, the beauty mark that rested so tantalizingly just above her mouth. In the tropical glare from the sun, with the verdant bloom of the jungle behind her, her fragile beauty took his breath away. "I have to do this," he said, more roughly than he wanted to. "For both of us."

"I know."

The roar of the outboard motor made them jump.

Reluctantly, she felt him release her hand. Tony and Earle were waiting. And in Cuzco, Kevin Howard was probably waiting, too. She turned away before he could see the beginning of her tears.

By the time she turned back, he was gone.

ON THE WAY BACK to her cabin, her ankle gave out again.

She pulled herself up sharply, waiting for the pain to subside, then veered across the compound to Tony's quarters. She'd left the bandage she'd brought with her from Cuzco in his cabin. For the next few days, she was going to have to take it easy. She might even take Selena up on her offer to look at the sprain. Anything was better than the poorly staffed clinic in Maldonado.

The bandage was on the table in the corner, right where she'd left it. As she turned to go, she glanced toward the bathroom. The door to the medicine chest was partially ajar. She stopped, shivering, struck by an uncomfortable feeling of déjà vu. That was how this whole thing had started, with the first message on her mirror: *I'm watching you.* She slammed the cabinet door shut before her mind could replay any more of it.

There was no mirror in the cabinet.

She stared uncomprehendingly at the bare metal for a moment, her brain supplying her with one explanation after another. Jorge had taken the mirror away to be cleaned. Jorge had broken the mirror and was in the process of replacing it. Tony had broken the mirror.

Or a piece from it.

She backed away, shaking her head in horror. It couldn't be. Not Tony. As she moved blindly toward the door, her heel caught on something propped against the wall. She spun around, moaning when she saw what it was. The missing mirror. A jagged, half-moon had been broken from the edge of it.

Not Tony. The words built into a mantra as she fumbled in her shirt pocket for the piece of mirror she'd taken with her from Earle's cabin. Trembling, she inserted the fragment into the jagged edge of the mirror. It fit perfectly.

It had been Tony all along.

Her mind was racing now, delving up the inconsistencies in the events of the past few days. The messages. The accidents. The tenuous bridge linking them both. All this time, she and Buck had been looking for a single man, when they should have been looking for two. No wonder Earle had appeared so bewildered when they'd accused him of both crimes. He'd been telling the truth.

The mirror toppled to the floor, shattering. *Seven years bad luck,* some remote part of her brain reminded her. Did that include the five years she had already spent buried in the jungle with a man she thought she could trust?

With a man she had trusted. Until now.

She dug the heels of her hands into her eyes, forcing herself to think clearly, forcing herself to see Tony not as the man who had left Hollywood with her, but as the man he had obviously become. Increasingly resentful of his role as handyman cum troubleshooter at the lodge. Increasingly hostile toward the guests. Increasingly enamored of her.

One by one the pieces of the puzzle slid into place. Tony had had ample time to dig the pit in the swamp forest during his many forays into the jungle and he could have easily sabotaged the boat in his off-hours. He had probably planted the cigar fragment and the baseball cap, too, to implicate Frank and Earle, to make her believe that the accidents were tied to the messages she'd been receiving, to make her turn to him.

The wheels in her mind spun wildly. Was that when his frustration and jealousy had finally surfaced? With the first message? Her thoughts suddenly tumbled. Or had Buck been the impetus?

Her reasoning took one more terrifying leap before she lunged for the door. Buck had been his target all along!

She collided with Jorge on the front steps.

"Miss Monroe," he began brightly, holding up a sheaf of registration forms.

"Not now," she gasped. She had to get to her cabin. It was too late to stop Buck and Tony on the river, even if she had had a serviceable boat, which she didn't. But she could radio through to Maldonado. The authorities there would have someone waiting to meet them on the dock. She prayed Buck would be safe until then.

That thought died when she saw what was left of the radio.

Tony had been thorough. She moved dazedly through the debris scattered across the room, barely recognizing the broken tubes and shattered console. Anything that hadn't been twisted or bent had been ground into the floorboards as though their destroyer had been delirious with rage.

The telegraph key was wedged beneath the legs of the table. She reached for it slowly, then let her hand drop back to her side, amazed to realize she had been tabulating the damage, weighing the number of replacement parts she kept in the supply hut.

Tony had probably seen to them, too, while they'd been grilling Earle. It would take her hours to fix the radio. Days. She bowed her head as the last stubborn shred of hope left her. She would never get it fixed.

And meanwhile, somewhere on the river, fate was playing out its hand.

Chapter Fourteen

The telephone in Jimmy Cochrane's hotel room was clumsy and old-fashioned, but it worked. He checked it for any recent electronic additions before he dropped it onto the table in front of Earle. "Dial."

Earle did as he was told, stammering as he identified himself to the person on the other end of the line. Several minutes later, he put down the receiver. "They said he'd get back to me." He glanced nervously over his shoulder at Buck. "It won't be long."

"It better not be," Jimmy said, sticking his face close to Earle's. "Or you and I are going to have to break off diplomatic relations."

"Jim," Buck warned, without turning from the window. His contact had taken a room at the back of the hotel, facing an antiquated air duct and a line of washing, most of which was obscured by the light rain that had met them when they landed in Cuzco. The stewardess had told them the sudden change in weather was normal for this time of year. It was also depressing as hell.

Jimmy joined him at the window. "What's wrong, buddy boy? Missing your ladylove?"

"Leave it alone," Buck warned.

"Okay, okay. You'll feel a lot more like celebrating after we nail this guy."

"We haven't nailed him yet."

"Just a matter of time, buddy boy. Just a matter of time. Once Howard ID's this Speer character, you can contemplate your little ladylove all you want." He glanced toward Earle. "That's more than I can say for him."

Buck followed his gaze.

As though aware he was now the topic of conversation, Earle jerked to attention in his chair. A drop of nervous perspiration sparkled on the end of his nose. He'd started to sweat heavily the moment they'd boarded the plane to Cuzco and he'd simply never stopped. By the time they reached the hotel, his shirt looked like it had been used to drag the river.

Buck grimaced. "Do something about that, will you?"

Jimmy sucked a back tooth thoughtfully. "What do you suggest?"

"A little less veiled innuendo, for one."

Jimmy grunted. "He's going to have to deal with a lot more than innuendo when Washington gets hold of him."

"They're not interested in small fry like Earle Godot," Buck replied, shaking his head. "Speer's the one they're after. I doubt if they'll even want to talk to Godot once Kevin Howard makes the ID."

Jimmy shrugged, glancing back at Earle. "You're the boss, boss. What do you want me to do with him?"

"Buy him a drink and put him on a plane back to Canada." Buck worried the minute hand on his watch. "Why hasn't Howard called back yet?"

"It's only been a few minutes. He'll call. You've got to learn to relax a little." Jimmy tipped his cowboy hat back on his forehead and grinned at him. "Like me."

Relax, Buck thought grimly. The only thing he felt capable of doing right now was putting his fist through the wall. He forced out a lungful of air and tried to clear his thoughts, concentrating on a few relaxation techniques his ex-wife had tried to teach him. It was no use. As soon as he managed to quell one nagging doubt, it was replaced by another. And all of them seemed to revolve around Catherine and whatever role she unwittingly played in Kevin Howard's grand scheme of betrayal.

He ground his teeth together as his apprehension grew. Jimmy, his eyes closed, was spread across the bed. Earle had relaxed, too, if his rapidly drying shirt was any indication. Buck stared unseeingly out the window, numbering the unknowns. A single mistake could sink this entire operation. And with it, whatever future he might hope to have with Catherine.

The trouble was, he'd already made the mistake. The coil of tension in his stomach told him that much. What it didn't tell him was *where* he'd slipped up.

The strident bell on the telephone nearly put him on the roof.

"Jordan," he barked, yanking up the receiver. The sound of the familiar voice on the other end of the line brought his pulse rate back up to the danger zone. By the time he slammed the receiver down, he was swearing.

"Well?" Jimmy demanded, the freckles standing out on his pale face. "What's the verdict?"

"Four hours. He wants to meet me at a place called Kunka. Know it?"

Jimmy nodded. "It's an old Incan site on a hill above the city. I can probably find a place nearby to cover you."

"Uh-uh. He wants me to come alone. If he sees anybody else, the deal's off."

Jimmy shook his head slowly. "I don't like it."

"It's either that or he walks."

"Then let him walk."

"I can't do that," Buck said, though that was precisely what he felt like doing. "Washington's put too much time and effort into this operation. If Howard wants me to come alone, then I come alone."

Jimmy snorted. "Then at least wait until I can find you another piece. You know Howard better than anyone. He could turn on you like *that*." He snapped his fingers. "I'd feel better if you went in armed."

The gun. That was another thing Earle Godot had never adequately explained. What had happened to his gun? The walls were starting to close in on him again. He had to get some air.

Buck snapped a jacket off the bed, jamming his arms into the sleeves as he headed for the door. "You've got four hours." After that, he was going to be on a boat back to the Phoenix. A very fast boat. And to hell with Washington, the Serpent, Kevin Howard and anyone else who stood in his way.

CATHERINE QUICKLY inventoried the contents of her knapsack before she zipped the bag closed. Flashlight. Water bottle. First-aid kit. The last item on the list was the only one she hoped she wouldn't need.

She swung the bag over her shoulder, gingerly flexing her right ankle as she did so. In the high-topped, close-fitting walking boot, the sprain was barely noticeable. But after ten miles, even the finest leather wouldn't be able to hide the injury. By that time, she hoped it wouldn't matter. She would be at Quester's Inn, and Buck would be safe.

"I want Jorge on the riverbank at all times in case another boat comes by," she instructed Enrique, pulling a sharp-edged machete down from the supply shelf. She tested the blade against her finger and nodded. Tony had sharpened all the knives the week before. She supposed she ought to be thankful to him for that. Without the knife, she would never make it through the tough vines and broad-leaved vegetation she would face when she left the trail.

"If Jorge does reach Maldonado before I get to Wolf's, he's to give this to the authorities," she said, handing Enrique a letter in which she had outlined her concerns about Tony. "They'll know what to do."

Her horror at finding the smashed radio and her paralyzing fear for Buck's safety hadn't lasted long. When the initial shock had worn off, she had decided to attempt the hike to Wolf's lodge for help, despite Buck's suspicions about the man. At least by confronting the odds, she could give Buck a fighting chance. If she stayed at the Phoenix, he had no chance at all.

She noticed that Enrique studiously avoided touching her fingers when he took the letter from her. Since she'd first appeared in the kitchen, without the veil, he'd treated her with an awestruck deference that she didn't quite know how to handle. It was almost as though he expected her to glow or, worse, perform some sort of miracle equal to the one which had restored her face.

It was a reaction she would have to get used to, she told herself. After today, Catherine Monroe no longer existed.

"I'll return as soon as I can," she said, striding toward the door.

"And the others?" Enrique asked timidly, keeping his distance. "They saw Señor Buck taking Señor Godot away. They are already asking questions."

"Tell them—" She hesitated, a dozen different stories flitting through her mind. She discarded all but one. "Tell them the truth."

At the edge of the compound, she turned around for one last look at the lodge. Enrique was still in the doorway to the supply hut, gazing after her. At this distance, he appeared to be genuflecting.

KUNKA.

According to the guidebook he had been studying, the site had been named after the Quechuan word for neck. He hoped it didn't mean his. Buck shifted uncomfortably in the front seat of the tiny rental car and surveyed the area. From

Jimmy's brief description, he had expected a huge, abandoned Inca fortress on the outskirts of the city. Instead, the tiny road sign pointed to a large limestone boulder that sat in a small hollow a dozen yards from the road. Behind it, in the cradle formed by the Andes, Cuzco simmered in the purple haze of early evening.

He started the car engine and rolled onto the rough, dirt side road that served as a parking lot. Two stoutly built Indian women and a disinterested llama in the field next to the site followed his progress as he neared the rock, but made no effort to approach him. Apparently it was a little late in the day to drum up the tourist trade. Or maybe it was the grim expression on his face that convinced them to keep their distance.

He circled the boulder twice on foot before he found the small doorway that had been fashioned out of a natural crack in the rock. Jimmy had told him it led to a series of subterranean tunnels. He moved closer, clicking on a small flashlight. The feeble beam did nothing to calm his nerves. At this point in the game, a bank of klieg lights couldn't calm him. He could deal with the dark. It was the man waiting for him in the dark that unnerved him.

He eased through the narrow opening. Almost at once, the tunnel began to descend, the rock walls polished and uncomfortably close. He caught himself counting the number of bends in the passage, as if the total could somehow tell him how far he had come and how far he had to go. He soon gave up trying; beneath the earth, direction meant nothing.

A current of cold air brushed his cheek, bringing with it a whiff of eucalyptus smoke from the hills outside. Someone—it may even have been one of the women he'd seen earlier—was cooking dinner.

"Rice and beans," he muttered, using the menu to stave off the first wave of claustrophobia. "Roast chicken and sweet potatoes." He ran out of Peruvian dishes long before he ran out of tunnel.

Something rattled behind him.

He twisted toward it, stabbing at the darkness with the flashlight beam. Nothing. Even the cooking smoke was gone. The air seemed to grow danker and darker as he stared down into the tunnel, as if the molecules themselves had begun to coalesce.

He walked on, nerves jumping, wishing he had brought the gun. After several hours of wheeling and dealing with a couple of black-market types, Jimmy had finally come through with a weapon, although it looked more like an assault rifle than anything Buck could easily carry with him. An American-made assault rifle, no doubt, he thought with black humor, courtesy of your friendly, neighborhood snake in the grass. He'd been forced to leave it behind at the hotel. For the first time, he wondered if that had been a mistake.

Behind him, something rattled again.

He whirled around. He was no longer alone.

Buck sucked in his breath as he stared at the apparition materializing in the narrow recess he had just passed. His lungs, and every other major organ in his body, seemed to be malfunctioning.

The man acknowledged his shock with a slight nod of his head. "You by yourself?"

"Yes." He could barely form the word. He cleared his throat. "Yes."

Kevin Howard nodded, apparently satisfied. "Then keep going. The tunnel widens out a little farther down. We can talk better there."

Buck obeyed, resisting the impulse to check back over his shoulder as he walked on. Howard was there; he could sense him. Hell, he could almost smell him. His overheated imagination snagged a twenty-year-old fragment from his memories: the pungent odor of his own blood as it poured from his belly that night. For some reason, he couldn't shake the feeling that he was about to relive the whole hideous episode.

The tunnel widened into a roomy, dead-end cave. Buck played the flashlight beam cautiously around the walls and ceiling, checking for unwanted guests. They were alone. His light picked out a broad, low rock shelf on his right that spanned the entire length of the chamber.

"Altar," Kevin said, laying his own flashlight on the wide ledge. The diffused light carved hollows in his narrow cheeks and turned his close-set eyes to slits. A two-inch scar across his chin had not been there twenty years ago.

"Local legend says the Incas performed ritual sacrifices down here," he continued, looking around him. "Strange bunch of people, the Incas. They built an entire empire using only three laws: don't lie, don't steal and don't be lazy." His thin lips turned up in a ghastly grin. "No wonder they lost it all to the Spanish."

"I didn't come here for a history lesson," Buck said stiffly.

"Think of it as a bonus." Kevin produced a package of cigarettes from his shirt pocket. "You still a smoker?"

"No."

"Smart." He lit one, took a long drag and coughed out a lungful of smoke. "But then, you always were. Too smart to get yourself involved in that mess back at the base. What did you think you were trying to prove that night—that you were some kind of superhero?" Another fit of coughing wracked his wiry frame. He recovered slowly, wiping a string of spittle from his mouth. "Even a superhero has to bend to the will of the masses. Supply and demand, Buck. That's the lesson we have to learn from history."

"I assume you're referring to the arms thefts," Buck said, sarcasm lacing his voice.

"The thefts. The gun deals. The exchange of information. You want the name of the Serpent. I want—well, you'll see." He picked a piece of tobacco from his tongue. "We all come out a little bit ahead."

"Try telling that to Neil Taylor."

Kevin's voice turned ugly. "I had nothing to do with Taylor's death."

"Just like you had nothing to do with sending those messages to his daughter."

His face creased into a sly smile. "You finally discovered her little secret, did you? It took you a little longer than I thought it would, even using that wimp Godot as a go-between."

Buck stared at him. "You mean you wanted me to find out about Catherine's background?"

"I did everything but spell it out for you. I even tried to clue you with a title from one of her films when I found out you were in Cuzco. She tell you about that one?"

"No."

He sneered. "I didn't think so. You used to be quite the ladies' man, Buck. What's wrong? Losing your touch? Or did the veil throw you?"

Buck's fist caught him just under the jaw. Kevin went down hard, the cigarette bouncing out of his mouth onto the stone shelf beside him.

"Get up," Buck ordered hoarsely.

Kevin barely managed to make it to his feet when Buck hit him again. This time he deflected most of the blow with his shoulder, dropping into a defensive stance as Buck continued to advance on him.

"You want to take me out?" Kevin spat out a mouthful of blood. "You think that's gonna make up for what we've been through? Then come on, take me out." He grinned, beckoning.

They circled each other warily. It was hardly an even match. Buck had at least fifty pounds on his opponent and a good three inches, but right now he wasn't thinking about fighting fairly. He was thinking about the blood and the bullets and the sleepless nights.

Buck landed another punch, then he jerked back as Kevin's foot lashed out, catching him in the hip. He grunted and feinted left, driving his elbow into the side of Kevin's head as the other man rushed him.

They fell back together onto the stone altar, Kevin scrabbling wildly for Buck's eyes. Buck caught him on the side of his head with another flurry of punches. Two more blows dropped him like a stone.

"Go on," Kevin gasped, struggling to get to his feet. "This is what you want, isn't it? Payback for that night?"

And more, Buck thought darkly as he moved toward him. At the last moment, he managed to pull his punch. Howard wasn't worth the effort. Nothing was, if it meant losing sight of his goal. He'd told himself when he took this assignment that he was in it for the honor. Well, it wasn't the honor, he realized. He'd come down for an explanation, for an apology, for some sign from Kevin Howard that he regretted what he'd done to him all those years ago.

But that didn't matter anymore. Catherine was the only thing that mattered.

He dropped back, breathing hard. "Get up. Now."

Kevin stood, gauging Buck's expression in the dim light. "If it makes it any easier for you, I regret that night almost as much as you do," he said, the sheen of fear in his eyes slowly dissipating. "Maybe more."

Buck's derisive laughter reverberated throughout the cave. "I'll bet. In case you've forgotten, I was the one who spent six hours in surgery after you shot me."

"I got my own sob story," Kevin snapped back, plucking his cigarette from the dust. "Try twenty years on the run." He sucked fiercely on the cigarette, the red tip glowing like the eye of an angry god. "After I made that telephone call to the base hospital, the Serpent thought I'd sold out. He'd been suspicious of me even before the robbery. I thought if I winged one of the boys who came to investigate the break-in, he'd be satisfied." He turned on Buck. "But you had to be a hero. You had to try to stop me." He spat on the ground in disgust. "I had no choice after that but to run."

"You could have turned yourself over to the authorities," Buck said.

"Which ones?" Kevin asked. "Taylor? I read in the newspapers that he was on the payroll himself. I didn't know who to trust." He ground the cigarette beneath his heel. "At first I went north, to Canada. Caught a freighter out of Vancouver. The Serpent's men were right behind me. I finally lost them in Manila. From there, I worked my way to South America and this happy corner of the globe." He looked around him, as though visualizing the length and breadth of the country. "I figured Peru—who the hell was going to look for me here?"

The implication of his last remark hit Buck like a body blow. "You mean one of the Serpent's men traced you to Cuzco?"

"After twenty years? I prefer to think of it as dumb luck," Kevin replied, scowling. "I recognized him in the market a couple of months ago. Big, stupid son of a gun. I think he spotted me, too. After that, I knew the city wasn't safe."

"Why didn't you run again? That seems to be your speciality."

"I got a family now," he said slowly. "Kids. I can't leave them behind and I sure as hell can't take them with me. So I decided to cut a deal—the name and location of the Serpent for the military's guarantee of safety for me and mine."

Buck went cold, thinking of Catherine. "And you decided to throw in a little harassment and intimidation for old time's sake?"

Kevin sneered. "You still don't get it, do you?" His head suddenly swiveled to the right, his eyes narrowing.

Buck heard it, too: the sound of a leather shoe scraping across the smooth stone of the tunnel.

"I thought I told you to come alone!" Kevin hissed.

"I did." Buck took a step toward the black mouth of the tunnel. Some sixth sense made him rear back. "Get down!" he yelled, hurling himself at Kevin seconds before the first shot rang out.

He rolled as soon as he hit the floor, then lunged for the flashlights. In an instant, the cave was plunged into total darkness.

"Keep down," he gritted again, hoping the bullet hadn't found its mark. There had been no sound from the other side of the cave since he'd extinguished the lights. "I'm going to try to draw his fire."

He didn't know whether his informant had heard him or not.

Another bullet slammed into the rock face above his head, the third whining high and to his left. The gunman was shooting blindly, Buck realized, probably hoping to lay down as many shots as he could before the rapid fire attracted outside attention. That, and the fact that he hadn't come equipped with his own flashlight, could only mean that their assailant was unfamiliar with the cave. And that could work to Buck's advantage.

He groped for the edge of the altar, ducking low as another deafening series of shots ricocheted off the tunnel walls. Rock chips flew everywhere, nearly as dangerous as the bullets themselves. Buck didn't realize he'd been hit until he tasted the first trickle of blood. He probed the soft flesh in front of his right ear, wincing as his fingers encountered more blood. Not a bullet hole, he thought with some relief, but it would probably need a few stitches to close.

Quietly, he pulled himself onto the altar, dropping low as soon as he could. There'd been no sound from the tunnel since the last flurry of shots, but his instincts told him that the gunman was still out there somewhere, listening, waiting, playing for time. Buck wriggled silently to the tapered tip of the stone ledge. From what he remembered of his earlier survey of the cave, the altar extended narrowly into the mouth of the tunnel. He could use that knowledge, especially if he was right in assuming that the gunman was operating in strange territory.

His right hand closed over open air. He'd reached the end of the altar. The smell hit him almost immediately. Nervous sweat. And not his own. He was close enough to his prey now to determine what the man had had for supper. Onions and garlic. Lots of garlic.

The odor grew stronger. The man had shifted positions. He was probably no more than two feet in front of him. Buck slowly inched to a half crouch, willing Kevin to move, to sneeze, to reach for a cigarette. All he needed was something to work on. The muscles in his calves began to cramp as the seconds slowly stretched into minutes.

Come on, Kevin, he willed silently. *Do something!*

Kevin Howard coughed.

Their invisible assailant moved.

That was all Buck needed. He launched himself from the altar, catching the gunman as he squeezed off another shot. The impetus took them both into the far wall.

"Kevin!" Buck yelled, kicking himself free. "I need—" *Help.* But he didn't. He realized that as soon as the body rolled limply to one side. The intransigent rock of the tunnel had done his job. He worked his way up the man's prone form, groping in the dark for a pulse. His thumb registered a strong, steady beat. At least he'd have someone to interrogate.

"He dead?" Kevin asked, coming up behind him with a flashlight. He rode the feeble beam hopefully over the unconscious form on the stone floor.

"No." Buck dropped the gunman's wrist. "Just out cold. He'll have a hell of a headache when he wakes up." He motioned Kevin closer. "Shine that on his face."

Kevin complied silently.

The man was a stranger.

A fit of coughing suddenly doubled Kevin over.

Buck spun around. It wasn't the nicotine this time that had closed Kevin's throat. Even in the dim light, he could see that his informant was red-eyed with fear.

"Know him?" Buck demanded.

Kevin shook his head, his entire body shaking.

"Look again." Buck grabbed the front of Kevin's shirt and yanked him to his knees. He twisted the unconscious man's head from side to side, Kevin's terror growing more obvious with every motion. "He's Spanish," Buck ground out, "probably from around here. You know this city. You must have seen him before."

He tilted the gunman's head to the side. Black hair, hooked nose. "Who is—" Buck's jaw dropped suddenly as he made the connection. Hawk-nose. The man who tried to kill them was the same man who had chased Catherine through Cuzco.

"Serpent," Kevin spat out. "He's one of the Serpent's people." He knocked Buck's hand away. "He must have followed you here. I told you to be careful. Now neither one of us is safe." He began to scuttle into the cave.

Buck dragged him back. "Who is he?" he barked. "I want his name! Who is the Serpent? Is it Speer? Is it Wolfgang Speer?"

"I don't know what you're talking about," Kevin choked out. "I don't know any Speer."

"Dammit, then who?"

Kevin's answer shocked him.

Chapter Fifteen

She had been a fool to think she could do this alone.

Catherine drove the blade of the machete into the nearest tree, sagging wearily against the handle as the blade bit and held. She had intended to rest for a few minutes, leaning against the knife, but the longer she lingered, the less she wanted to move at all.

Her ankle was a red-hot seam of pain.

She shifted her weight slightly, lowering her right foot slowly to the ground. The movement brought on a wave of nausea. She took a deep breath and applied a bit more pressure. This time the agony was almost unbearable, forcing a low moan from her lips. If she could barely touch the toe of her boot to the ground without screaming, how could she hope to walk another four miles? Or five?

She shuddered as the numbers played tag in her head. It had been another five miles five miles ago. She had to face the inevitable. She was hopelessly lost.

She twisted her head to one side, sweat beading on her forehead as she contemplated the thick jungle growth. She'd made good time at first, taking the lagoon trail as far as the lake, then cutting across country to hit the last few miles of the trail that led through the swamp forest. She'd planned to keep the swamp on her left all the way to Quester's Inn.

At that point, she'd even anticipated reaching Wolf's an hour before her best estimate.

That hour had shrunk to fifty minutes, then forty, then thirty, as she began hacking her way through the jungle. Then, even thirty minutes had become an unattainable dream. She'd forgotten how circuitous and how arduous a task breaking trail could be. When they'd first opened the lodge, she had had two good feet and Tony by her side.

Now even her body betrayed her.

Her gaze shifted to the pale sky visible through the thick fingers of vegetation above her. In the few minutes that she'd spent ruing her condition, the light had changed. How long before the sun set? How long before the eerie jungle night made walking with even one good foot virtually impossible?

Not long at all. The whine of a mosquito brought her out of her bleak reverie. She slapped listlessly at it, then pulled the machete free from the tree trunk. She'd walk as long as she could, then find some safe spot to spend the night. Maybe even now Jorge was speeding toward Maldonado. Buck was probably already safe.

She clung to that thought as she took her first tentative step. Then the next. And the next. *Buck was already safe.*

The fire would consume her if she thought anything else.

"WHAT DO YOU MEAN, there's not another plane out tonight?" Buck slammed his fist into the ticket counter. In the deserted airport terminal, the noise echoed like a gunshot. A bored-looking security guard leaning against the far wall hitched up his pants and began to stroll over as Buck continued his tirade. "I've told you, I have to get out of Cuzco! I have to get back to Puerto Maldonado! Now! Tonight!"

The olive-skinned woman behind the counter looked at him with open hostility. "*Señor,* as I have already told you, the last commercial flight left at noon. There is nothing that flies to the frontier this late in the day."

"What about that one?" Buck punched a finger toward a military transport that had lumbered onto the runway. He was well aware of the scene he was making, but right now nothing would keep him from getting back to the Phoenix.

Nothing short of a long night spent in a hot, Peruvian prison, he amended hastily, eyeing the security guard who had joined them at the counter. Getting arrested was not going to bring him any closer to the jungle.

The security guard cocked his head and watched the dun-colored plane roll to a stop. "This one is reserved for the natives," he explained carefully, scratching his chin, "who cannot afford regular flights." A silver front tooth flashed. "Others, *gringos* like yourself, are expected to use the domestic airlines."

"Aren't there private planes?" Buck insisted. "Who can I see to charter a two-seater?"

The man shrugged. "It is late, *señor*. All the pilots have gone home."

"I can book a flight for you tomorrow," the woman behind the counter suggested listlessly, her fingers tapping the computer keyboard. "The first open seat I have leaves at one-thirty."

Too late. Buck's mind tortured him with the thought. It was probably already too late. Even if he managed to charter a plane, he still faced a three-hour trip by boat up the Tambopata River. By the time he reached the lodge, Catherine could be gone. Or worse.

His imagination closed down at that point, preventing him from suffering through other worse-case scenarios.

"Look," he said, his voice taking on a reasonable tone, "I need a plane. Now." He leapt for the impossible. "A float plane if you have it. If not, anything that has wings and a motor. I can pay—"

The security guard's eyes lit up.

Buck turned to him slowly. "—as much as you ask."

He'd said the magic words. The security guard thumbed his jaw. "I have a cousin, *señor*," he said finally. "Maybe he can help you."

THE HEAVY DRILL of Tony's footsteps kicked up a flock of macaws from one of the trees beside the boardwalk. He ignored their aggravated screeching and continued the long walk down to the dock.

Halfway to the stairs, he noticed the blood on his fingers. He shrugged, using the tail of his shirt to wipe his hands. By the time he reached the powerful motorboat idling beside the shore, he'd erased all trace of his conversation with Enrique and of the violence that had accompanied it.

The boat edged toward the end of the dock, and Tony climbed in.

"Well?"

"She's gone."

"Gone?" The old man in the stern of the boat was in no mood for riddles. "Gone where? How?"

Tony shrugged again. "Enrique was the only one I saw, and he wasn't doing much talking. I finally had to persuade him to give me the information." He said it simply, without malice, as though he'd expected a fight and welcomed it.

"And?"

"She left on foot last night for Quester's Inn." He glanced at the river. The air was still tinged with lacy remnants of early-morning fog. In an hour or two, it would be gone, replaced by a heavy mantle of tropical heat. He shifted uneasily in the boat, already anticipating the grip of the sun. "She should be there by now."

The old man followed his gaze. For a moment he said nothing. Then he sighed. "Let's go get her."

CATHERINE RAN OUT of water just after dawn.

It was the perfect conclusion to the worst night of her life, she thought with disgust as the threw the plastic bottle back into her knapsack. Since she'd left the Phoenix the day before, she'd had no sleep, little liquid, and only the mosquitoes had eaten like kings.

She jammed the pack across her shoulders, scratched at a semicircle of bites on her upper arm and picked up the machete. A moment later, a palm leaf sailed through the air. It was followed in quick succession by two more leaves and a tough, snaking length of vine. She blew a wisp of hair out of her eyes and raised her arm for another blow. She was drunk with exhaustion and she knew it.

And she didn't care.

That giddy, abnormal feeling had seen her safely through the last twelve hours and, if she was lucky, would see her safely through the next twelve. Long enough to reach Wolf's. She charged a small sapling. Long enough to confront Tony. She decapitated a clump of ferns. Long enough to make her way to Buck.

She paused, her breath coming in short, hard gasps. Sweat dripped like acid into her eyes. But it wasn't real. None of this was real. The only sane thing in her life right now waited for her at the end of the jungle. And if it took the last ounce of strength she had in her, she was going to make that rendezvous.

And then let the chips fall where they may, she thought, steeling herself for what lay ahead. She thrust forward, the blade of her knife glinting dangerously.

Let them fall where they may.

FROM THE AIR, the Tambopata River looked like a mild-chocolate ribbon.

For the fifth time in as many minutes, Buck checked his watch. From the moment they'd lifted off the tarmac at Cuzco, the gesture had become almost habitual; so had the impatient frown that flickered across his face. "How long until we land?" he yelled over the roar of the engine.

The young man at the controls of the small plane flipped up the detractable lenses of his aviator glasses. "Shouldn't be more than a few more minutes, man," he hollered back. "There's an abandoned airstrip on this side of Quester's Inn. Hasn't been used in years, though Wolf still keeps it cleared. He had it cut when he opened up the place. I guess he figured on getting a lot of company." He grinned soundlessly and jabbed a finger toward Buck's side of the plane.

Buck glanced down. He saw it almost at once: the bleached white scar in the green chest of the jungle. His gaze moved a little to the right, settling on the fringed line of rooftop that marked Wolf's lodge. In between lay at least a quarter mile of dense, tropical vegetation. Fifteen minutes' walk if he was lucky, he calculated quickly. Thirty minutes or more if he was not. The tension he had been carrying in his head and neck ripped, like a barbed weight, into the rest of his body.

Warily, he eyed the kid at the controls. He was an odd combination of native Indian and European: dusky-skinned, big-boned, his hair as orange as the carrot he'd just bitten into. Buck hunched lower in his seat.

His companion chomped happily. "Like I said earlier, man, this is the closest I can get you to the Phoenix. You'll have to get someone on the ground to take you the rest of the way."

Buck nodded, mentally adding another hour to the journey, *if* Wolf was home and *if* he was in a hospitable mood. His posture worsened.

His companion continued to chew, occasionally checking the gauges in front of him as he prepared to land. The engine coughed once as they skimmed through a low cloud, and Buck jerked upright. "Problems?"

The kid tapped a dial and grinned. "Nothing I can't handle, man."

"Where'd you learn to speak English?"

He looked pleased with himself. "I spent two years at UCLA."

It figured. Buck winced and held on as the ground rushed toward them.

THE LIGHT PLANE disappeared before Catherine could catch more than a glimpse of it. It had been small and unmarked. Two pale faces bobbed at the windows before it vanished behind the trees. Probably lumber barons doing another survey of the area, she thought. Or worse, treasure seekers.

She gritted her teeth and limped on. The exhaustion-induced euphoria had finally evaporated, taking with it the mind-numbing stamina that had enabled her to use her right ankle. Now she was simply used up.

She stopped to get her bearings. She had stumbled upon one of the trails that branched out from Wolf's lodge just after sunrise. Since then, she'd made up for lost time, despite discovering that she had overshot the lodge by several miles during her midnight ramble. She refused to think what those extra miles might have cost her, or what they might have cost Buck.

The trail ended abruptly in the clearing behind Quester's Inn.

For a moment, all she could do was murmur a garbled prayer of thanks. Then she dropped the knapsack to the ground and dragged herself up the steps to the lodge.

The place was empty. Totally empty, she discovered, as she wandered from one echoing room to another. She moaned softly at the implication. If Wolf and his guests were gone, then the boat was gone, too. She'd come halfway through hell for nothing.

Her mind leapt for the only other avenue still open: the radio.

The radio room was at the back of the lodge. She'd seen the system only once, many years earlier. Wolf had added several new components to boost its range and efficiency, she noted as she sank into the operator's chair. She snapped a toggle and was rewarded with a slight hum. Encouraged, she reached for the microphone.

A hand on her shoulder stopped her.

She spun around.

Tony stood framed in the light from the doorway. "Move away from the radio," he ordered bluntly.

For a moment, she could only stare at him while her shocked senses calculated the pain and betrayal of the last twenty-four hours. She had been through so much, she had come so far, only to lose it all now, in this sad little room, in an arms dealer's lodge, on the other side of paradise.

"Move away from the radio," he repeated. "Please."

She half rose in her chair. "Where's Buck?"

He continued to stare at her.

"I asked you a question!" she hurled at him. "Where's Buck? Did you leave him at Maldonado? Did you—" her voice cracked unexpectedly as the finality of the situation broke over her "—did you hurt him? Tony, answer me!"

His broad shoulders twitched, as if he were throwing off a weak moment. "I put him on a plane to Cuzco."

"You're lying."

"He's telling the truth." For the first time since he'd entered the room, the man behind Tony spoke out. "Mr. Jordan was quite safe the last time we saw him."

Catherine gasped. "Uncle Rudy?"

Rudolpho Montoya waved a manicured hand in Tony's direction. "Make yourself useful," he ordered abruptly. "I want to talk to my niece alone."

"Stay right where you are!" Catherine cried out, launching herself from her chair. The pain in her ankle was almost her undoing, but she managed to grab on to the arm of the chair as she appealed to her uncle. "Do you know what he's been doing lately?"

Rudy put up his hand. "We'll talk about that." He nodded at Tony. "Go."

"Stay!"

Tony hesitated for a moment, glancing between them.

Rudy's voice hardened. "We need some privacy, Tony, for God's sake. Take a look around. Keep an eye out for the pilot of that plane we saw earlier. And make sure Speer and his guests don't show up before we've had a chance to have our little chat."

Scowling, Tony gave a curt nod before disappearing through the doorway. A minute later, Catherine felt the slight tremor of the floorboards as he thundered down the steps.

Catherine glared at her uncle. "What's going on? And what are you doing here? You know you're not supposed to travel."

Rudy sighed. "It was necessary. Tony knew I was coming. I made the reservations when he telephoned me from Cuzco. He picked me up at the airport when he came into Maldonado. He's been telling me some very disturbing things about you and a man named Jordan." His eyes, redrimmed with fatigue, roamed her face.

Rudolpho Montoya had always been a handsome man, with a sultry Latin charm that even the jowls and pouches of middle age could not take away. His recent bout with heart disease had changed all that. Catherine saw it in the way he winced when he walked toward her, in the slight trembling of his hands, in the less than perfect posture. There was something else there, too, something that hovered beneath the warm veneer of his smile, something that had nothing to do with his current ill health. It was almost—Catherine struggled to name it—disappointment, as though by coming to the lodge, she had somehow broken faith with him.

"You've taken off the veil," he said, nodding slightly. "I approve. I never liked that idea of yours."

"You haven't answered me," she persisted, perplexed.

"All in good time." Two unhealthy blotches of color had appeared high on his cheeks. He lowered himself stiffly into the operator's chair, his gaze never leaving her face. "You look more like your mother every time I see you. Maria would be proud."

Catherine knelt beside him. "You shouldn't have come. You know what your doctor told you after your last attack. I could have handled this thing with Tony alone."

He patted her hand. "It's not as simple as that. Tony did the right thing in alerting me to the situation."

"Situation?" She laughed hollowly. "He's fallen in love with me! He's been acting crazy!"

"He's been following orders."

"What are you talking about?" she demanded. "Whose orders?" The words seemed to crumble on her tongue as she read his response in his face. "You mean *you* were behind it?" she said, incredulous. "The pit in the swamp forest? The accident on the river?"

Rudy shifted his weight slightly. "Tony knew I wanted Jordan warned off. I left the details up to him. I was furious when I found out he'd mixed you up in it. He might have killed you." He fingered a lock of her hair. "Maria would never forgive me for that."

"Maria's dead!"

"I promised her I would always look after you."

"Is this what you call looking after me? Scaring me to death? Harassing my guests?" Her shock was rapidly giving way to anger.

His eyes lost their look of nostalgia. "Jordan's hardly a guest. Do you know anything about him?"

"Do you?" she shot back.

"He's a threat to us," he said simply. "Just like that man in California was five years ago."

She attempted to stand, grinding her ankle into the side of her boot in exasperation. The pain was enough to clear her head. "Buck is nothing like David was," she said, gripping the armrest.

"Baby, he's everything like David was. And more."

"He loves me."

"Is that what he's told you?" His gaze turned thoughtful. "Maybe he does. But that won't stop him from getting what he came down here for. He'll expose us if we're not careful."

She heard it this time, his use of the plural, as though both of them had something to hide. At the back of her consciousness, a terrible thought began to take shape.

His head came up sharply at her shocked silence. "You already know about Jordan." It was a statement of fact.

She nodded.

"And you know why he's really here."

She nodded again, running her tongue over her parched lips. "He's after a man called the Serpent. He thinks it's Wolfgang Speer." There was no need to say any more than that. She could see by his eyes that he was familiar with the story. Her next sentence rolled out thickly, as though the words had formed a logjam in her throat. "Is it Speer?"

His gaze turned sorrowful. "I think you know the answer to that one, too."

"I need you to say it!" She grabbed his shoulders. "Say it! Is it Speer?"

"No. I'm the one your Mr. Jordan wants."

She shuddered, backing away from him. He'd made it sound so matter-of-fact, as though he was admitting to a parking violation instead of tearing down what little she had left of her life. Her past. Even the lies had been built upon lies.

"Do you know what you're saying?" The tears had started. She dashed them away angrily, fighting for control. "My father was killed because of you!"

"A mistake. A terrible, terrible mistake." He rose to his feet, shaking off the palsy that had made him seem so vulnerable. For a moment, he appeared as commanding as he was twenty years ago. "I had a man at your house the night your father was shot. It was late. You were sleeping. You never even knew he was there. He threatened to hurt you unless your father went to the base in the truck with the rest of my men and gave them the keys to the weapons lockups. Your father also told the military police that the intrusion alarms were malfunctioning. I'd thought of everything."

She stared at him. "Then it wasn't treason."

"Maybe not to you. I'm not so sure the military would have seen it that way," Rudy said, pausing. "Sometime after midnight something went wrong. There was a shooting."

Buck's, Catherine realized.

"Your father tried to get away during all of the confusion. My men panicked. By the time I heard about it, he was dead."

Shuddering, Catherine drew in a breath, the memories from that night burning through her. She'd awakened to find herself alone in the house. The neighbor next door had finally given in to her frantic pleas to go to the base, but by that time it was all over. Her fingers fluttered to her face. She could still feel the pull of her father's lips where he'd kissed her before putting her to bed that night. It had been the last time she had seen him alive.

Rudy reached for her hand. "The military convicted him after that—I didn't. I planned to tell you everything eventually."

She jerked away from him. "When would that have been, Uncle Rudy? When I was too old to care anymore?"

"When I thought you were able to handle it." A look of reproach came over his face as he studied her. "You changed after the deaths of your parents. You became less open, less trusting. Sometimes I was afraid to leave you alone."

"I was dying inside," she blurted out. The tears were starting again. She let them fall. "I had no one. You were always attending some medical lecture somewhere." *Or had he been dealing arms?* Her breath seemed to catch in her throat as the innocence of those years slowly tarnished. "I didn't really know who I was or what I wanted until I started to act. And then I met David." And it all came unraveled.

"He was expendable, you know."

She thought she'd misunderstood him. "What?"

"Crane. He was expendable." Rudy watched her closely, as though gauging her reaction to this new piece of information. "I needed a body to satisfy the investigators. I already had someone working in the Office of the Medical Examiner to ensure the remains were identified as those of Catherine Tremaine."

She shook with the news. "You mean David wasn't dead when you reached the canyon house that night?"

"He would have lived if he had received medical attention. I made sure he didn't."

It was like looking into the mouth of a shark. "I don't even know you," Catherine whispered, groping blindly behind her. Her hip struck the edge of the table. She shifted direction toward what she hoped was the door, her attention riveted on him.

"I did what I had to do to protect you," Rudy insisted. He did not seem aware that she had moved. "Just as I'd promised your mother I would."

"You protected yourself!"

"I made sure we were still able to be a family! It's what you needed! It's what you begged me for the night that David died!"

"I wanted sanctuary!"

"And that's exactly what I gave you." He indicated the lush tropical vegetation outside the open window. "And I can do it again. We can leave here immediately. I've got a plane waiting for us at the airport. By tomorrow night we can be anywhere. Australia? Africa? We can open another lodge if you'd like. We can start completely from scratch. I'll get rid of Tony. He's outlived his usefulness, anyway. It will be beautiful."

She stopped in her tracks. "I won't run anymore."

"You don't have a choice," he said gently. "This is a multibillion-dollar operation. I have people who depend on me, customers who are expecting their merchandise. I won't disappoint them. Jordan's probably already met with Kevin Howard in Cuzco. Our cover's been blown. The entire operation is in jeopardy."

She shook her head. "No."

"Then I'll have to get rid of Jordan."

She gasped.

"Choose," he said. "One or the other. If we change your identity again, Jordan's information will be next to useless. I can go underground. If he doesn't have access to you, he won't be able to get to me. Otherwise, I'll have to plug the leak at this end. He's in Cuzco now. I've got a man there who can silence him before he talks."

She had to force herself to take a breath. "And what if *I* talk?"

He regarded her fondly. "You won't. You're Maria's daughter. And blood is always thicker."

The door suddenly flew open. "It's Jordan!" Tony shouted, gesturing behind him. "I spotted him coming up one of the trails!"

"I thought he was in Cuzco!" Rudy snarled, grabbing Catherine by the wrist before she could move. "Get rid of him. We'll take the boat. You can meet up with us later."

"No!" Catherine screamed, catching sight of the weapon Tony pulled from his belt.

She hurled herself at him just as the gun went off.

Chapter Sixteen

Buck was at the edge of the compound when he heard the shot. He broke into a run, trying to isolate its location. The sound had been distorted by the high, thick walls of the jungle but it seemed to have originated in or around Quester's Inn.

He checked the dormitories first. Nothing. From the looks of the few personal possessions scattered around, Wolf's guests had taken another overnight trip up the river. The supply shed behind the inn was empty, too. He bounded up the steps to the main building, his apprehension growing as the minutes ticked by. He hadn't heard so much as a whimper since the gunshot.

He found them in the radio room, huddled together on the floor.

There was blood everywhere.

Tony jumped to his feet as soon as he saw Buck, but Catherine stopped him before he could take more than a few menacing steps. "It's over," she screamed, grabbing his pant leg. Her voice dropped to a whisper as she looked down at the man who lay bleeding in her arms. "It's over."

Tony slumped against the wall, wiping one bloodstained hand across the front of his shirt. The other still held the gun.

"Mine?" Buck asked, yanking it out of his grasp.

Tony shrugged as if the question was not worthy of him.

Buck emptied the chamber before handing the gun back. "Keep it," he said curtly. "Think of it as a souvenir." Then he knelt beside Catherine. She was a mess, her hair snarled, her clothes torn and dirty. There was an insect bite reddening on one pale cheek. But at least she seemed to be unharmed, physically. He didn't know what state her emotions were in.

"He's dying," Catherine murmured unevenly, trying to wipe away some of the blood that trickled down her uncle's face from a cut on his temple. His eyes were closed. She continued her gentle ministrations although they were cosmetic at best. There was nothing else she could do. She had already examined the bullet wound below his heart. Blood oozed from it every time he took a breath. "I thought you were dead, too," she said numbly, looking at Buck.

"So did I." He traced the curve of her lower lip with his thumb, then glanced at Rudy. "Your uncle?"

She swallowed hard, nodding. "He was waiting for me when I reached the inn. After you left the Phoenix, I found a broken mirror in Tony's cabin. He'd used it to construct the trap in the swamp forest. I thought his feelings for me and his jealousy of you had finally reached the breaking point. I had to warn you. There was no boat available and he'd destroyed the radio—" Her gaze flickered to Tony.

"So you decided to hike across country," Buck finished for her. "You could have died out there." *Or in here.* The thought grated across his consciousness.

"How did you know where to look for me? Did you talk to Enrique?"

He shook his head. "I haven't been back to the Phoenix since I met Kevin Howard in Cuzco. I chartered a plane to get here."

She trembled at the mention of his informant's name. "Then you know."

"That your uncle is the Serpent? Yes."

Her uncle stirred. Tony stepped away from the wall but, at a warning glance from Buck, resumed his position. His face still wore the customary look of defiance, but some of the vitriol had gone out of his eyes.

Rudy's gaze focused first on Catherine, then shifted to the left as he realized there was someone else with her. "How did you get away?" Even though he was dying, his voice was a blunt instrument.

"The goon you sent after me overestimated his skills in the dark," Buck said. "Hawk-nose is one of your uncle's men," he added for Catherine's benefit. "He and I tangled again in Cuzco."

She looked puzzled. "If he was working for my uncle, then why did he try to kill me in the market?"

"He wasn't after you." Rudy coughed harshly, grimacing. A fleck of bloody foam appeared at the corner of his mouth. "His orders were to keep an eye on Jordan. He was at the airport when you flew your guests to Cuzco the first time, and the second time when Jordan flew in alone. When you separated that day in the restaurant, the fool decided to follow you. Against my instructions." His voice lost its gritty edge as he regarded Catherine. "None of what happened had anything to do with you."

"The accidents?" she asked, looking to Buck for confirmation. "The messages?"

"The accidents were intended for me," Buck said. His brief conversation with his informant after he identified Hawk-nose had cleared up a few things. "Your uncle learned that I was coming to the Phoenix to make the rendezvous with Kevin Howard almost before I did." He clenched his teeth. There'd obviously been a breach in security somewhere along the line. That was a leak he planned to have plugged as soon as he got back to Washington. "Rudy wanted to scare me away without alerting you to the fact that I was down here to get information about the arms robberies. He couldn't kill me outright, not without raising a few suspicions from the local authorities, so he arranged for a few accidents.''

"And I just happened to get in the way,'' Catherine murmured. "What about the messages?''

"Those were a little gift from my informant to the Serpent.'' Buck shook his head. "Howard has been running so long, he's gotten paranoid. He told me he recognized Tony one day in the market in Cuzco.''

"I recognized him, too, the little yellow weasel,'' Tony muttered. "I should have offed him right there.''

"But you didn't,'' Buck informed him. "You waited for instructions from Montoya in California like you'd been told to do. And by that time, Howard had had you followed to the Phoenix. From there, it was only a matter of time before he made the connection. Rudy was the Serpent. Catherine was Rudy's niece. He dug a little bit more and found out about Catherine Tremaine and Catherine Taylor. Howard may be a weasel, but he's one smart weasel, and he's got a lot of contacts in interesting places.''

"He thought he'd blackmail me,'' Rudy rasped as another fit of coughing shook his body. By the time he regained his breath, his voice was much weaker. "He didn't think the military would hold up its end of the bargain. If the deal fell through, he wanted to make sure he had an ace in the hole. He could expose Catherine. He made sure that I knew that. He thought the messages would pressure me into leaving him alone. He chose the Phoenix as the rendezvous site for the same reason.''

"Flexing his muscle,'' Tony spat.

"But you never learned about the messages until Tony notified you from Cuzco,'' Catherine protested. "By then I'd already received the first two.''

"Howard's mistake,'' Rudy choked out. He was having trouble breathing now. His skin seemed almost transparent. Catherine tried to loosen the buttons of his shirt but he clasped her hand frantically. "No time," he whispered. "No time."

"Howard thought you'd turn to your uncle when you started receiving the messages," Buck said, finishing the story quietly. He put his hand on Catherine's shoulder to steady her. "But instead you turned to me."

Rudy nodded weakly, his eyes wandering to the left and then to the right before he finally found Catherine's face. "You never—" he shook from some hidden reservoir of pain "—you never got around to answering my question. Would you have come away with me like I'd asked you to? Or would you have let me go after Jordan?"

Catherine's throat closed. For a moment, she could only stare at him, her fingers gently tracing the noble sweep of his brow. So like her mother's. So like her own. How could all those years with him have come to this? Somehow she managed to break through the pain long enough to answer him. "I would have put on the veil."

He smiled sadly. "Do you love him that much?"

Her voice shook as the realization suddenly took hold of her heart. "Yes." Buck's grip on her shoulder tightened at her words.

Rudy nodded, as though he had never doubted it. A small, thin sound escaped his lips as he tried to form another sentence, but whatever he wanted to say was lost in a violent paroxysm of pain. Catherine held him until the shaking stopped, her world draining of all color, all memory, all emotion. When his eyes finally closed, she found she could not even weep.

"WHAT WILL HAPPEN to Tony?" Catherine asked later, on the dock. They had already loaded her uncle's body onto the boat for the trip down the river to Maldonado. Then there would be the questions from the Peruvian police and, after that, the arrangements to bury him on the ancestral family estate outside Lima. She could not see herself bringing him back to the States to inter him next to the graves of her parents, despite what he had told her back in Wolf's radio room. *Blood was not always thicker.* She lowered her head. How could love be the source of so much pain?

"There'll be an investigation," Buck told her, watching the emotions rage across her face. He hadn't touched her since they'd left the inn, but he'd wanted to. Oh, how he'd wanted to. He looked away before he could act on the urge, putting up one hand to shade his eyes from the glare off the river, determined to give Catherine as much time as she needed to sort through her emotions.

"Kevin Howard has already promised to testify. I think Tony will, too, once he's had a little time to think. He was probably on your uncle's payroll right from the start. That's how he knew Kevin Howard. It wouldn't surprise me if Tony was with your father the night of the shooting."

Catherine shuddered, glancing up the trail to where Tony was staring moodily into the jungle. "He probably monitored my movements when I lived in Los Angeles. Then he came down to Peru after the fire to keep an eye on me, too, at my uncle's request."

"Probably."

Wearily, Catherine brushed her hair back from her face. "What about the weapons my uncle was selling?"

Buck shrugged. "Without leadership, your uncle's arms empire will probably crumble, unless some kind of a power struggle occurs from within its ranks. There's always the possibility that someone else will try to take the Serpent's place. If he does, we'll be ready for him."

"And my father?"

"The military will reopen the file on the events surrounding his death," Buck continued softly. "And I'm sure the Office of the Medical Examiner will do the same with that of Catherine Tremaine. Once they learn about the extenuating circumstances, the threat to your life when you were a child, your father's attempt to stop the Serpent's men, your later breakdown, you'll both be exonerated." His mouth twisted. "The media may be nosy, but it's also sentimental. You're going to be the darling of the press when you come back to America. If you come back." The last words were added as an afterthought.

She ran the toe of her boot across the dock as she considered her options. "I'll have to keep the lodge open for another week until Reverend Woolsey and the Wheelers check out." She owed them that much, and a full explanation as soon as she returned to the Phoenix. Selena would probably be enthralled. At least they'd all been spared the sight of Tony's attack on Enrique, although under pressure from Buck, Tony had admitted striking Enrique only once. Still, the thought was enough to sicken her. "After that, the lodge goes up for sale. Maybe Wolf will be interested. He's wanted to expand operations for a long time."

"Are you sure you want to sell?"

She sighed. "I can't hide down here forever. And once the story breaks, the trails will be crawling with reporters. The environment's too fragile for all of that. Maybe Wolf will let me come back now and then for a visit."

Buck reached up and drew one finger across the soft, flushed skin of her cheek. He knew how much she was giving up. "He'll probably issue you a special invitation."

"Probably." She took a deep breath, savoring the unique perfume of the jungle. The air seemed to radiate with the cries of the birds, the languorous flight of the butterflies, the slow pulsing of all the hidden places in the green woods. "After all of this, California is going to seem so strange."

"Who said anything about California?"

Her heartbeat accelerated at the lazy smile that spread across his face. "Where else can I go?"

"I know a much nicer place in the Colorado Rockies. It's a little remote, of course. Nothing but blue skies and crisp mountain air. I can't provide you with a swamp forest or anything like that, but I can guarantee you the most spectacular snowfalls in the winter, the brightest wildflowers in the summer. I think I can even promise you a deer or two outside the bedroom window in the mornings.''

She smiled, playfully suspicious. "Yours?"

"Mine." His dark eyes never left hers. "It's a couple of hours outside Denver. Of course, you'd have to put up with a few inconveniences. There's no telephone, for one."

She took a step toward him. "I don't have anyone to call."

"And there's no television, for another."

She took a second step. "I never watch it."

"And then there's me." He met her halfway, pulling her into his arms. "I'll be there all day, every day. Summer. Winter."

"Spring and fall?" she murmured.

He looked solemn. "Those, too."

"What about the nights?"

"Especially the nights." His voice dropped to a husky whisper. "Do you think you could get used to all that?"

"How soon do you want an answer?"

"I'll let you know." He kissed her once, twice, his mouth moving tenderly over her lips. Above them, a single macaw wheeled, like a messenger from heaven, across the sun-washed sky.

"Time's up."

She wound her arms around his neck, smiling.

Valentine's Day was the best day of the year for
Dee's Candy and Gift Shop. Yet as the day drew closer,
Deanna Donovan became the target of
malicious, anonymous pranks.

A red heart was pinned to her front door with a dagger.

Dead roses adorned her car.

Soon, she was being stalked by her unseen admirer.

Suspicious of everyone, Deanna has nowhere to turn—and no
way to escape when she is kidnapped and held captive by her
Valentine lover....

#262

Cupid's Dagger

by Leona Karr
February 1994

You'll never again think of Valentine's Day without feeling a
thrill of delight...and a chill of dread!   CUPID

HARLEQUIN®

INTRIGUE®

The mystique of mummies and Egyptian jewels come to life in Dawn Stewardson's Harlequin Intrigue duet:

You're in for a surprise when an ancient sarcophagus is opened—but the occupant is *not* a centuries-old mummy but a murdered young woman.

Don't miss these Intrigues:

THE
MUMMY CASE

Available now!

and

THE
MUMMY BEADS

February 1994

My Valentine 1994

Celebrate the most romantic day of the year with
MY VALENTINE 1994
a collection of original stories, written by
four of Harlequin's most popular authors...

MARGOT DALTON
MURIEL JENSEN
MARISA CARROLL
KAREN YOUNG

Available in February, wherever
Harlequin Books are sold.

HARLEQUIN ®

VAL94

NEW YORK TIMES **Bestselling Author**

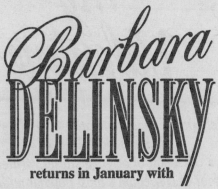

Barbara
DELINSKY

returns in January with

THE REAL THING

Stranded on an island off the coast of Maine,
Deirdre Joyce and Neil Hersey got the
solitude they so desperately craved—
but they also got each other, something they
hadn't expected. Nor had they expected
to be consumed by a desire so powerful
that the idea of living alone again was
unimaginable. A marrige of "convenience"
made sense—or did it?

B0B7

HARLEQUIN®